LYING LOW

LYING LOW

A JANE AVERY MYSTERY

CYNTHIA ST. AUBIN

THOMAS & MERCER

Text copyright © 2018 by Cynthia Olsen

Published by Thomas & Mercer, Seattle

www.apub.com

Amazon, the Amazon logo, and Thomas & Mercer are trademarks of Amazon.com, Inc., or its affiliates.

ISBN-13: 9781503904316
ISBN-10: 1503904318

Cover design by David Drummond

Printed in the United States of America

This book is dedicated to the endlessly talented and patient Kerrigan Byrne, my critique partner and bestest friend (and whose books you should totally read). For sitting beside me in the trenches and making even that seem like the only adventure worth having. You are the GutterBear to my TrashPanda. I love you senselessly.

Chapter One

There was a man in my bed.

There was a *naked* man in my bed.

After two years in dry dock, a naked man in my bed should have been a good thing. A splendid thing. A fan-fucking-tastic thing. And that might have been true.

If the naked man in my bed hadn't been dead.

Very dead.

Very dead, and totally not my type.

Skinny, for one thing. Pale as a mushroom and the kind of dirty that makes it difficult to tell arty-coffeehouse hipsters from a borderline homeless dude washing up in McDonald's bathrooms. Where you're not sure if the stiffness in their beard is barber's wax or a couple of days' worth of cold grease from dumpster pizza. If the rat-brown clump of hair had been artfully arranged to fall just so across his forehead, the effect was somewhat compromised by the pin-neat hole directly between his eyebrows.

The sort of hole a .38 caliber bullet would slide through right nicely, by the looks of it.

"I gotta say, I wouldn't have thought he was your type." Officer Bixby, a couple of inches taller than I and several times more muscled, is a totally different type: a bro.

An earnest bro.

An honest bro.

But a bro nonetheless.

He also happens to be a former patrol cop, recently on loan to help the homicide unit after an unfortunate run-in with a bullet made writing traffic tickets a difficult prospect.

He's actually not a bad guy to have around despite his habit of always turning up when shit's going down in my life.

Which is to say, often.

"My type?" I asked.

"Yeah," Bixby said. "For some reason I can't see you with the type of guy who does manual labor."

"Well, he *isn't* my type," I said. "But you're wrong about the manual labor. I mean, Jesus, Bixby. Look at his fin . . . gers."

I regretted the words the second they were out of my mouth.

Not because it was a lie, which I had recently sworn off, but because fingers were kind of a—forgive me—*touchy* subject with us. Ever since Bixby wandered into the path of a bullet that was meant to lodge itself in my head, he'd labored under the delusion that the loss of his right index finger and thumb as a result of the aforementioned bullet was entirely and irrevocably *my* fault.

No mention of the charmingly homicidal debutante who had arranged for the bullet in the first place.

"What I mean is, he doesn't have any calluses on his palms or fingertips." I pointed to the bloodless, waxy hands secured to my bedposts at the wrists with kitchen twine—the sight of which brought a pang of guilt. Not because the poor dead sap had been secured with it, but because a roast chicken hadn't. Yet another example of my obvious domestic failings. "Just because his fingernails are dirty doesn't mean he worked with his hands. There are lots of things that could explain that," I continued.

"Such as?" Eugene Kappas, a fortyish police detective with a dandelion fluff of curly brown hair and more than a passing resemblance to John C. Reilly, looked at me across the expanse of the rumpled bedclothes. He'd been quiet while he sorted through the pile of laundry next to the bed with latex-gloved hands, looking for shell casings and sending judgy glances in my direction.

So I hate doing laundry.

Truth be told, there were far more prevalent opportunities to level judgment against my general person. Like the fact that this was not the first time I had been surprised by a corpse chillaxing somewhere in my place of residence.

The first time it happened, I had been ten years old.

I had come stumping out of the bedroom at the back of the trailer shared by my mother and me, eyes still crusted with sleep. No sooner had I opened the bathroom door and flipped on the light than I saw a foot sticking out from behind the daisy-bespattered shower curtain.

A man's foot.

Waxy pale. Long hairy toes. A pill of dark lint stuck to the pinky toe, which was bereft of the nail. The flesh just above the ankle compressed in a ribbed pattern where once there had been a sock. A dress sock, I reasoned, because of the lint's dark color.

Details, Janey. You never know what you'll need to remember later. Even at ten years old, my mother's admonitions had already taken up residence in my ear.

When I poked the foot with the nonbristled end of a My Little Pony toothbrush and it didn't move, I decided it was time to have a conversation with my mother.

I found her in the kitchen, barefoot and wearing the bathrobe I had picked out for her at Goodwill the previous Christmas, chosen because it was the precise color of the powdery green dinner mints I loved to shave with my teeth. She cradled a silver mixing bowl in the crook of one arm, whisking up pancake batter in time with the cranium-crushing thump of Norwegian death metal.

"Momma?"

She looked up at me and beamed. "Morning, sunshine! You want maple syrup on your pancakes, or peanut butter?"

"Peanut butter." I propped my chin on the breakfast bar, scooting a half inch over when the peeling wood-patterned laminate cut into my skin. "How come there's a man in the bathtub?"

"Fucktrumpet!" The bowl slipped in her hands, sending a small tidal wave of batter splashing up. She set the bowl down, hurried around the counter, and knelt before me, pushing the sleep-tangled hair away from my face. "Oh, Janey, I'm so sorry. I thought I locked the door. Are you okay?"

"Sure," I had said, a little confused at her strong reaction. "But what's he doing there?"

"You remember how Mommy told you about the bad men?"

I nodded enthusiastically.

"Janey versus the Bad Men" had always been my favorite bedtime story. Long lurid tales during which I, wearing a cape and lots of sparkly spandex, routinely exploded heads like watermelons and made flaming hedgehogs shoot out of bad men's butts.

Mom had always let me pick which powers I wanted.

"Well, a bad man came to our house last night and wanted to hurt us. But Mommy hurt him first."

"What will happen to him now?"

"Well, now he'll stay right where he is while we eat our pancakes. Then later this afternoon, Mommy will put on a movie for you and make him go away. How about that?"

"Why can't I watch you make him go away?"

Mom took me by the hand and led me to the sagging orange-and-brown plaid couch I had named Eustace.

"Janey, do you know what a *witness* is?"

Something about the sound of it tickled my memory. An idea swam close enough for me to snatch it. "Like when people bring their friends with them to *People's Court*?"

"That's right," my mom had said. "It's someone who sees a particular thing happen, so they get asked about it later. Well, sometimes it's better *not* to see some things because then if you get asked about it, you don't have to lie."

Lie.

This one syllable washed me in hot, stinging shame.

It was a word that rode home in my backpack on notes from teachers. A word flicked at me like spitballs from the other kids in my class. A word adults liked to point in my face like fingers.

"Jane?"

My head snapped up as the cloud of memory evaporated, dumping me back into the present moment where yet another dead body needed handling.

"I'm sorry," I said. "What was that?"

Detective Kappas gave Bixby a knowing smile. "You were about to enlighten us as to what other circumstances could have caused the dirt under his fingernails."

"Digging his way out of a shallow grave," a male voice interjected.

This comment—totally plausible but completely unhelpful—was supplied by the room's newest occupant.

Shepard.

A.k.a. my self-appointed bodyguard / personal security expert / babysitter.

A.k.a. six feet five inches of *gimme-gimme-gimme*, wrapped in fatigue pants, wrapped in *yum*.

Shepard was the one-name moniker he had adopted during his days as an army sniper.

The other descriptions were those I had assigned him after figuring out I wasn't likely to learn the rest of his name despite the fact that I once handcuffed him naked to a shower. Which I realize sounds much kinkier than the truth of the matter.

You know, one of those perfectly understandable incidents wherein the person who has been appointed to guard your body ends up getting in your body's way and needs to be temporarily bound to a bathroom fixture.

We've all been there, am I right?

Nevertheless, that incident, and several others like it, had established a somewhat combative and adversarial relationship between me and the man with the unenviable task of keeping me out of trouble.

"Who is this guy and why is he here?" Kappas asked, shooting a look at Bixby rather than Shepard, whose presence he seemed determined to ignore.

Shepard stayed silent, leaning back on the heels of his combat boots and regarding Kappas with all the respect a cobra has for a cockroach.

Since Bixby didn't immediately answer, I blundered ahead. "Detective Kappas, this is Shepard. Shepard, this is Detective *Eugene* Kappas." Childish of me, perhaps, to enjoy a slight jab at the expense of his name, but fitting, I thought, for a man who insisted on poking through my panty drawer with the end of a pencil.

"First name or last name?" Kappas asked, glancing up from his pad.

"Yes," I answered.

Kappas's already-beady eyes narrowed a fraction.

"Shepard has a certain . . . *understanding* with the governing body of the Denver PD." A grudging acceptance—if not admiration—colored Bixby's voice as he explained.

"You mean he has special permission from the chief?" Kappas asked.

"More like from the governor of Colorado," Bixby said.

"Look, I don't know what kind of shop you're running here, but this isn't how we do things back in Chicago. Without everyone observing regulations and a clear chain of command—"

"I don't make the rules," Bixby interrupted. "Or the special dispensations. My assignment is to help you get acclimated, and that's what I'm doing."

"Relax, *Eugene*," Shepard said, peeling himself away from the wall. "You'll get the hang of things."

I shot Shepard a look that I hoped said something like *bite your tongue* but may or may not have been something more like *I'd like to bite your tongue.*

It's easy for nonverbal messages to get crossed when there are 295 pounds of grade A beefcake in your peripheral vision.

I cleared my throat as much to dissipate the growing tension as to drag attention back to myself. "As I was about to explain before Shepard graced us with his own unstudied theories regarding the aforementioned fingernails—"

"Lawyers," Shepard muttered, casting an eye roll in the direction of the two people in the room also likely to disapprove of my chosen profession and its attendant verbal posturing.

I decided to let the insult slide rather than correct him, as that would mean admitting that I wasn't *technically* a lawyer until I passed the bar. A fact the prestigious firm that had taken me on as a part-time unofficial associate had been consistently reminding me of as I scheduled—and rescheduled—exam dates, following my mother's disappearance.

"About the dead dude's nails," I said, choosing smallish words with vengeful specificity. "I was thinking more along the lines of a job that requires a lot of typing."

"Typing?" Bixby, who had a habit of finding poses that allowed him to flex his muscles when Shepard was around, reached down for the edge of my down comforter with one stiff, latex-gloved hand.

"Didn't you ever have to write a twenty-four-page paper in one night while you were in college? I mean, there you are, writing snacks at hand, scraping cheese dust from your teeth, and some gets under your nails, and then you type and you type while regretting every decision that led you to this moment and cursing yourself for being a procrastinating whore, and ten hours later, you look like you've been working under the hood of a car all your life. You know?"

They didn't know.

"You sure you didn't know him?" Bixby asked, lifting the edge of the comforter. "Uh-oh."

"Uh-oh?" I asked, leaning around Bixby's broad back. "What *uh-oh*?"

"If you didn't sleep with him, then what's this?" Bixby pointed to the stiff, dried blob on the edge of the down comforter. The edges had begun to flake.

"Don't tell me I'm the only one who eats tapioca pudding in bed."

"Pudding?" Kappas squatted down near the stain to get a better look. "That doesn't look like pudding to me."

"It's pudding, I assure you. Taste it if you don't believe me."

I thought I might have seen Kappas gag at the suggestion, but I couldn't be certain.

"See, this is why I don't eat in bed at all," Bixby said. "I don't like crumbs."

"Ah," I said triumphantly. "But pudding doesn't have crumbs."

"Neither does salami," Bixby pointed out, gently folding back the comforter. "Because holy shit was this guy packing."

"Please," I scoffed, peering over Bixby's shoulder. "If you've seen one, you've seen them—whoa."

And whoa it was.

"Well, that solves one mystery," Bixby said.

"Which one would that be?" his partner asked.

"Why Miss Avery slept with him in the first place."

"I did *not* sleep with him!" The blast of air from the conditioning vent overhead was chilly on my face, revealing just how red and damp with perspiration my face must be.

Smooth, Jane. Very smooth.

"In fact, I've never seen him before in my life. All I know is I arrived home from the nail salon to pack for a last-minute flight, came into my bedroom to grab my carry-on bag, and *boom*. Dead guy."

"Uh-huh," Eugene Kappas said, his voice espousing the same unconvincing tone employed by the driver's license dude when I insisted that I'm five feet five inches, 125 pounds, and have brown hair and blue eyes.

The brown and blue part just about anyone can vouch for, though I'd prefer to think of my eyes as glacier indigo and my hair like the deepest espresso.

The five-feet-five part requires several pairs of woolly socks and the 125, an act of God or cutting all carbs.

Both of which would qualify as a miracle in my book.

"And was Mr. Shepard going to accompany you on this flight?"

"No *mister*," I said. "Just Shepard. And no. He was going to see me safely to the airport."

"And what is his relationship to you?" Kappas skewered me with eyes that were the strange bluish gray of a newborn's.

A panicked pause.

Not because I didn't know, but because I didn't want to say.

Because saying, "Shepard is a former US Army Special Forces sniper turned bodyguard/babysitter hired to keep me alive while also preventing me from causing a metric shit-ton of trouble for Archard Everett Valentine," would create more questions than answers.

Because Archard Everett Valentine was a reformed thief, a suspected mistress-murderer, the gazillionaire architect who gave the keynote address at my law school graduation, and most recently, the man help-ing me search for my missing mother—whom he had hired to do a little private detecting for him before she vanished.

Because Valentine had once upon a time been granted immunity for testifying against a violent, homicidal psychopath and learned how to protect himself from people who wanted him dead.

Because Valentine had recently been offering similar protection to my mother.

Because Valentine was, even now, waiting for me in a parking lot across the street.

Because.

"Personal security specialist," I blurted.

A canyon appeared in the fleshy outcropping of Kappas's forehead as he jotted something down on the battered notepad in his hand.

"Speaking of which," Shepard said, graciously changing the topic, "maybe if you actually used the security system I put in place, people wouldn't be able to dump dead bodies in your bed."

My hands found my hips, the place they frequently visited when I was in direct proximity to Shepard. "*Maybe* if you hadn't installed a system that requires the Rosetta stone and an old priest and a young priest to arm, maybe I would."

"Easy to arm, easy to disarm."

"The Gospel according to Saint Shepard," I muttered.

"Where were you headed?" Detective Kappas was still down on his knees, running his gloved fingers under the edge of the bed. A patch of sweat darkened his dress shirt between his shoulder blades.

"Pardon?" I asked, quickly wresting my attention from the way Bixby's arms filled out the sleeves of his dress shirt as he—carefully and with considerable effort—pulled out my sock drawer.

"You said you were on the way to the airport. Where were you headed?" Kappas repeated.

Shepard and I traded a glance.

A simple question, right?

The trouble is, no question is a simple question when you'd prefer to answer it with a lie.

Because I do lie.

Or I did.

Like, all the time and shit.

After the recent imbroglio wherein I'd landed myself in the crosshairs of a multiple murder plot hatched by the dean of my law school and the parents of my former valedictory nemesis (and current coworker), Melanie Beidermeyer, I had made up my mind to turn over a new leaf. Or perhaps a new forest, given the level of personal alteration this would require.

No more lies.

No more fibs.

No more prevarication, exaggeration, or fabrication of any kind.

"Seattle," I said.

"What's in Seattle?" Kappas asked.

"Maybe my mother."

For the thousandth time in the twenty minutes since I'd read it, the words from the personal ad in the *Mile High Grapevine*, a favorite local gossip rag for Mom and me, circled in my head.

Intelligent Brunette Seeks Rescue.

Even if it hadn't been our prearranged contact code should we need to communicate with each other incognito, I would have felt her in the words that followed. The gently mocking tone that colored her every word.

> Looking for a partner in crime to share in occasional adventures and recreational flaying. If you enjoy walks on the beach and the smell of patchouli oil, you might just be the person I'm looking for. Find me before it's too late.

Before it's too late.

Words universally dreaded in the English language, because what follows them can never be good.

Exactly *how* bad remained a topic of mental debate for me, subject to change by the day, the hour, or even the minute sometimes. Thanks to a letter she'd left for me at Valentine's loft, I'd moved beyond the belief that she was being held against her will as I'd suspected in my first panicked moments after she disappeared. But the idea of her being on the run by either choice or necessity or some tangled combination of both brought me little comfort.

"*Maybe* your mother?" Kappas slicked the word in a thick coat of sarcasm.

"She's missing."

Missing. Disappeared. Vanished.

Words I had gotten used to saying. All equally true and untrue when it came to describing the massive rift my mother's absence had caused in my world.

I'd been living with her absence the way you chew around a rotted tooth: always aware of it, never entirely free of its ache or certain when it might send up a sudden stalk of misery to steal your breath away.

Of course, this wasn't the first time she'd up and poofed out of sight. My life—or as much of it as I could remember—had been pock-marked with such orphaned stretches.

A couple of days here. A fortnight there.

Only I had always been in on the plan. Privy to the details.

Not tasked with searching for the cast-off clues of a hasty departure, followed by a possible abduction, followed by revelations of blackmail and murder. What had initially looked like my mother making herself voluntarily invisible now appeared to be a far twistier proposition.

And I, curious soul that I was, had determined to find out exactly what had happened if it killed me—*metaphorically speaking*, I felt the need to add as my eyes flicked back to the deceased human in my bed.

"And your mother's name?" Kappas shifted on his battered leather shoes like an ungainly ship listing in the tide.

"Alexis Avery," Bixby said. "She's a private investigator."

As much as I wanted to, I couldn't fault Bixby for being all eager beaver about knowing these things.

After all, he'd been the officer who investigated my mother's car when I found it with the driver's-side window broken out in the parking lot after she'd disappeared from my graduation from the University of Denver's Sturm College of Law a little over a month ago. He'd been the one who informed me that a background check revealed that my mother, along with the legal records that generally confirmed a person's status in the world, had mysteriously and utterly vanished. She had covered her tracks so well that she disappeared without a single trace.

Until the personal ad she'd placed.

She needed help.

She needed *me*.

And here I was, stuck in my apartment with three men. Well, four technically, if you counted the dead guy—and that seemed like the least I could do, considering—while my intended travel partner sent me increasingly tersely worded texts.

Where the fuck are you?

I hadn't answered him.

He was the kind of man you didn't answer unless the answer was a good one.

Then two minutes later: If you're not here in five minutes, I'm leaving without you.

Hold your wad, I hastily texted back.

"Who is that?" Bixby's partner asked.

"A friend," I said.

"And what's the friend's name?"

Goddamn cops and their fucking specific questions. It was so much easier to lie when the truth could be vague as shit.

Shepard again caught my eye, giving me a look that was either *don't you dare say* or *let's do butt stuff.*

Again, nonverbal cues have never been our thing.

"Archard Everett Valentine," I said.

I've never been in any gathering where an extended beat of silence doesn't follow his name.

"You were going to Seattle with Archard Everett Valentine?" Kappas asked.

I gathered by the wolfish gleam overtaking his blunt and blocky features that he'd already heard of Valentine, new in town though he was. "Yes," I said.

"Are you aware that he was a suspect in a recent homicide?" Kappas pressed.

Oh, I was aware all right. I'd been the one who had originally discovered the charred and smoking corpse of Valentine's mistress, Carla Malfi.

"*Was,*" I emphasized. "If I remember correctly, all charges were dropped."

"All *those* charges were dropped," Kappas said. "There are still several pending investigations where his name is prominently featured. If I were going to Seattle to look for my missing mother, that's not the guy I'd be taking with me."

I guess that depends on your mother, I thought but didn't say.

Because *my* mother had been doing some private detective work for Valentine in exchange for his protection. Protection from whom, exactly, Valentine insisted I needed to ask her myself if and when we found her.

A task he was eager to complete not, I suspected, out of some benevolent need to help a young, desperate, and eternally irritating human like myself out of a bind, but because he needed the information she had disappeared with when she had dropped—or was snatched—off the grid.

When Valentine's name flashed on my phone's screen, I considered sending it directly to voice mail, then decided I might have better chances playing for time if I answered it.

"Hello?"

"The parking lot of your building is crawling with cops. You need to get out of there before any of them see you." Even angry, Valentine's voice was a lot like the man himself: hard-edged, smoky, and probably laced with scotch.

"They've kind of already seen me," I said. "In fact, there are two of them looking at me now."

"What? Why?" A measure of the anger in his tone decreased in favor of alarm.

I sighed, heavily put upon by my own newly adopted scruples. That was the trouble with this no-lying policy. It applied equally to everyone.

"So, there's this dead guy in my bed."

Silence. "Come the fuck again?"

"There's a dead guy," I repeated. "In my bed."

"And you called the cops *before* you called me?"

"Actually, the cops were already here. They were investigating a break-in next door, and I sort of screamed and they came running."

I could literally *feel* Valentine deciding whether he bought this. Irony, considering it was 170 percent truth, however improbable it might seem.

"And neither you nor Shepard thought it appropriate to give me a heads-up?" Valentine's words were short. Clipped. Spoken through teeth mostly clenched.

At least I wasn't the lone target of Valentine's ire. Shepard, who Valentine employed to do a variety of shady things of equally shady legality, had a relationship with Valentine as tense as my own due to the former sniper's hands-on approach where I was concerned.

Partly because Shepard couldn't seem to keep those hands off me.

A prospect as panty-melting as it was problematic.

I had mostly managed to head him off at the pass, so to speak, by elucidating all the problems that would be created by our canoodling. Which is why we'd only gotten as far as occasional tonsil hockey.

Which I never think about, in case you were wondering.

"It's not that we didn't think it was appropriate so much as I didn't want to," I said into the phone. "And I didn't want Shepard to either. So I asked him not to. And he didn't." I glanced at Shepard, who by this point was doing a lot of shifting around on his combat boots and clearing his throat and similar masculine posturing.

"Do you want to remind him that I sign his fucking paychecks?"

"Paychecks aren't everything," I said.

"What else is there?"

"A general sense of well-being. Helping your fellow man. And also, the persuasive power of tits."

Notorious snatch-hound that he was, Valentine hadn't a leg to stand on here and we both knew it.

"And is Shepard looking at yours?"

"Not *now*," I said. "That would hardly be appropriate since they're processing a crime scene and all. The cops. Not my tits. My tits are wearing the exceedingly sensible button-up shirt and cardigan I chose for traveling. Wrinkle-free, they're meant to be. Again, the clothing, not my tits. Not that I'm saying my tits are wrinkly. Because they're not."

Once again, I had managed to draw the attention of almost every male in the room. A decent accomplishment, considering the dead body in everyone's line of sight.

"Speaking of traveling, I was under the impression that we were going to be doing some. My pilot has been waiting on the tarmac for twenty minutes now."

"We are," I said. "Just as soon as I'm done answering questions here."

"Questions like, what is *this* doing in the trash by your bed?" Bixby stood on one side of my bed, holding the limp sheath of a discarded condom aloft.

"And what is *this* doing in your nightstand?" His partner stood on the other, the butt of a gun pinched between his latex-gloved fingers. My heart lurched at the sight of it, a .38 I'd affectionately named Face-Gravy for its ability to reduce the average cranium to so much meat soup.

"Be careful," I said. "It's loaded."

"I'll say," Bixby said, holding the condom at eye level. "It looks like a damn softball in a sock."

"I was talking about the gun," I said.

"What gun?" Valentine growled into the phone.

"The one the detective just found in my nightstand."

"The detective just found a gun in your nightstand?" Somehow, it sounded even worse when Valentine said it.

"And a used condom," Shepard announced.

"I *will* shoot you," I hissed over my shoulder.

Bixby's partner raised an eyebrow at me.

"Hypothetically," I clarified. "I did not shoot that guy. I did not have sex with that guy. I feel like no one is giving the proper weight and consideration to these points I'm making."

Valentine sighed. Long, gusty, and tired. In my mind's eye, I could see him massaging the fine, high bridge of his patrician nose. "You know what?" he said. "This is actually a good thing."

"How is this a good thing?"

"Because I almost let you on my private jet. Disaster follows you fucking *everywhere*. Do you have any idea how hard I've had to work to clear my name after Carla?"

After Carla.

My life had been divided into those periods as well.

Before I had seen the charred remains of Valentine's mistress, Carla Malfi, and after.

Death will do that.

It changes people.

It changed me.

That Valentine had been cleared of her murder didn't necessarily matter in the court of public opinion. The accusation would forever cling to him like the acrid smoke that had billowed up from her body.

"Just give me thirty minutes," I said. "I'll get this sorted out. I promise."

"No, Jane. It's better if you stay here. See what you can find out from the *Mile High Grapevine* about how the ad was placed. I'll chase the leads in Seattle."

"No," I said, panic beginning to claw its way up my throat. "Don't you leave me, or so help me, I will shoot you and bury your body in the desert!"

Bixby and his partner blinked at me.

Shepard just shook his head, face pressed into his palm.

This is what happens when I tell the truth.

A literal facepalm.

"I meant, like, leave me, on a plane," I whispered to the room at large, my hand pressed over the phone's mouthpiece. "This isn't a relationship thing."

"You have a permit for this?" The plastic evidence bag crinkled as Kappas carefully worked it over the gun's barrel.

I frowned with my whole face as my own self-adopted motto echoed in my head.

The truth. The whole truth. Nothing but the truth.

"No," I admitted. "I don't."

Bixby's partner looked at him as a knock at the bedroom door announced the arrival of a full complement of crime scene technicians.

"Cuff her," Kappas said.

I didn't ask the usual questions because I already knew the answers.

Reasonable suspicion.

That was all they needed to take me into custody.

There was a dead man in my bed. A used condom in my trash. An unregistered weapon of the same caliber that killed him in my nightstand.

I was, as they would say in law school, royally fucked.

As Bixby unclipped his handcuffs from the leather pouch on his belt and walked toward me, I heard my mother's voice in my head.

That tumble of smoke and silk that I'd always found so comforting. Like she'd had a lifelong cold. Like she should be singing the blues to accompaniment of a stripped-down guitar.

Run, Janey, she urged. *Run.*

And a few weeks ago, I might have.

A few weeks ago, that voice had been louder than my own thoughts, more solid than my own reason.

But without it finding its way into my ear every day, it had grown quiet.

A whisper. An echo.

I let Bixby cuff me.

"They won't be able to keep you," Shepard said, squeezing my shoulder as I passed. "I'll pull some strings."

And there was comfort in it. In hearing him say it, though I well knew the laws that would or wouldn't set me free.

He pulled strings.

I yanked chains.

Neither was likely to help me now.

Chapter Two

Jail is a lot like any other government agency.

Cold, gray, and populated by the world's most wildly unenthusiastic employees.

From the bored officer who yawned as he scanned my fingerprints to the sour-faced bruiser who didn't take kindly to my asking her, "What's my safe word?" when she groped me with latex-gloved hands.

And no one, *no one*, seemed at all impressed by my attempting to find a good angle for the mug shot.

Not that angles were of much help by that point.

I had cried just a tiny bit in the back of the police cruiser.

And by *just a tiny bit*, I mean *bawled like a bitch*.

An act that surprised no one so much as me.

My mother hadn't raised me to be the kind of candy-ass who cries in the back of a cop car. In fact, I have what I might describe as a healthy disdain for authority figures in general.

So I couldn't for the life of me figure out why I lost my shit until after I was processed and lying on my cot in the county clink. I say *cot*, but *concrete slab with a mattress on it only slightly thicker than your average maxi pad* would be more accurate.

I had been lying there, contemplating the ceiling, when realization finally congealed in my brain.

The cop car.

Those red and blue lights filtering through my shrinking pupils, their flashing waking up a memory as suddenly as a seizure. Images long since buried in the parts of my brain I didn't let out at parties.

I had been ten years old the first time my mother was arrested.

We were living in California at the time, in a small, perpetually dusty trailer park on the outskirts of Death Valley, where the scorpion population far outstripped the pool of potential playmates for a girl my age.

I'd been out in the yard—a small patch of sunbaked gravel, when the police car came crawling up the road. No, not crawling. *Crunching.* Because the anemic driveway that served as the trailer park's main drag was mostly paved in the cat litter the trailer park residents threw down to soak up engine oil from their constantly broken-down vehicles.

I had looked up from the frying pan my mother let me use to bake mud pies in my "oven"—the rickety wooden staircase attached to our trailer's front—and knew *shit was about to get real,* in my mother's parlance.

I quickly slid the mud-filled pan in between the second stair and the third, or *the bottom shelf,* as I liked to think of it. The temperature was already set to broil.

In Mojave, California, it was always set to broil.

"Momma!"

Her face was there, floating in the darkness beyond the screen door. Though it was late in the afternoon, the trailer's few windows admitted little daylight and our electricity had been shut off a few weeks before.

We'd been "camping" since then, lighting small fires in the old woodstove abandoned by our trailer's previous resident to ward off the cold desert nights. I slept curled into my mother on the mattress we shared, always the little spoon.

As the cop car rolled to a stop outside our trailer, my mother pushed the screen door open, the hinges shrieking in protest.

The stab of admiration I felt upon seeing her had been sharp enough to steal my breath. Joanna Alexis Avery didn't stand like a woman on the hand-built staircase of a trailer. She stood like a queen. Shoulders back. Head high. Eyes silvered by the bleached sand of the sparse desert landscape. Her dark hair whipping around her face by the scorching Santa Ana winds.

"You remember when we talked about plan B, Janey?" she had asked.

I nodded with all the seriousness my ten-year-old self could muster. "Yes, Momma."

"Good girl."

Chalky dust settled around the patrol car like a sinking cloud as two men stepped out. Small-town cops. One older than he should have been. The other, heavier.

"Good afternoon, ma'am."

My mother said nothing. And this, too, filled me with a strange sort of pride. She wasn't like one of those people on TV, always asking stupid questions like, "What seems to be the trouble, Officer?" or "What is this all about?"

"They didn't say there would be a kid." The heavier officer had already begun to sweat, dark rings blooming beneath the armpits of his khaki shirt.

The men exchanged a look that felt like they were tossing a coin.

The older of the two cleared his throat. "Alexis Avery, we have a warrant for your arrest."

Of course, she didn't go quietly.

And according to plan B, neither did I.

While the younger of the officers attempted to wrestle my mother into the back of the cop car, I shrank into a little ball and dialed up the wailing.

"Poor little thing," the older officer said, approaching me the way you might a wounded animal. "Is your daddy home?"

"I don't have a dad." Despite the rabid fiction I'd already become somewhat infamous for perpetrating, this part was true. Just a few weeks earlier, my fourth-grade teacher had sent me home with a very strongly worded note when, on Family Day, I proudly told a rapt rug full of my classmates how my mommy had "gone to a sperm bank to get squirted with a turkey baster of baby batter because men were too much damn trouble."

"Do any other grown-ups live at home?"

"Uh-uh."

"We're going to have to take her with us. Farrell, put a call into Child Protective Services," the older officer called over his shoulder to his partner, who yelped as my mother sank her teeth into his forearm. "Come on, darlin'."

I peeked from between my folded arms, waiting until his shoes were close enough, just as my mother had taught me in our many, many rehearsals of plan B.

And then, as soon as they were, I sprang to my feet.

"Blow me, you bloated goat-wanker!"

To this day, I don't know what shocked him more: hearing those words come out of a little girl's mouth, or the length of PVC pipe (left over from one of my mother's many "science projects") that I hiked up between his legs as hard as I could.

Then I ran.

I ran as hard as I could, slowing only to slip through the small gap in the chain-link fence that separated us from the desert.

The deputy was in no shape to give chase. Not only because he was both older and slower, but also because his nards were still located somewhere in his abdominal cavity.

I was well hidden by the time his partner climbed over the fence. So well hidden that he walked right by me as he muttered to himself about sending someone from Child Protective Services back to collect me.

Only when the sun sank below the scrub brush and the insect choir began its evening vespers did I crawl out from under the rusty truck skeleton, pocked by years of target practice.

Dirty and tired, my skin salty with pure child's sweat, I crawled through the back window of the trailer's one bedroom, landing squarely in the middle of the bed we shared.

And promptly had a small meltdown.

My plopping down had thrown up a wall of my mother's scent from her pillow, and I realized for the first time that I was really, truly all alone.

I had lain there curled into a ball, sobbing helplessly into her pillow until a sharp rap on the trailer's front door sent me scrambling into the closet like a frightened rabbit. Another, louder knock followed by someone shouting—

"I brought you extra blankets."

I sat up straight on my cot, startled out of my memory and into the present, where Bixby stood in front of my cell's bars, a small stack of linens in his arms. And impressive arms they were still, though his recent injury had put an end to his regular routine of bench-pressing small cars and large barbells.

"How very thoughtful of you." I shuffled over to him in my prison-issued slippers and collected the blankets, which were thin enough to be passed through the meager rectangular slot used for food trays. "So where's your new best friend?" I asked, hugging them to my chest.

"Back at the precinct filling out paperwork."

"And he let you out all by yourself?"

"He doesn't own me, you know."

"Could have fooled the shit out of me." Giving him my back, I made the exceedingly short journey over to the cot and dropped the blankets onto it, then plopped down heavily next to them.

"Look, Jane. I'm really sorry about all this."

"Not as sorry as I am." The bitterness of my own laugh left me feeling centuries old and hollow.

"I've been talking to Kappas about you."

"Oh yeah?"

"Yeah. He's really not a bad guy, you know."

"Detective Eugene Kappas can tongue-punch a badger's ass."

"Speaking of badgers, I wanted to ask you something."

"That's got to be one of the weirdest segues in the history of jailhouse conversation."

"You remember the day . . . the day we met?"

This was a kindness on his part. Calling it *the day we met* instead of *the day your mother went missing*.

"Vividly," I said, despite the month that had passed since the fateful day of our first acquaintance. The day of my law school graduation.

"Remember when I was processing your mother's car, and you said that she broke out of jail to see you play Left Badger in a school play."

"Chicken Little," I supplied.

"Right," he said. "Though I still maintain that there weren't any badgers in *Chicken Little*."

"Please tell me you didn't come here just to continue that debate."

"No," he said. "But it's related. I asked you then what she'd been charged with, and you said that information should be readily available to me."

"Your memory is admirable, Bixby, my friend." I flopped back on the cot and propped my hands beneath my head. "Consider yourself gold-starred."

"Here's the thing, though." Bixby picked at a spot of chipping paint on the bars with his nonbandaged hand. "That information isn't readily available to me. All your mother's records had been conveniently deleted, if you'll remember."

"I remember."

"So what was she charged with?"

"Why does it matter?" I asked the ceiling. "That was a long time ago."

"Just a matter of personal curiosity."

"Your personal curiosity?" I asked. "Or Kappas's?"

"Mine," he said, though his gaze didn't quite meet my eyes.

I got up from my bunk and walked over to the bars.

To his credit, Bixby didn't step back when I approached. He even leaned in when I crooked a finger toward him.

The bars were cold against my face. Their metallic scent mingled with the lingering ghost of Bixby's aftershave. Evidence of his impeccable and elaborate personal grooming rituals.

"Murder," I whispered. "My mother was wanted for murder."

I watched Bixby's face for signs of how this information had been received. Cop that he was, he gave little away. His eyes stayed fixed on mine, his mouth serious.

"Did she do it?"

I sighed. "That, my dear Bixby, is a story for another time. And by another time, I mean a time when there aren't bars between us and cameras around us. Assuming that ever becomes a reality in my life."

"Your chances of that might be a lot better if you didn't insist on associating with known criminals and reprobates."

"Those criminals and reprobates happen to be the best chance I have at finding my mother."

"Maybe if you didn't have such a combative relationship with the police—"

"Maybe I wouldn't have such a combative relationship with the police if they hadn't almost gotten my mother killed!" I was irate, my fists clenched at my sides and my pulse pounding in my ears.

"What are you talking about?"

"Just forget it." I paced the abbreviated length of my cell, failing utterly to expend the burst of adrenaline that had left me shaky and hollow.

"Please, Jane. I really want to know."

"Four," I said.

"Four?"

"Four is the number of cops who were tried and convicted of corruption as a result of my mother's arrest and subsequent trial."

"What kind of corruption?"

"You fucking name it. Extortion. Perjury. Internal payoffs."

Bixby was silent, staring at my cell floor like he was the one on the wrong side of the bars.

"So you tell me, after the very people we were supposed to trust betrayed us at every turn, why I should place my faith in them?"

"Because not all cops are like that," he said.

"No," I said. "But all *humans* are like that. Everyone has their price."

"Even you?" Bixby asked.

"Even me."

"And what's yours?"

I didn't even have to think about it. The answer was there, ready always in my mind and on my tongue. "There's nothing I won't do to find my mother. Nothing."

Wisely, Bixby carried that line of conversation no further.

"Well, despite the fact that all cops are untrustworthy pigs, this one has spoken to his contacts here at the jail and asked them to take extra-good care of you."

"I'm not sure what *extra-good care* represents, but I appreciate it."

"Is there anything you need?" he asked. "Do you have any questions I can answer?"

A sudden surge of goodwill toward the terribly earnest eight-fingered dude-bro standing in front of me banished the hurricane of my rage. Or at least placed me close enough to its eye that I felt almost like myself, if only for the briefest moment.

"I do, actually," I said.

"Fire away—er—maybe that's not the best choice of words."

"I thought cops had to be clean-shaven. How is it you get to wear a goatee?"

"Special permission from the chief of police." He raised an expertly manscaped eyebrow at me. "Any other pressing questions?"

"Just one. Exactly how long does it take you to shape your goatee?"

"Really? You have a willing officer of the law in front of you and this is what you want to know?"

"I don't need exact numbers," I said. "Just, you know, ballpark it for me."

Bixby sighed and shook his head. "Have a good evening, Jane."

"Do you have to use special attachments?" I called after him. "What about product?"

"Good night, Jane."

He paused at the end of the hallway, waiting as one of the security gates buzzed open for him.

The sound of it sliding home provided the coda for this nightmare of a day.

I flopped backward on the cot and buried myself beneath the mound of scratchy, pill-balled blankets, praying sleep would find me before the memory did.

Murder. Murder. Murder.

My brain skipped back to the word again and again like a scratched record before adding its own unwelcome refrain.

Like mother, like daughter.

Chapter Three

I had spent a lot of time picturing myself in courtrooms over the last three years.

Of course, in these vivid fantasies, I was usually wearing a killer suit and gracefully pacing the length of the jury box, my hair in a sleek chignon as I stunned a jury slack-jawed with my *Law & Order*–worthy closing argument.

I'll tell you what I had never pictured—being the one in county jail–issued orange, sitting behind the defendant's table at my own arraignment, a stone-faced judge glaring down at me.

I'd only ever connected with the term *railroaded* in the most oblique way, but now it made frightening sense.

In the two days since I had been taken into custody, I could feel myself sliding toward a guilty verdict like a steam engine had been pushing me down greased tracks.

Foolishly, hopefully, and with a naïveté I had no right to after studying cases with far less compelling evidence than my own, I had reassured myself that any minute now, one of the guards would come marching down the hall, and I'd be released.

And in no small part because I hadn't actually killed anyone.

I mean, that *had* to be a thing at some point, didn't it?

Unfortunately, my attempts to convince Detective Kappas of this had failed miserably.

As had whatever strings Shepard had promised to pull.

Unless, of course, those strings had been an extra roll on my dinner tray and two phone calls instead of one.

A smarter woman, and perhaps a saner one, might have used those phone calls to reach a lawyer.

It wasn't like I didn't know any. On the contrary, the trouble was that I knew too many.

As an unofficial associate at one of Denver's most prestigious law firms, spreading the word that I'd been arrested wasn't exactly in the best interest of my career.

They find one dead guy in your bed and suddenly you're *that girl charged with murder.*

Not exactly the reputation you want following you around when you eventually plan to make a living at this whole law thing.

So, I hadn't called a lawyer.

I had called Valentine.

Of course, after I had finished asking if he had any leads on my mother and suggesting that he engage in extensive acts of self-sodomy for leaving for Seattle without me, Valentine had offered to send his own lawyer to represent me.

I had politely thanked him but declined, citing the fact that there are certain lawyers whose counsel you only employ when everyone already knows you're guilty, and I didn't have much use for one of those in my present situation.

My hand shook as I took a sip from the sweating water glass in front of me, the shackles on my wrist clinking as I brought it to my mouth. I glanced around the courtroom, a cavernous space with more polished wood than a museum of carpentry and blessedly free of anyone I knew.

Well, anyone but Detective Kappas, whom I covertly flipped a double-barrel bird to like the grown-ass independent woman that I am.

"This docket number 238-2-17, the *People v. Jane Marple Avery*, murder in the second degree."

Second degree. That was something, at least.

The court clerk handed a sheaf of papers up to the judge, who licked her thumb and flipped through the top few pages before squinting at me through the bottoms of her bifocal lenses.

"I understand that you've insisted on representing yourself in this matter, Miss Avery?" she asked.

"That is correct," I said.

"Splendid," Judge Alvarez said without enthusiasm. "And how do you plead?"

"Not guilty."

My mouth was open, but the words hadn't come from me. Someone at the back of the room had beaten me to it.

I turned as a whoosh of murmurs rose from the benches behind me, the solid clunk, clunk of the judge's gavel effectively cutting them short.

Sam Shook strode down the center aisle, his leather briefcase in one hand, an armful of papers in the other.

A strange rush of comingled gratitude and dread squeezed tears into my eyes at the sight of a familiar face.

The gratitude: it's my supervisor!

Dread: it's my supervisor.

Shook whisked into the cocounsel chair next to mine, dragging in his wake the scent of cologne and soap and clean wool. He gave me a small tired smile before setting his belongings down on the table.

The judge raised an eyebrow, seemingly not certain if she wanted to scold him or spank him.

Shook had that effect on women.

"Please state your name for the court records." Judge Alvarez leaned forward in her seat, bosomy in her black robe.

"My name is Sam Shook. I will be representing Miss Avery."

Shook's accent confirmed the origins hinted at by his honey-colored skin and wide dark eyes. That gentle Indian tilt of the tongue that turned *w*'s into *v*'s and panties into putty.

"I was under the impression that Miss Avery would be representing herself."

"She has since reconsidered that strategy," Shook said.

The judge set the papers down, her mouth flattening into an unamused line. "She's reconsidered in the last thirty seconds?"

Sam looked at me.

There was a question in that look.

Unlike Valentine or Shepard, it mattered to Sam Shook whether I had an opinion, and what that opinion might be.

He had come uninvited, my brilliant—if slightly dreamy—legal mentor, but I still had a choice.

"I've always been a quick reconsiderer," I said.

"All right. Proceed, Counselor," the judge said, motioning to the table where the prosecution sat, cologned and coffeed, smoothing the lapels of his suit jacket.

Even if District Attorney Vick Wiggins hadn't been the asshole ultimately responsible for charging me with murder, I'd still have wanted to dick-punch him on sight. Maybe it was the sandy blond hair of a uniform color that suggested a Just for Dudes dye job, blow-dried and hair-sprayed into a perfect Superman wave curling over his forehead. Or perhaps it was his face—the manufactured caramel of expensive spray tans and cheap leather. Then again, perhaps it was his smile—revealing teeth twice as large and twice as white as any human had business owning.

When he spoke, the Shatner-esque cadence of his words had the practiced quality of someone who had rehearsed them to himself in the small leather cockpit of a Mercedes on his way to the courthouse. "Because of the brutal nature of the crime, people request"—dramatic pause—"remand without bail."

"This is preposterous." Sam exhaled a lungful of air. Something between a sigh and a snort. "My client has no criminal record whatsoever. No prior offenses. She was the valedictorian of her law school class and has many friends in the local community in addition to gainful employment. She poses no flight risk."

That word, *valedictorian*, streamed light into my soul the way sunbeams climb through high cathedral windows. It had only recently become something I could lay claim to as the college had taken its sweet time correcting the error even after the revelation that Melanie Beidermeyer had been awarded the honor erroneously as part of the plot between her mother and Dean David Koontz. The fact that Melanie herself had been blowing the dean in a misguided attempt to earn what her mother had already arranged for had *somehow*, mercifully, been swept under the rug. As had Melanie's involvement in the files reported missing by her mentor, Kristin Flickner, before her untimely death at the beringed hands of Grace Beidermeyer.

I know, right?

And so, I swallowed my pride along with a sizable lump of bullshit and kept my mouth shut. In exchange I got my rightful valedictory honors, and she got to keep her job.

You're welcome, Melanie.

"Furthermore," Shook continued, "the case against my client is entirely circumstantial. Mr. Wiggins has failed to establish any motive or concrete physical evidence tying Miss Avery to the crime itself."

"More concrete than the victim being found in the defendant's apartment?" Wiggins theatrically brought his finger to a chin cleft that I suspected had more to do with a plastic surgeon's scalpel than genetics. "Or being shot with the same caliber gun—*unregistered gun*—that Miss Avery had next to her bed where he was found?"

"I'm sure Mr. Wiggins is well aware that Miss Avery's is not the only .38 in the world. No proof has yet been established that Miss Avery's gun was indeed the weapon used in Lucas Logan Bell's murder."

Lucas Logan Bell.

There was something maddeningly familiar about that triptych of syllables. Like a politician or a serial killer.

Detective Kappas had said it many times in the hours-long interrogation sessions at the police station. Then, as now, an alarming jangle of recognition followed it.

Where had I heard it before?

"We're still waiting on the ballistics test results." Wiggins pronounced the word *ballistics* with the kind of avid relish only a district attorney could summon.

"Well, perhaps if you had waited for those results before charging Miss Avery, I might be more sympathetic to your cause, Mr. Wiggins. As it stands, Mr. Shook"—the judge turned her attention to our table, pausing to reach up and toy with her white lace collar—"I am inclined to agree with you."

And that was no small part of Shook's charm. Getting people to agree with him.

In addition to turning granite-faced judges into coquettes, apparently.

"The court finds that Miss Avery poses no immediate threat to herself or the community, nor is she a flight risk. Bail is set at fifty thousand dollars." The judge brought her gavel down on its stand as punctuation.

We had been dismissed.

Wiggins gave a frustrated sigh and began jamming his papers into piles, muttering under breath that I was certain would smell like hollandaise.

"It doesn't matter," I whispered to Shook. "It could be fifty thousand or fifty million. I don't have it."

Shook didn't smile often, but when he did, I half expected a choir of fat cherubs to descend from the heavens, plucking their gilded harps and harmonizing on a single, heartrending note.

He reached into his pocket, withdrew a small slip of paper, and unfolded it.

A check.

A blank check.

I had a sneaking suspicion that I knew what the name at the top would be even before I glanced to confirm it.

Another three-name progression around which my life had begun to swing.

Archard Everett Valentine.

"Fortunately, you have friends who do," Shook said, all dimples and straight white teeth.

Friends who do.

Friends.

Friend.

The word had always felt spinier in my mouth than its rounded letters would suggest.

Friends are just people who haven't screwed you over yet, Janey.

One of my mother's more frequent assertions.

Did I have friends now?

Is this what friends did for you? Stand by you when all others flee? Defend you when others accuse you?

The two uniformed guards who had been responsible for transporting me to the courthouse hovered in the aisle, gently making their presence known.

"Looks like my ride is here," I said.

Shook nodded to them deferentially. "I'll be sending someone over to post your bail. You'll be out as soon as the paperwork is completed."

"You won't be coming to do it yourself?" A thin arrow of disappointment speared my chest. Somehow I had assumed his heroics would extend all the way to the scene where I flew into his arms, tears of gratitude streaming down my face as the heavy metal prison door clanged shut behind me.

At least, that's how it would have happened on *Law & Order*.

Or any decent Lifetime movie.

Shook ducked his head, a delicate expression of regret flowering on his face. "Unfortunately, I will be unable to as I have to catch a flight."

"A flight?" I asked. "To where?"

"Seattle."

My heart leapt beneath the coarse orange fabric over my chest.

"Why? What for?"

"I'm afraid the events of this weekend rather expedited the importance of the patent dispute case the firm has been engaged in."

"The 3-D microchip printing technology?" I asked, rather impressed with myself that I'd managed to produce the term. I'd been involved in several briefings wherein my eyes had glazed over once the words *Git repository* and *source code* had been mentioned. "Why? What happened?"

Shook's dark brows drew together as he searched my face. "Do you not remember?"

I scraped my memory for some connection between the facts of the case and my current circumstance but came up blank. "Remember what?"

Shook leaned in close, his breath sending a swarm of goose bumps down my arms as he whispered in my ear. "Lucas Logan Bell. The man who was found in your bed. He was the project's principal engineer."

Chapter Four

I felt my face doing what a wad of dough might if you spiked it on the end of a stick.

The revelation set off an avalanche of memories, the particulars of the case sifting through the screen of my memory.

BitSled, the Denver software development shop, claimed that theirs was the rightful patent governing the software for 3-D microchip printing technology. Trouble was, Oxbow Group, a larger and wealthier shop based in Seattle, claimed the exact same thing.

And this happened right about the time that the intellectual property forecasting engines determined the technology would be worth approximately $10 billion within two years.

BitSled had engaged our firm to file suit against Oxbow Group, and Shook, my mentor, was the lead litigator on the case.

Which meant that Lucas Logan Bell, as BitSled's lead tech dude, had spent a decent stretch of time answering Shook's famously sharp questions.

My mind flashed back to Bell's body. The details seared into the backs of my eyelids.

The pale flesh.

The grubby fingernails.

Usually, I'd allow myself a moment (or seven) to enjoy being right about his profession, but this had somehow been overshadowed by his being found naked and dead in my bed.

"I didn't sleep with him." The need to clarify this to Shook was suddenly as overwhelming as it was urgent. "I never even met him."

"I believe you," Shook said. "Just as I believe that you didn't kill him. But the fact that you were associated with a case in which he would be a key witness—"

"I know," I interrupted. TV shows generally got one thing right concerning cases like mine. Any solid connection between the accused and the victim, however tenuous, is bad.

"We do have one advantage." Shook dropped his voice and glanced around the courtroom, probably to make sure that Wiggins—or one of his small army of polished minions—wasn't lurking behind a nearby bench eavesdropping.

"What's that?" I asked.

"Wiggins obviously isn't aware of this particular connection yet, or he most certainly would have mentioned it. All the more reason to expedite the discovery phase of the BitSled case. Depositions must begin as soon as possible."

"Sure," I said. "Of course. As soon as I'm released—"

Shook reached out and patted the back of my hand. "Jane, as always, your dedication is admirable, but under the circumstances, it would be best for you to remain here in Denver."

"But you're my mentor," I insisted. "I'm supposed to shadow you, remember?"

"I do indeed, my protégé. But we feel it would be wisest for you to remain here. Lest it seem that your leaving is in some way related to this case."

I felt Gary Dawes in that *we*. The whole of his wrong name–saying, boob-ogling, penis-nosed, good ol' boy presence.

The founder of the law firm where I had interned and now served as junior associate had never liked me, as witnessed by the fact that he'd called me Jennifer the entire time I'd been in his employ.

Not that a superior disliking me was all that unusual. My misanthropic tendencies and legendary lack of patience for other people's bullshit tended to score me more enemies than friends, and for the most part, that never bothered me. It was the people like Dawes, whom I had tried and failed to charm, who sent my undies crawling up the canyon, so to speak.

"You're going to be taking all the depositions yourself?" I asked.

"Not by myself, exactly." The pause. The subtle sideways flick of his leonine eyes.

Guilt.

Which for Shook meant that whoever would be going with him was someone I wouldn't be happy about. And in our firm, that could be whittled down to one person.

"No," I said. "Not *her*."

"Since Kristin's death left Melanie without a mentor, Dawes thought perhaps it might be beneficial for me to mentor you *both*."

I drew air in through my nose and let it out of my mouth on a gusty sigh.

Smell the roses, blow out the candles.
Smell the roses, blow out the candles.

Nope. No good.

Blood shot up into my head along with a flash of limbic anger. I brought both of my shackled hands to my face, so I could press my index finger against the vein that commenced pulsing by my eye at the mere mention of Melanie's name despite our recent tenuous truce.

Maybe *truce* isn't the right word.

What do you call a relationship where one party (Melanie) promises to never try to sabotage you personally and professionally again and the other party (me) promises to try to overcome a laundry list of insults and grudges both real and imagined?

That.

We had that.

But *that* didn't seem like much at the moment.

It wasn't exactly because Melanie's mother, Grace Beidermeyer, had at one point tried to kill me, nor that the same mother and Dean David Koontz robbed me of the valedictory honors that had been rightfully mine. It wasn't even that Melanie was filthy stinking rich, constantly dressed in designer duds, or previously had a charming habit of pointing out my deficiencies in both attire and personality to anyone who happened to be in earshot.

It's that Melanie Beidermeyer was so damn . . . blonde. And beautiful. And bubbly.

And a multitude of other adjectives beginning with *b*. And also *D*. Two of them, in fact.

And now, Melanie's double Ds would be aimed solidly at Shook. *My* Shook.

I mean, he wasn't *my* Shook. Not in the biblical sense.

There had been no hanky. No panky. Not that the thought of either and/or both hadn't occasionally wandered into my head.

But I respected him enough to keep that distance.

Hell, I *liked* him, and I had sort of made a lifelong habit of not liking anyone. Now I'd have to share him not with just anyone, but with Melanie Fucking Beidermeyer.

What would become of our morning jam sessions? Our chats over coffee while trolling the neckbeards on the *Walking Dead* Reddit boards?

Would Melanie be part of those now too?

I could see it already.

Shook, behind his desk, sharing the coffee he'd brought from home because neither of us could abide Judy the paralegal's gritty caffeinated mud.

Melanie, complimenting his *Walking Dead* mug with the AK-47 handle.

Melanie, leaning across the desk just so, an expression of rapt interest pasted on her face.

Melanie, laughing at his jokes. That throaty chuckle that seemed to go straight to men's heads as the blood went straight to their cocks. Talking to him in her sweet-tea-on-the-veranda southern drawl.

The laughing. The leaning. The lash-batting.

All things I have never in my life been good at.

My heart turned small and cold in my chest. "So everyone's going to Seattle without me. I get it."

"Who is *everyone*, exactly?" Shook asked.

"You, Melanie, Valentine."

"Valentine is in Seattle? Why?" Concern drew his dark brows to the crease in the center of his otherwise smooth forehead. And I knew why.

Shook, after all, was still Valentine's divorce lawyer, and Valentine's divorce was still going hideously.

"Why don't you ask him?" I said. "You'll both be there."

Bratty? Sure.

Pouty? You bet your ass.

But after forty-eight hours in a holding cell and only intermittent conversations with Detective Kappas for relief, I was kind of done peopling.

"I'm afraid I don't understand why this is upsetting you so. Does it bother you that Melanie is going?"

Now why did he have to go and ask me a question like that? One that answering honestly would tell him much more than I would ever be comfortable with.

"Yes," I said. "Yes it does."

"I assure you, it is no favoritism on my part. I only want to make sure I discharge my duty to both of you."

Why did hearing this make me feel like I'd just been sucker punched in the gut?

I stuck my arms out so my transport officers could move my handcuffs into their behind-the-back traveling position. "I appreciate you showing up today," I said. "Doing your duty and all."

"Jane, that's not why I—"

"Good luck with the depositions," I said, turning to my armed escorts. "I'm ready. Let's go."

"I'll check in with you as soon as we've landed," Shook called after me.

I shuffled away at the processional speed allowed by my ankle restraints, refusing to look over my shoulder.

Never look back, Janey, my mother's voice echoed inside my head. *You might find something to regret.*

———

The *someone* Shook sent over to post bail turned out to be Shepard.

That everyone in the administration area jumped up from their desk and scattered like cockroaches when he stepped through the door was just icing on the shit sandwich.

When the last *t* was crossed and *i* dotted, they buzzed open the door to the Denver County Jail's small gray antechamber, where Detectives Bixby and Kappas were waiting for us.

"Shit," I said to Bixby. "Not you again." I felt a small filament of warmth at our standard greeting.

"Nice to see you too," Bixby said, his standard reply.

"Did you think of something else to arrest me for in the last hour?" I tugged the sleeves of my cardigan down over the red marks on my wrists where the handcuffs had been.

"We're not here for you. We're here for him." Kappas jerked his nearly nonexistent chin at Shepard, who folded his arms across his considerable chest.

"Why?" Shepard asked, veteran of impenetrable one- and two-word answers.

"Just to talk," Kappas said. "We have a few questions."

"About what?"

"About a lot of things."

"I already gave a statement at the crime scene."

"Oh, this isn't about the murder Miss Avery is charged with. It's about the recent shooting of your ex-wife's lover. Though the details of the crimes are oddly similar, actually. One shot. Right between the eyes." Kappas mimed a gun with his hand, clicked with his tongue as his stubby index finger landed between his own bushy brows.

I felt my face go numb, a high-pitched buzzing in my ears.

Detective Kappas was looking at me. Gauging whether I had known this by my reaction.

I hadn't.

I *had* known Shepard had a criminal record.

In fact, Bixby had told me about Shepard's criminal record shortly before he lost a couple of fingers to a sniper's bullet.

A sequence that had caused me considerable consternation at the time.

In the wake of several unwelcome revelations that followed, Shepard had extended the invitation to peek at his alarmingly long rap sheet and I had surprised myself by telling him I didn't want to know. Whatever he had done, whoever he was before I'd met him, I wanted to let him keep that.

God knew we had lied to each other. I to him and he to me. Resuming a working relationship had meant giving each other a clean slate.

And now we had his-and-her murder allegations.

"So what do you say?" Kappas asked. "Can we talk?"

"It's not a good time." Shepard shouldered past him. His face had gone mask-tight, his mouth set in the hard line I had come to know and dread.

Kappas grabbed Shepard's forearm.

Several employees beyond the bulletproof window gasped, their hands floating to their mouths.

Shepard's jaw tensed, the cords rising beneath the smooth skin of his neck. He glared down at Kappas's fingers, his gaze looking like it might incinerate them on sight. "*Don't* put your hands on me."

I didn't realize I had been holding my breath until it came whooshing out when Kappas released his grip. "Quite a temper," he tsked, wagging an index finger at Shepard before dropping his hand back to his side. "Especially when I'm just trying to help you. You've had enough run-ins with the law over the years that I would think you'd be eager to help us in eliminating yourself as a suspect."

"And talking with you is going to accomplish that *how?*"

"We just need a quick rundown of your alibi. Nothing major. We don't even have to go to the police station. We can talk right here. I'm sure they'd let us borrow a conference room."

"And Jane could sit in?" Shepard glanced over at me, something like worry in his eyes.

"I'm afraid not," Kappas said. "We can't reveal the details of our investigation. And particularly not to someone who's been charged with second-degree murder in a separate case."

"And *I've* been charged with her safety," Shepard said. "I'm not leaving her alone."

Kappas spread his hands to the cinder-block walls surrounding us. "It doesn't get much safer than this building. Metal detectors. Guards. Closed-circuit cameras. Tell me you have a facility half as secure as that."

Shepard wouldn't tell him, but he did. He maintained a healthy network of safe houses with tech twice as sophisticated as what the state allocated to its prison system.

But that's not what was on his mind, and I knew it.

Shepard wasn't so much worried about people getting into the jail as he was about trying to keep me from getting out.

Without his supervision, of course.

Dollars to doughnuts said that Valentine had tasked him with trying to keep me here in Denver, and Shepard had already been thinking about exactly how he would make that happen.

"Could you maybe handcuff her to something while we're talking?" Shepard asked. "A file cabinet or something bolted to the floor?"

"I'm afraid that won't be possible." Bixby shifted on his feet, drawing himself up to his full height—several inches shorter than Shepard despite his best efforts. "Now that she's posted bail, we can't legally hold her here anymore."

"What about you?" Shepard said, pointing to him. "You could keep an eye on her."

"Why does anyone need to keep an eye on me?" I asked.

Shepard and Bixby exchanged a commiserating glance that I cared for not at all.

"No can do, bro," Bixby said. "As part of this investigation, I'll need to sit in on the questioning."

"I'm not your bro."

The only reasonable thing to do here was put Shepard out of his misery. "Go," I said, sitting down in one of those industrial chairs that always seemed to have bits of food and finger grease woven into the fabric of the armrest. "I'll wait for you."

Shepard considered me with narrowed eyes. "If I leave you here, you're not going to run away?"

"I absolutely positively swear I will not run away," I said, holding my hand over my heart.

"Don't worry," Kappas said, nodding to the desk attendant who buzzed the door open for them. "This won't take long."

Shepard followed them in, the door closing heavily behind them.

As soon as it clicked closed, I stood, smiled at the attendant, and strolled out.

After all, I had promised I wouldn't *run*.

And I was a woman of my word.

Recently.

Chapter Five

Shook's expression when he saw me standing at the end of his aisle on the plane was somewhere between mild shock and total panic. Which on him looked charming as fuck.

"Jane?" Shook asked. "But how did you—where did you—I thought you were—"

At the mention of my name, Melanie, who was stationed in the window seat, looked up from her iPad abruptly.

"Why, Jane! What on earth are you doing here?" she said, pressing cotton candy–pink lacquered nails to a blouse of the exact same hue. Like Shook, her voice still betrayed some of the accent derived from her origins, despite what I was certain had been a concerted effort on her part to lose it. It was the kind of gentle twang that conjured wraparound porches, sweet tea, and copious amounts of hair spray.

Hair spray that Melanie never seemed to need because her hair was always already fucking perfect.

"My job," I said. "We work for the same firm, remember?"

Melanie grinned at me, fuchsia lips tipping up into a smile that looked almost genuine. It was a quality of hers I admired, albeit grudgingly, this ability to put on a happy face despite having two parents in prison. I reminded myself that that same smiling mouth also had Dean David Koontz's dick in it at one point, and I felt a little better.

"Well, of course I remember, honey," she said. "I just didn't think you'd be joining us is all."

Was it surprise I was hearing in her voice?

Or disappointment?

"Well, here I am," I said. "Lucky for me the flight was delayed, isn't it?"

The passenger behind me cleared his throat, irritated at my holding up the show.

"Well, my seat's back by the bathroom," I said. "Last-minute ticket and all that."

Shook looked from me to Melanie. A protracted glance during which he was deciding something.

"Melanie, would you mind if I sit with Jane?" Ever polite. Ever respectful.

"Mind? Why would I mind?" Melanie asked, wearing a face that looked like she'd just sniffed a dirty diaper. "I'm sure you two have a lot to discuss."

"Thanks, Mels," I said, using the nickname I'd overheard one of her sorority sisters employing once upon a time.

Shook retrieved his laptop bag from the bin overhead and stepped into the aisle in front of me. "Would you like me to bring your bag back?"

"No," I said. Mostly because I didn't have one. Time hadn't allowed for me to do anything but hire an Uber straight from the jail to the airport. I had my phone, my wallet, and the clothes I was wearing. The rest, I'd have to improvise.

We abandoned our assigned seats and found two together directly across from the bathroom, lucky me, and slid into them. Shook gave me the window seat, taking the middle for himself.

"How did you know which flight we would be on?" he asked.

The answer to this was as complex as it was unseemly.

"Well, you know Judy hates me, right?"

Judy, the firm's steel-haired, iron-twatted paralegal, made a habit of finding new and inventive ways to sabotage me professionally. Mixing up my appointments, losing the paperwork I'd given her to copy, et cetera.

Shook didn't bother to deny it. "She does seem to address you with a certain . . . coolness."

"She once booked me a flight to Detroit when everyone else was traveling to San Antonio."

"That was an unfortunate incident, yes," he said, the barest trace of a smile playing about his dusky lips.

"And you remember that time she sent me a meeting invite for an appointment with a judge who didn't exist in a courthouse that was demolished ten years ago?"

"Perhaps she hasn't provided the most reliable assistance to you on certain occasions," he conceded.

"Your talent for understatement is truly astounding," I said. "Anyway. She makes appointments and meetings private so that only the people she's invited can see the details. One evening after she'd left, I logged in to her computer and gave myself administrative access to her Outlook calendar so that I could check what the actual travel arrangements and appointments were."

"How were you able to log in to her account? I find it unlikely that she would have willingly shared her password with you."

"I had a hunch." And that hunch had gotten me in on my first try.

IhateJaneAvery.

Case-sensitive, of course.

"I see," Shook said.

What *I* could see was Sam Shook working around to a way to ask me what the hell I thought I was doing here—in the politest possible terms, of course.

I elected to save him the trouble.

"Look, I know you wanted me to stay in Denver, but there is no way I can just sit by while you and Melanie investigate the case that's directly related to the murder someone is obviously trying to frame me for."

"Are you certain that was your motive?" Shook asked.

"What do you mean?"

"I mean, are you certain it wasn't just the fact that Melanie was accompanying me that motivated you to come?"

"Yes."

No.

Maybe.

Is it a lie if you don't know the true answer yourself?

Shook shifted in his seat, refolding his abnormally long legs, a real liability when you're flying economy. His boarding pass fluttered out of his shirt pocket, landing on the floor between us.

Sahem Ashook.

His legal name, but not the name he used to practice law.

I sometimes forgot that he'd stripped the name he'd been born with of several vowels in order to convey what he described as *the right impression.*

"I promise I won't be any trouble. I just want to sit in on the meetings. See what I can find out. I'll be quiet as a mute mouse. You won't even know I'm there."

"I highly doubt that." From the bemused expression on his face, it was impossible for me to tell how he meant it. "And anyway, trouble seems to find you whether you want it or not."

"You're not wrong about that."

"Not wrong." A sly little grin tugged at the corner of his mouth closest to me. "Jane Avery, have you ever in your life said the words *you are right*?"

"I'm sure I have." I reached up and aimed the air-conditioning nozzle down at my face, only moments away from fanning myself with the catalog hawking solar-powered foot massagers and robot butlers. Something about being this close to Sam Shook, breathing the same air, made me feel a little dizzy. "I just don't remember when. Or to whom."

The plane lurched backward as we pulled away from the gate.

I watched the world through the small porthole of double-paned safety glass, waiting for that breathless moment marking the transition from earth to sky.

Sam's dark head had tipped back against the headrest, his eyes falling closed, his breathing regular. I looked at the long, dark lashes feathered against his prominent cheekbones. The way his skin darkened just below his eyes. The tender creases of his eyelids. He had lovely lips, Shook did. Not overly full, but beautifully formed.

For a split second, I could imagine exactly how they'd feel pressed against mine. How and where they would meet, those two different and distinct shapes coming together.

Then I had to look away.

There's something terribly vulnerable about people when they sleep.

Everyone except for my mother, who, in the few times I'd not conked out before her, managed to retain her characteristic stubborn-chinned resolve even then.

I wondered where my mother had been sleeping lately.

If she had been sleeping.

We'd always been a pair of insomniacs. Falling asleep not in our beds, but together on the couch, the flicker of vintage cartoons painting our faces in Technicolor. Her head at one end of the sofa, mine at the other, one well-used quilt covering us both.

She always made sure I had most of the blanket we shared on those long lonely nights. Just as she'd always made sure to check the window and door locks no fewer than three times before we settled in.

Better safe than sorry, Janey.

Safe and I were no longer on speaking terms.

Sorry I understood all too well.

I leaned my head against the window, feeling the cold from the stratosphere chill my cheek. Wind pushed a scrim of tiny droplets against the glass. A preview of the gray Seattle skies we were hurtling toward.

I only hoped that my mother was under them too.

That it was *toward* her that I was flying.

I'm coming, Mom, I told the universe at large.

I'm coming.

Chapter Six

A mere four hours later, and I was already contemplating homicide.

Perhaps it's not the most flattering thing to admit about myself, that I was already considering the violent murder of a man I'd just met while having been officially charged with the murder of another, but fuck it.

I'd vowed to tell the truth, hadn't I?

His name was Tyler Dixon, and I was going to kill him.

My would-be victim was the Lucas Logan Bell equivalent at Oxbow Group, and he'd managed to insult me no less than four times in the first five minutes of our acquaintance.

I'd been sitting in the chilly corporate conference room, making notes on an actual by-God yellow legal pad when I had the distinct feeling that I was being watched.

And by watched, I mean stared at.

And by stared at, I mean eyeball-slapped.

I looked up to find the *man*—and I use the term in the loosest sense possible here—in the seat next to mine regarding me with all the affection usually reserved for a turd in the punch bowl.

"Am I the only one who doesn't know who the hell she is?" he asked, rocking his chair back onto its hind legs, hands jammed into the kangaroo pouch of his black Pac-Man hoodie.

This question prompted Curt Allen, Oxbow Group's chief technology officer, to make the formal introductions.

Tyler's first comment to me had not been *hello* or *how are you*, but "The print on your skirt makes your hips look wide."

Then, there had been the doughnuts. Which I, in a gesture of kindness, had picked up as a potential bribe for the software development team Shook informed me we would be meeting. Tyler's contribution: "What are you, some kind of plebe? This is Seattle. We eat Top Pot doughnuts here."

But what really sealed his fate was what he said to me after Melanie arrived with an armful of breakfast burritos and her shirt unbuttoned enough to show a solid two inches of cleavage, both of which the team fell on like a pack of hungry jackals.

Tyler's whispered assessment: "Don't you find it difficult to work with her?"

Me (thinking he might be redeemable after all): "Because she's so bubbly you want to kick her veneers in?"

Tyler: "No. Because she's more attractive than you in every way."

Me: *Smell the roses, blow out the candles. Smell the—*

Tyler: "What kind of perfume are you wearing?"

Me: "I'm not."

Tyler: "Could you?"

And so on.

As far as the rest of the development team, they mostly reacted to our presence the way a colony of prairie dogs would to stray coyotes wandering through their camp. Big eyes. Lots of head ducking and chattering.

"So, there were two copies made of BitSled's Git repository." Shook, who sat at Curt's left near the head of the table, held up two long, slim fingers.

"What does *G-i-t* stand for?" I asked.

Next to me, Tyler sighed, dropping his head into his hands. He had the kind of neat Poindexter side-part that made you want to reach over and give him atomic noogies. Well, maybe it wouldn't make *you* want to do that, but you could very well be a more emotionally developed human than I am.

Don't judge me.

"*Git* doesn't stand for anything," Tyler said to the polished wood veneer of the table. "Linus Torvalds named the concept after himself, referring to himself by the English slang word *git*. Which I'm assuming you're familiar with the meaning of."

"Idiot," I said. If he assumed that I was providing the meaning of said word, more's the pity.

"What exactly is a Git repository?" Melanie, who had only picked the sprinkles off the doughnut in front of her, had her iPad out and was taking notes with a sparkly pink stylus.

"A Git repository is a distributed software control system using internal index files and unidirectional cyclic graphs to tightly pack the codebase and allowing multiple teams to concurrently commit and share code with full version control," Tyler rattled off with dispassionate efficiency.

Melanie cleared her throat. "Thanks, sugar. Now, could someone *else* explain to me what a Git repository is?"

But the honor of explanation went to Curt, some kind of tech-nerd tribal law, perhaps.

"So, a repository is a way of tracking a file and any changes that happen to that file. Have you read *Harry Potter*?" he asked gently.

"I watched the movies," Melanie said.

I thought I detected a slight shift of disappointment in Curt's features. "Right. Well, think about a repository like Gringotts bank. When you walk in, a little goblin writes your name down in the logbook. With me so far?"

Melanie nodded, leaning forward with her hand tucked under her chin and her boobs riding up another solid inch from resting on her forearm.

I would have sworn I could hear the succession of ten small thumps beneath the table as each and every developer present popped wood.

"Well, after your name is recorded in the logbook you go to the counter, where you set down everything you plan to put into your vault. Another little goblin counts and records it, then writes that in the logbook too."

"Oh," Melanie said, her mouth an exaggerated oval. "So, just like the Gringotts goblins record you and your deposit, a repository maps who made what changes to the codebase, when they made them, and exactly what those changes were?"

"Exactly!" Curt said, seeming pleased.

My antennae perked up as I glanced at Melanie with narrowed eyes. She had rattled that off just a little too easily.

"So, we know two copies of BitSled's Git repository were made," Shook said, bulkily steering the ship of conversation back to the facts of the case. "We have one of those copies in our possession. The other is, as of this time, unaccounted for."

"I know this is a silly question and maybe you can't answer." Curt slid an expensive-looking pen through his thumb and forefinger, drawing them down the surface before flipping it and beginning again. "But is there a reason BitSled's principal engineer didn't accompany you? I thought surely he'd be the one to review the code. Even if the firm did employ an outside forensics investigator." Curt's small dark eyes flicked to the straight-faced suit at Shook's side.

Meanwhile, the mere mention of the words *principal engineer* was enough to send a cold bead of sweat crawling down my ribs. I quickly sandwiched my elbows to my sides to cover any potential pit-stains as my heart hammered in my chest.

"I'm afraid he was . . . unable to join us," Shook said. "Though he had already provided us all the information we need to conduct discovery."

"So *that's* why we're here?" Melanie leaned forward on the table, the contact hiking her boobs up toward her neck a further inch. "To look for the missing copy?"

I cleared the wad of fear from my throat, sitting up straighter in my chair. "No," I said. "We're here to compare our copy of the BitSled code repository to Oxbow Group's repository."

"And why would we do that?" she asked, using the sugary-stupid tone she employed whenever anyone in possession of a dick was present.

"Because then we'll know exactly who arrived at the technological solutions first, and how they did it," I said. "And, we'll also be able to tell if Oxbow Group's repository happens to resemble BitSled's code in any ways that are problematic."

Tyler snorted beside me. "You didn't know that *Git* wasn't an acronym, but you knew that?"

I turned my torso to face him fully, leaning in much farther than I knew he was comfortable with.

"I like to surprise people with my competence," I said.

Truth was, I'd done some mad googling using the airplane's Wi-Fi while Shook slept. I've never been able to sleep on planes and the presence of a certain exceptionally attractive seatmate hadn't helped that situation in the least.

"I'm certain you will not find that Oxbow Group's code resembles BitSled's in the least," Curt said. "Tyler is the most scrupulous record keeper I've ever worked with. Nothing happens in that codebase that he doesn't know about."

"Before we begin to review the code, I believe Mr. Smith had a couple of questions he would like to ask," Shook said.

Mr. Smith was the kind of man who looked like his face might shatter if he ever attempted something so frivolous as a smile.

I half expected a puff of dust to appear when he cleared his throat.

"Has the repository ever been rebased?"

Curt looked not at Mr. Smith, but at Melanie, already anticipating the question forming on her features. "Rebasing the repository is like magically creating a thousand goblins and having them each rewrite a log entry with what *you* tell them to. And no," he said, turning to Smith. "Our repository has never been rebased."

"That's not true," Tyler said.

I felt the vibration in the bottom of my seat when his chair at last thumped down onto all fours.

Curt's cheeks colored a rosy pink. "That's right. I think I'd blocked out the whole Jimmy Hinson affair."

A rash of snickers broke out among the engineers at the table.

"What is it?" Shook asked. "Who is Jimmy Hinson?"

"Jimmy was one of our JavaScript developers," Curt said.

"Was?" Shook glanced at me. A quick flick of the eyes anyone else might have missed. For a split second, I thought our minds must have gone to the same place. That perhaps Jimmy's employment as well as his life had been ended by a bullet to the head.

"Yes. He resigned after the incident that resulted in our needing to rebase the repository."

More snickers.

"And what was the incident you're referring to?" Smith asked.

"Horse porn," one of the developers at the end of the table said. "Jimmy accidentally uploaded his entire collection."

The developers took turns lobbing the titles at each other like tennis balls.

"Cunt-ucky Derby."

"Ridin' Dirty."

"Brokeback Mountin'."

"Fifty Shades of Neigh."

One of the snickers broke into full-on laughs when someone whinnied seductively.

"That couldn't have had anything to do with why he quit." Tyler's voice was an odd mix of sulky and disgusted.

"So he *did* resign?" Smith asked, jotting notes on his pad. "He wasn't fired?"

"It's a surprisingly easy mistake to make," Curt explained. "Anyone can do it with a single line of code. There are no safeguards. No double checks."

"And who was it that rebased the code after the *incident*?" Smith asked.

The room fell silent, the last pained neigh dying an abrupt death on the air.

"I did," Tyler said.

"You'll find that my principal engineer kept excellent records," Curt said almost defensively. "Everything you need to know about the rebasing is there and ready for review. Isn't that right, Dix?"

"Dix?" Smith asked.

I squelched an involuntary laugh of my own. The appropriateness of its phonetic pronunciation hit me with full force.

"Short for Dixon," Tyler said, cutting his eyes to Smith. He glanced back at Shook, his head twitching short and sharp toward the right. "This is the best you could bring? This idiot can't even follow a conversation and he's the one who's going to review *my* code repository?"

It had often been my experience that extra helpings of smarts didn't leave much room on the plate for social skills. But I was beginning to suspect Tyler might be on a different spectrum entirely. Come to think of it, *spectrum* might have been the operative word.

"Mr. Smith is the most respected data forensics analyst in the city of Seattle," Shook said. "He came most highly recommended by several clients we've represented in the past."

"Respect comes from people, and people are stupid."

I bit down hard on my lip, hoping it mirrored the dismay I saw on the faces around the conference room table.

I'd actually had this thought on a regular basis, but Tyler actually *said* it.

Like, out loud.

"Perhaps we should take a brief break and reconvene in fifteen minutes." Leave it to Shook to suggest the thing most likely to defuse a tense situation.

Tyler was on his feet and out of the conference room first. He moved with a kind of pigeon-toed shuffle that let me know his Vans sneakers would be worn on the insides. Just as I knew that his stoop-shoulder posture was an attempt to make himself smaller in a world whose currency didn't interest him in the least.

Melanie reached down and plucked her wallet out of her purse, turning delicate shoulders to Shook. "I think I'm going to get myself some coffee from the café downstairs. Can I pick up something for you?"

The pleased expression on Shook's face filled me with a sudden and murderous rage.

Why didn't *I* think to offer to get him coffee?

Because you're an asshole, came my brain's instant reply.

Apparently, it wasn't just my conscious self that had committed to telling the truth.

"That would be most appreciated, Miss Beidermeyer," Shook said.

"Now, now." Melanie gently poked a finger at his bicep, a part of Shook I may or may not have daydreamed about tenderly palpating for shape and lickability on occasion. "It's Melanie. You are my mentor after all."

I hoped they hadn't heard my knuckles crack as my fists tightened.

"Okay, Melanie. I'll have a quad shot latte, please. What about you, Jane?" Shook asked, volunteering Melanie to get something for me by extension.

"None of that rocket fuel for me," I said, painfully aware of my tendency to become a twitching, spastic head case with the addition of even minimal caffeine and/or sugar. "Sugar-free vanilla steamer or whatever they have like it."

"Isn't that pretty much just hot milk?" Melanie asked, her giggle inviting Shook to do the same.

I folded my arms across my chest, drawing myself to my full height much like I'd seen Bixby do in Shepard's presence. "It's been a stressful couple of days."

"Well, all right." Melanie slung her pink Prada purse over her shoulder. "Be back in two shakes of a lamb's tail."

"Okeydokey," I said, simultaneously mimicking her brightness and wishing the aforementioned lamb a virulent case of syphilis.

"Are you all right?" Shook's eyes were the textbook configuration known as concern.

"Fine," I said. Then, remembering my promise, "No. Not fine. I'm exhausted and brain-dead and more raw than a hooker's twat on payday."

"Your mother?" he asked.

I nodded, then quickly summarized the personal ad and everything that had happened since I'd last updated him on the status of my mother's ongoing absence. "Which reminds me," I said. "I need to go make a call."

"Of course." Shook stepped out of the way, chivalrous as any knight. "And Jane?"

I looked back at him from the carpeted corporate hallway. "Yes?"

"If there is anything I can do." That smile again. "Anything at all."

"Thank you," I said. "I appreciate it."

I wandered over to a maze of abandoned cubicles and sat down, eyeing my phone like a big fat spider in my palm.

To google the number I needed, I was going to have to turn it on. And when I turned it on, I was going to have a message from Shepard, and that message was going to be not pleased.

I took a deep bracing breath and punched the button.

Three messages.

What the actual fuck?

U said u wouldn't run away. What happened to "I'll wait for u"

I thought you weren't fucking lying anymore?

I didn't run, I walked, I typed with infinite patience and honesty. Also, I didn't say *where* I would wait for you.

The reply winged back fast enough to startle me when the phone pinged in my hand.

I will find u.

And though his message was stalkery enough that my skin should have crawled, it only succeeded in producing sympathetic twinges in my lady bits. All save for the *u*, which had my lady boner all *exeunt stage left*.

But I knew he was right.

Shepard would find me.

He always did.

Sounds fun, I texted back, feeling feckless and smart-assy. Can't wait.

That's because you don't know what you're waiting for.

I closed my text app, punched up the interwebs, and tracked down the *Mile High Grapevine*'s customer service number.

An automated recording answered, the polite female voice instructing me to listen carefully as menu options had changed.

After pressing 4 several times and ending up in a phone routing hole, I opted for 3 on the next round. A tired female voice answered on the second ring.

"Hi," I said, relieved to have reached a human. "Is this the *Mile High Grapevine* administrative offices?"

"Yeah."

"Great," I replied. "Can you connect me to the classified and personals department? I keep getting dropped in a hole when I try and reach it through the automated system."

She let go of an irritated sigh. "Fine."

I heard a click, then another equally unenthusiastic female voice came over the line.

"Classified and personal ads, how may I help you?"

"Hi," I said, "I actually have kind of a strange question for you."

"No, you may not include a picture of your genitalia with your ad."

"That's actually not—"

"And no, I will not tell you what I'm wearing."

"I don't want either of those things."

"Oh," she said, sounding both piqued and relieved. "Then what's your question?"

"I need to find out about a personal ad that was run in the Saturday afternoon edition of the paper."

"You have to follow the instructions provided in the ad to contact the person placing it. You don't do that through us."

"That's just the thing," I said in a hurry, sensing her finger hovering over the disconnect button. "There weren't any."

"We get thousands of ads every week. There's no way I can—"

"I think the person who placed it might be in serious trouble." A beat of silence. "Please," I pleaded.

"What is the text of the ad you're referring to?"

"The title was 'Intelligent Brunette Seeks Rescue.'"

"Hold on," she sighed. Then, "Yes. I've located that ad."

"I'd like to know the name of the person who submitted it."

"I'm afraid I can't give you that information."

I could feel my blood pressure rising. A spike digging behind my left eyeball. "Can you at least tell me how it was placed?"

"We received the submission via our website."

My heart leapt. "Do you have an IT department you could connect me to? They might be able to give me an IP address."

"I could connect you," she said, "but it would be a waste of your time. They're not authorized to give out that information either."

"Could you please just transfer me?"

There was silence, then a click and a high, nasal male voice. "What?"

"Well, hi there," I said, conjuring Melanie's syrupy accent to the best of my ability. Hell, it had worked on other people who possessed penises. "I was wondering if you might be able to help me with a little something."

"All vendors need to go through the sales department," the voice said.

Then the motherfucker hung up on me.

The dial tone stung in my ear.

The potential lies I could have told to get the information I wanted gathered in my head like gloating ghosts. I could almost hear their wavering voices.

If only you hadn't abandoned us, Jane. We would have helllllped yooooou.

"Fuck," I growled. "Fuck fuck *fuck*."

"You did that all wrong," a disembodied voice said.

I stood, peeking over the cubicle wall in the direction the voice had come from. I had been mistaken. The cubicles weren't *all* abandoned. One held three monitors, one keyboard, one chair, and Tyler.

"Never try sexual persuasion with tech support guys. They don't get laid enough. Try offering to level them up on *World of BattleCraft* or work in a few obscure fandom references." Tyler didn't look up from the configuration of screens, two of which flashed a proliferation of dialogue boxes and other kinds of technological wizardry that I couldn't even begin to guess at. The third showed a first-person shooter game where Tyler was currently decimating any number of unsuspecting opponents. Beneath his flying fingers were two separate keyboards that didn't look so much like keyboards as they did the control panel of a spaceship glowing red and blue.

"They let principal engineers game at work?"

"I'm not a principal engineer," he said, typing something into one of the black boxes with his left hand while pulling off a headshot with the right.

Ambidexterity.

I'd known this was a thing but never actually seen someone with that particular talent. It was odd and a little discomfiting. Like stumbling across a unicorn in a cow pasture.

"What are you, then?" I asked.

"I'm a genius who happens to earn his living by tech."

"And humble too," I said.

"Humility is an artifice of the weak-minded. When you're as good as I am, you don't need it."

"You're that good, huh?"

"Better," he said. "Hyperhidrosis or poor hygiene. Which is it?"

"Which is what?"

"The perspiration. You were sweating profusely. Your hands left fog prints on the conference room table. Also, I can tell by the wrinkle patterns on your shirt and skirt that you've sat in them longer than twelve hours, which suggests more than one day of wear."

"What are you, the Asperger's answer to Sherlock Holmes?"

"Yes," he said, directly acknowledging what I had begun to suspect. "Only less derivative. Oh," he added almost conversationally, "it's not hyperhidrosis *or* poor hygiene that had you sweating. It's because of this."

His fingers stopped abruptly as he sat back from the desk.

To my abject horror, what appeared on the center of the three monitors was my own puffy, mascara-streaked face with a black box containing a series of letters and numbers just below it.

My mug shot.

Chapter Seven

Several more images of me surfaced behind my mug shot.

Me at the airport. Me stepping off the airport curb to the waiting taxi. Me inside this very building, waiting for the elevator.

I could taste the panic on my tongue, coppery as an old penny.

"How?" I asked.

"Facial recognition software," Tyler said. "I wrote a program that compares sixty-seven points of craniofacial recognition to any images available both on the Internet and on a grid of security cameras."

"But how did you get an image of my face to search by?"

"I took your picture in the dev meeting."

He had had his face in his phone the entire time. It wasn't difficult to imagine him angling that phone at me when I was paying attention to some other bit of conversational fluff.

"Aside from my mug shot, why are the only images from security cameras in Seattle?"

"Because I've only been able to plug the code into the backend of certain local security companies."

The subtext behind what he'd just said could have choked a horse. Or a hooker. Or even a horse hooker.

"Okay, but seriously, do you have any idea how illegal this is? This represents a violation of so many rights and laws, I can't even begin to name them all." Though I dearly wanted to. Something about being in

Tyler's presence brought out the need to spit facts and figures, titles and subsections. To prove I knew even one thing he didn't.

"It's proprietary," he said. "For my personal use only."

"Nope. Still doesn't make it legal."

Tyler shrugged. "So sue me."

"Someone could."

"They'd lose."

"And why is that?"

"Because I'm smarter than they are."

"Doesn't that depend on the lawyer?"

"No."

Because he truly believed he was smarter than everyone.

In my head, I had begun to tally his comments in one of two columns: *Asshole* or *Sociopath*. I mentally put a tick mark in the latter.

"So why did you write the program anyway? Are you some kind of weird voyeur?"

"I'm *the* weird voyeur."

"This is probably not something you should tell people."

"Why not?"

"Because they might just get the impression that you're not exactly right in the head."

"They think that anyway."

"Maybe if they knew *why* you felt the need to write a software program like this, they wouldn't think those things." And by *they*, I meant *me*.

"It's not worth explaining."

"Because it's complicated?"

"Because I don't think you're bright enough to follow me."

Before I could contemplate how much Tyler might benefit from a swift slap to the back of his head, I heard voices down the hallway. I searched the strange terrain of his keyboards, slapping keys as I whisper-hissed at him. "Put this away! Now!"

"Don't!" His voice ratcheted up to the high, thin decibels of panic. "Don't touch!"

Our hands collided as we both slapped. Me at the keyboard, him at my fingers.

And because the universe is a dick, Curt and one of the other developers chose precisely that moment to walk around the corner. So I did the only logical thing a girl could in that circumstance.

I sat on Tyler Dixon's desk.

Positioning myself directly in the line of sight between Curt's bifocals and Tyler's screen, then quickly laughing and ruffling Tyler's hair. "So tell me, do you compile your own kernel or—"

They stopped.

They stared.

"Oh hi!" I conjured a casual ease I didn't feel. "We're just having ourselves a chat." And a minor apoplectic fit, on Tyler's end. "We'll catch you back in the conference room, yeah?" I said by way of gentle dismissal.

"Um . . . yeah," Curt said. They walked away robotically, faces screwed up into strange, discomfited expressions.

I turned to Tyler once they were out of sight, quickly sliding off his desk. "Why did they look like they'd just seen an eight-legged goat?"

Tyler pointed to one of the "No Trespassing" signs on the cubicle's exterior wall. On the bottom, someone had taped a handwritten addendum: *No touching. Anything. Ever.* An asterisk on the word *touching* led me to the bottom of the sign, where additional words had been added in a slightly smaller script: **This includes equipment as well as the developer using it.*

"Sorry," I said. "I didn't know you had a thing."

"I have a lot of things," he said. "Beyond that, you might want to consider your lack of foresight next time you do something like that."

"My lack of foresight?"

"Your underwear. Or lack thereof. Did you kill him?" Tyler was already typing again, chains of numbers sliding across the shining surfaces of his eyes. "Lucas Logan Bell." Impatience threaded tightness into a voice already an octave higher than the men I listened to on a regular basis. I wasn't keeping up. "Did you kill him?"

"I didn't. And I also didn't fuck him, if that was going to be your next question."

"It wasn't. Lucas Logan Bell never would have slept with you."

I steeled myself for the insult that was surely coming, the reason why no man in his right mind would copulate with a creature so unprepossessing as myself. "Unattractive?" I suggested, beating him to the punch.

"Female."

Little alarm bells sounded somewhere deep in my brain. "He was gay? How do you know that?"

"LARP."

"LARP?" I repeated. "Is that some kind of obscure sex cult or something?"

"Live action role-playing."

"And this is different from some kind of obscure sex cult because . . ."

"LARP is a game where the players actually act out the battle. Everyone has a character and weapons and abilities that they use to achieve a desired goal or target. The outcome of battles is governed by a specific set of rules mediated by the game master and the players."

"I see. And this is something both you and Lucas Logan Bell did?"

"Yes. We're in different kingdoms, but part of the order governing a shared geographical region."

"Kingdoms? There are kingdoms?"

"And duchies, and parks, and glades and households. Anyway, the governing leaders from one duchy will often interact with the governing leaders from another. Lucas was the champion for the Duchy of the Iron Mountains just like I'm the champion for the Duchy of the Inland

Ocean. That's how I knew him. And as far as how I knew he was gay, his battle tag is Lord BoneSmuggler. I made a solid deduction."

Excitement made my heart flutter in my chest.

If he was gay, then there's no way I would be sleeping with him, and if I wasn't sleeping with him, his being naked in my bed wouldn't make any sense in terms of my motive. I could give this information to Shook, who could get ahold of his gaming chat logs.

"*Unable to join us.*" Tyler mimicked Shook's lilting accent with frightening accuracy, if not his polite formality regarding Lucas Logan Bell's absence. "Shook must have been insane to bring you here when you've been charged with second-degree murder. You blowing him?"

It occurred to me then that I could desk-check Tyler's face before he'd have the time to react. I had a brief but satisfying vision of his white teeth scattered among the black keys.

"For your information, Shook didn't want me to come. I hopped a plane and came here without his consent. He would have much preferred for me to stay back in Denver."

"That makes two of us."

"What the hell is your problem anyway? Someone piss in your Cheerios this morning?"

"Asperger's," he said. "We already discussed this, or do you have some sort of short-term memory issue? Also, I never eat Cheerios. Breakfast is two eggs boiled for four minutes exactly. Two pieces of bacon. Two pieces of toast cut into triangles because that's the only proper way to eat bread as anyone with half a working brain knows."

This part I didn't disagree with.

"Look, for the purposes of the discovery and depositions, I would appreciate it if you don't mention anything about my legal situation to the team. I'm here because I need to find out exactly what Lucas Logan Bell was doing leading up to his death. Personally and professionally."

"I won't say anything," Tyler said.

"I know it's a big favor to ask." I dropped a hand on his shoulder, quickly removing it when he jerked like he'd been tagged with a cattle prod.

"Yes," he said. "It is. But maybe I'll need a favor from you." He raised his eyebrows at me. Licked his lips.

"Wait a goddamn minute. If you think I'm going to have sex with you—"

"Have sex with me? Where the hell did you get that impression?"

"From your face. You were all waggling your eyebrows at me and licking your lips."

"Involuntary," he said. "I have facial tics."

"Oh." It was only one syllable, but difficult to choke out past the plentiful helping of metaphorical foot lodged in my gullet. "Sorry."

"Don't be. I wouldn't trade my IQ for yours, even if it meant I'd have the ability to read and mimic nonverbal cues."

I'd give Tyler one thing. He sure as hell knew how to make people feel *not* sorry for him.

"And anyway, before we had sex, I'd need you to get a Brazilian. Your current configuration would be far too distracting for me to achieve the primary directive."

My cheeks were hot.

He'd seen up my skirt when I sat down on his desk. And it was a damn good thing that desk was so bare, because I was pretty certain I would have used the nearest available object to brain him with.

"Lucky for us both then that I wouldn't have sex with you if you were the last man on earth."

"Research suggests that scarcity isn't a sufficient motivator where sex is concerned."

"How about I wouldn't have sex with you even if you were the last man on earth and you had an eight-inch dick."

"Seven and three-eighths," he said. "But that's well above average as I'm sure you're aware."

"So geniuses measure their dicks? I kind of thought that was more within the douchebag purview."

"I like to be aware of how I fall statistically in any cross section of the population. Measurements are data, and data can be processed."

"Your face can be processed." I hadn't exactly said it out loud. Slightly more than to myself and slightly less than to him.

"What was that?" His perfect, straight-backed posture was at odds with the strange, puppyish aspect of his face. He was younger than I'd thought originally. Maybe younger than me.

"Nothing." I fought an urgent temptation to lick my finger and stick it in his ear, give him the mother of all wet willies. Anything to destroy the perfect kingdom of lines and angles he'd raised around himself. "Hey. What did you mean, you're sure I'm aware that seven and three-eighths inches is well above average? Are you implying I'm some kind of mattress-hopping cock jockey?"

Because this was what it was like to have a conversation with Tyler Dixon. There were so many large insults that you didn't catch the smaller ones until it was almost too late to bring them up.

Tyler sighed. Perhaps *sighed* isn't the right word for it. What's the word for *exhaled the draft of a soul so tired of explaining itself that it questioned the validity of existing at all*?

That.

He did that.

"Contrary to the impression you give off, I believe you're at least intelligent enough to have caught my meaning in that respect." His fingers continued their endless dance over his keyboard.

My fingers flexed hard at my sides. I raised a fist to my mouth and bit down hard on my knuckles—lest I drive them into his face. It wasn't so much decency that stopped me as a thought.

"This software of yours. If I were to provide you a picture of a face of someone who may or may not have been in Seattle, would you be able to run it through your system?"

"In theory," he said.

"And what would it take to convert theory into actual practice?"

"Depends on how bad you want it."

"For the sake of discussion, let's say very badly."

"This would be far more than a favor. There would have to be commensurate payment for services rendered."

"What kind of payment?"

He cocked his head at an avian angle. His eyes scanning me from head to foot with an intensity that summoned the sweat back to the valley between my shoulder blades, my blouse sticking to it. How an assessment of one's body could be at once frank and nonsexual, I had no idea.

"The kind I would prefer not to discuss at the present place and time," he said finally.

The back of my neck felt humid. My hands sticky. This typically happened when my body was trying to ward off some horrible idea my brain had laid hold of.

They often had differing opinions, the internal and external parts of myself.

"If the terms of payment have to be discussed at a separate time, when might the services be rendered?"

Tyler rocked back in his desk chair, the springs accommodating this movement far more successfully than the one in the conference room had. "If you would be willing to discuss the terms, say, later this evening at my apartment, the services might be rendered now."

My heart beat like bass drums in my ears.

Hadn't he only just minutes ago explained the reasons why he wouldn't be interested in having sex with me? Damned if this didn't sound like a date to do the dirty.

"And if I was amenable to the suggested course of action?"

"Text me the picture."

"I'll need your number."

Tyler rattled it off without hesitation, his voice dipping and rising with the singsongy lilt of someone who memorizes numbers far longer and more complicated than this one.

I saved it into my contacts, christening Tyler as Dicks, feeling the phonetic spelling of his name to be most accurate in this particular circumstance.

Quickly swiping through my photo album, I passed by pictures of my mother and me together as quickly as possible.

Finally, I came to one of just her.

She was sitting across the retro '50s breakfast table from me. The morning of my graduation. The morning *of*.

She was laughing.

One hand resting on her cheek, her other on her chest.

Sunlight streaming through the east-facing windows, painting her black hair gold. Making aquamarine cabochons of her side-lit eyes.

She was the mother I had known, or thought I knew, my whole strange life.

I attached the picture to the text message and sent it to Tyler.

His phone pinged, and he did some sort of mysterious magic with it before turning his attention back to his keyboard.

"Your mother?" It sounded like a joke the way he said it, but I somehow instinctively knew he hadn't meant it that way.

"Yes."

"What's her name?"

"Why do you need that for facial recognition software?"

"I don't," he said. "But there are other systems I can search along-side this."

I paused, already feeling a strange, reverent hesitation in the back of my throat. The syllables always felt sacred on my tongue. Like a password. Like a secret.

"Alexis Avery."

Tyler's fingers danced over his multiple keyboards in the silence.

"She's missing." It wasn't a question. He'd pulled up her missing person report.

"Yes," I said.

"Weird."

"It's weird that she's missing?"

"It's weird that she has no other records."

"Tell me something I don't know."

Tyler offered no further comment on this matter, a fact for which I was infinitely grateful.

"There!" The first surveillance image popped up behind the picture I had provided for her missing person report.

Goose bumps erupted on my arms and crawled all the way up to my earlobes.

It was her.

Her hair wasn't dark anymore, but platinum. A sleek bob angled just below her face. But it was a face I knew. The specific angle of her jaw, the place where my stubby child's hand had rested so often as I drowsed off to sleep. The cheekbones I'd always wished I had inherited. The strange silvery-blue eyes that I had.

It was the first real glimpse of her I'd had since the day of my graduation.

The rush of relief I felt that she was still alive was quickly displaced by something else.

A sense of strangeness. Of sadness. A face I knew so well already becoming foreign to me.

A feeling that time or a force equally as mysterious was trying to catch up with the disassembly that surrounded her disappearance. Making her into something different.

Some*one* different.

"When was this taken?" I asked.

"Two days ago," he said.

My heart sank. Forty-eight hours was an ocean of time where my mother was concerned. She could be anywhere by now.

"Where did this image come from? What camera?"

"At the corner of Union Street and Western Avenue. Right by Waterfront Park." Tyler furiously tapped at his keys. Stopped. Grunted.

"What?"

"This never happens," he said.

"*What* never happens?"

"This is the only image of her I can find. I usually get a minimum of five to ten. You saw how many I got for you, and you've only been in Seattle a few hours."

"So that means she wasn't here long?"

"Or that she's good at keeping her face hidden."

She was good at keeping a lot of things hidden.

"Can you zoom in?" I asked.

"Can I zoom in," he muttered, sounding insulted.

Suddenly my mother's whole figure filled the window, the surrounding brick wall and buildings sheared off the edges of the frame.

Motion was implied even in this still-frame shot. Her hands pressed out wide against the brick wall, chin angled toward one shoulder. Hem of a light spring raincoat whipping out behind her.

My mind rewound the scene, beginning with where she was. Leaping back to where she had been.

I saw her running, rounding the corner, flattening herself against the wall as she waited for whoever was chasing her to run past.

My mother, running from someone.

Our whole lives, I had never seen her so much as take a hurried step, outside of chasing me around the playground in my younger years.

If you're five steps ahead, Janey, then you never have to run.

But she was running now.

From someone powerful enough to scare her.

Chapter Eight

"Could you maybe do one more?"

"Could I *maybe* or could I *definitely*?" Tyler's unblinking gaze, when he chose to level it, made me feel like an ant under a magnifying glass. It wasn't mitigated by the usual social niceties humans had generally come to observe. No blinking. No quick sideways glance. No sliding off to your cheek or your hair to give you time to compose yourself. When Tyler looked at you, he *looked* at you. Taking you apart and putting you back together again with unabashed ease.

"Could you definitely?"

"Send it," he said.

I opened up a browser on my phone, seeing as I didn't have a picture of Valentine other than one snapshot I'd taken covertly from my vantage *behind* him during his keynote speech at my law school graduation. And it just so happened, it wasn't of Valentine's face. But the part in question had enough curves and angles that it seemed like there should have been *some* kind of software that could track it.

I snagged the professional portrait from the website for his architectural firm, Archard Everett Valentine and Associates, and texted it to Tyler.

Tyler stared at his phone for a beat longer than he had when I sent him the picture of my mother.

"You know Valentine?" he said.

Valentine.

He'd called him by his last name. Though I'd only known him for the space of a couple of hours, I recognized this as a sign of a fairly intimate acquaintance on Tyler's part.

"Of course I do. How do *you* know him?"

"He's been trying to poach me."

"Poach you?" I asked. "For what? Valentine runs an architectural firm. Why would he need a principal software engineer?"

"Poach me for BitSled. Apparently he's one of the chief investors in the Excelsior 3-D microchip printing project."

This shit was getting old.

Finding out things I should have known through people who had far less of a connection to the people concerned than I did.

First Shepard, who had apparently been married once upon a time. And now Valentine.

I knew he had investments, but I didn't know he was invested in this. Shook hadn't deigned to mention it either.

"Bingo," Tyler said, rocking back in his chair once again.

Valentine's face. Caught from several angles. Some of them at the airport, though at the part allocated to people who brought their own wings. Another in the grand marble entryway of a hotel. And a final one on a street bustling with pedestrian traffic.

"Huh," Tyler said.

"For a genius, you're not very good at using your words," I said.

"This last one. It's right across the street from where your mother was."

"When?" I asked.

"Now," he said.

Adrenaline hit my brain like a bolt of lightning. "How far from here to where he is?"

"Piss that way." Tyler jerked his head eastward toward the bank of windows. "About three blocks."

"Thanks." And then, for reasons neither of us may ever understand, I kissed the top of his head. Despite his ducking like a cat as soon as he realized what I was doing, my mouth planted firmly and made a loud smacking sound as I pulled away.

I tasted him on my lips as I sprinted to the elevator—an oddly intimate mix of shampoo, clean scalp, and the slightly fruity undertones of whatever kind of product he used to cement his hair into place. And when that elevator didn't materialize, I sprinted toward the stairwell, barreling into Shook as I slung myself through the door.

"Sorry," I puffed. "Talk later. Gotta go."

"Jane!" His voice was honeyed even when echoing in a space with so many sharp angles. "Where are you going?"

"To find my mom!"

God, how I hoped that was true.

———

One of these days, I'm going to show up somewhere, and someone is going to be happy to see me.

But that day wasn't today.

And that someone wasn't Valentine.

The restaurant looked like the inside of a ferry save for the herd of cherrywood dining tables and wall sconces. The wood-trussed ceiling was low, the windows broad. A carved dolphin eternally diving overhead.

He sat at a table for two adjacent to the long bank of windows that stretched nearly floor to ceiling, his gaze fixed on an excavating crane biting deep mouthfuls of earth out of part of the bay they'd walled off.

I wondered if the architect part of him got envious when he watched the big machines altering the terrain for new construction the way a sailor gets misty-eyed when a ship passes nearby.

He turned his head to me slowly. A gesture that led me to believe he'd seen my reflection in the window before he saw me in the flesh.

"I should have left you in jail." He picked up the tumbler and swirled it, amber liquid climbing the sides of the glass. Scotch, I knew from experience. A squat candle guttered on the table in front of him, trying to make the daylight romantic. "My own fault, I suppose."

"May I sit?" I asked.

"Can I stop you?"

"Not really."

"Then by all means." He motioned to the chair across from him, which I took. "Déjà vu," he said.

For we'd done this before.

Me, dropping in on him at some fancy restaurant or another where he was sitting alone, nursing a drink. Waiting for someone who wasn't me.

Shit.

That part had just occurred to me.

"Were you waiting for someone?"

"I am, as a matter of fact. But I doubt they'll be coming."

"Why's that?" I helped myself to a piece of crusty bread hiding beneath the linen napkin in the basket between us, buttering it thickly.

Prison bitches get margarine, as it turns out.

"The same reason for everything that seems to happen in my life as of late. Because of you."

"But see, if you would tell me shit, I wouldn't have to keep hunting you down and surprising you."

"What kind of shit?"

"Like how you just happen to be at the exact spot my mother was less than forty-eight hours ago."

Valentine had never been a man who gave away much, and this time was no exception. He relied in no small part on his stunning good looks to rob you of any questions you had meant to ask him.

He turned the whole force of it on me, letting a long dark lock of hair fall into his green eyes. For the first time, I noticed the scattering of silvery threads weaving themselves through the coffee-colored strands. The restless wave stole color from his eyes, leaving them a paler shade of their normal jade green.

Details.

Valentine was a man not often seen by daylight.

"How did you know that?" A small bright pinging sound chirped from Valentine's pocket. His phone, though he didn't seem overly interested in it.

"Tell me about BitSled," I said, ignoring his question.

A shadow passed over Valentine's face as a ferry horn sounded in the distance, calling out across the water. He reached across the table, rearranging the napkin I'd displaced when I sat down. Adjusting the handles of the forks, spoons, and knives until they were parallel.

"I have many investments, Jane. Technology just happens to be one of them."

A waiter arrived just then, placing a steaming bowl in front of Valentine, the bowl brimming with mussels. The shells clinked against each other as he set it down, wine-and-garlic-scented steam curling up from it in tantalizing ribbons.

Smelling the briny broth, I was suddenly ravenously hungry.

Whereas everyone at the dev meeting had opted to chow down on Melanie's breakfast burritos, I'd eaten a single glazed doughnut in an act of self-solidarity.

"May I bring you anything?" the waiter asked, glancing nervously from me to Valentine and back again.

"A dirty martini."

I felt his hesitation. It wasn't yet 4:00 p.m. I glanced meaningfully at Valentine's drink. What's good for the goose, and all that.

"Do you have any preference as to the type of vodka?"

"The kind that's not strained through a hippie's sock," I said.

"Of course," the waiter said before disappearing again.

"So," I said, pilfering one of the mussels from Valentine's bowl. "Why is it you were trying to poach Tyler Dixon from Oxbow Group?"

Valentine watched as I brought it to my lips, his eyes glazing over with interest or dismay as I scraped the mussel into my mouth and set the iridescent shell aside.

"Remind me why I should answer your questions when you don't have any panties to trade me," he said, tearing off a chunk of the bread and dipping it into the broth.

My mouth felt like I'd been sucking on a sand popsicle.

The incident in question had occurred on one of our previous impromptu meetings. Wherein I had showed up uninvited and needled him for information about his and my mother's working relationship, the mere existence of which had sent my world spinning off its axis. Valentine had balked until I agreed to provide him something by way of recompense, my lucky Wonder Woman panties being the promised price.

"And how do you know that I'm not wearing panties?"

"You walk differently."

"Differently how?"

"Like—" His phone chirped again, casting a small blue aura up from his pocket.

"Like what?"

"Like . . ." He picked up his drink, taking a sip before setting it back down on the table. "Like you know the entire world could reach its hand up your skirt."

But the entire world wasn't here right now. It was just him. Just Valentine.

Now Valentine's phone didn't just chirp, it jangled. A default ring-tone Valentine had never bothered to change.

"But you don't deny you were trying to poach Tyler Dixon for BitSled?"

"Why would I deny it? I've done nothing illegal."

In this particular circumstance, I added for him.

Valentine's phone began ringing in his pocket once again. He yanked it out, swearing under his breath. "Jesus Christ, *what?*"

He was silent a moment as the caller said whatever they'd meant to say into his ear.

"Yes, I'm aware she's in Seattle. My mussels are in her mouth."

Shepard.

He'd found me. He knew where I was.

"I was under the impression that you were going to keep her in Denver."

Another pause.

"And you believed her?" Valentine said.

"Tell him I didn't say *where* I would wait for him." I set down another mussel shell and nodded my thanks to the waiter, who slid the martini in front of me.

"Jane says she didn't say *where* she would wait for you," Valentine said, catching my hand as I reached toward the bowl a third time, holding it by the wrist.

Electricity zinged from his fingers all the way up to my shoulder socket. A jolt that brought with it an unbidden image and its attendant sensations.

What it might feel like to have this wrist and the other one just like it pinned to the wall above my head. The specific imprint Valentine's fingers would make as they compressed the delicate network of veins. The surprising strength of his grip.

Valentine deposited my wrist on the linen tablecloth, his touch lingering like a lead weight binding it to the table long after he'd released it.

"Shepard says that intentional miscommunication of information still counts as a lie," Valentine said, covering the phone's speaker with one hand.

"Ask him about lies of omission. Such as failing to mention that he has an ex-wife. Or that her lover was recently shot in the head."

Usually, the thin white line that appeared at the edges of Valentine's lips was both incited by and directed at me. Refreshing then, that it was Shepard who had earned it this time. "What the fuck is this about Carol's lover?"

So Shepard's ex-wife was Carol.

And Valentine knew her. Or knew *of* her.

Carol.

Carol would wear cardigans better than I. She would buy him handmade soaps and cook healthy and nutritious meals. Carol did the laundry in a timely manner and never had bullet casings in her panties.

Carol never threatened to shoot people or dressed up in panda costumes and booted mouthy little shits who pulled on her tail.

Carol had probably never handcuffed Shepard to the shower.

Which could be either a good thing or a bad thing, when I thought about it.

"Uh-huh." Valentine looked up at me. "She did?"

I tried not to squirm as I took a healthy swallow of my martini, relishing the shards of ice bobbing against my lips.

"Shepard wants to know what Detective Kappas was referring to when he said that you—fuck! Why am I playing go-between? You fucking work for me and Jane isn't even supposed to be here," Valentine snarled.

Men can do that, you know. Snarl.

"Just get here." Valentine disconnected and dropped the phone back into his pocket.

Shepard was on his way.

Which meant that whatever I intended to do, he'd find a way to make it harder.

"What did he say about Detective Kappas?" I tried to make this sound like the casual question it clearly wasn't.

"Apparently the ballistics results came back. The bullet in Lucas Logan Bell's head was shot by your gun."

"But that doesn't mean I was the one who pulled the trigger."

"I know that. You know that. Shook most likely knows it as well. But you can see where District Attorney Wiggins might find this fact of particular use."

"All the more reason that we need to find out who really killed him and why."

"Jane, there is no *we*."

It stung.

I knew it shouldn't have on both a personal and professional level, but it stung all the same.

"True," Valentine said. "Our purposes happen to intersect in this particular case, but we have very different ways of going about things, you and I."

"Fine," I said. "You want to play Lone Ranger, we'll play Lone Ranger."

"And what does that mean, exactly?"

"I'm just saying that two heads may be better than one, but my head is better than yours."

The waiter paused mid-drive-by.

"Don't look at me like that," I said to the tray-bearing hash slinger. "I meant the *head* as in the head on my shoulders. Not the head I give with my mouth. Which, by the way, is something I will *never* be doing for him."

"I don't remember requesting it," Valentine said.

"No? Too sauced to recall how you told me you wanted to fuck me?"

And he had.

In the back of his custom Rolls-Royce Phantom limo, on the way to the apartment where his late mistress had once lived while she was terminally ill, Valentine had argued his own case. Both for and against.

"I don't recall that particular conversation." Valentine sipped at his drink with the easeful nonchalance of a character in a Fitzgerald novel.

"Most likely because when we had it, you'd had about a dozen of these first," I said, pointing to his half-empty tumbler.

By now, our waiter was backing away with slow, measured steps. I was almost surprised he didn't hold his tray aloft like a shield.

"Possible." It was as close to an admission as Valentine would get. "I fail to see how this relates to the discussion of our working together."

"Despite you getting wasted and hitting on me, despite your giving me reasons to mistrust you at every turn, I've shared information with you. I've been willing to follow your recommendations in your timing and allow *you* to lead the charge even though it was *my* mother who was missing. I have sources too, you know. Did it ever occur to you that maybe, just maybe, I don't need your money, or your private jet, or your ex-military operatives and your alpha-hole douche moves to find shit out?"

Okay, so I'd left a few things out.

Such as how when, equally drunk, Valentine had tried to kiss me and I hadn't exactly tried to stop him. Or how his making such a brazen offer of wild gorilla sex hadn't exactly been unappealing to my lady bits, if not the rest of me. Or how I had been lucky enough to stumble across an evil genius software developer with whom I could trade undetermined favors for assistance.

"I never said you did."

"Well, I *don't*." I stood up from my chair, an abrupt gesture that rocked the table enough to send Valentine's carefully orchestrated silverware arrangement out of alignment. "And I'll tell you something else. I'm not going to find out just some of the shit, I'm going to find out *all* the shit. About you. About my mother. About BitSled. About the dead guy in my bed. And when I do, maybe I'll make you trade me *your* panties to know what I know. What would you think about that?"

I knew what the restaurant's *other* patrons thought about it.

Because they were staring right at me, forks paused midjourney to their open mouths.

With as much dignity as anyone with no panties and days-old clothes can muster, I stepped away from his table.

"Oh, what the hell are you all looking at?" I asked, snatching up a handful of truffled steak fries from one gawker's plate as I passed.

Because they don't have truffled steak fries in prison, and eating them now seemed like a prudent course of action.

Just in case.

Chapter Nine

"You are not putting those in my butt."

Those were five inches long, pointy, a blinding shade of purple, and they were in Tyler Dixon's hands.

I stood in his Bellevue living room, barefoot—because he'd had me take my shoes off at the door—and disbelieving.

"They don't go in your butt," Tyler said, holding them out to me. "They go on your ears."

"My ears?" I asked, taking them. Upon closer inspection, they were some kind of foam latex. About the consistency of a stress ball, with little channels at the bottom where they were meant to be attached. "You're a lot kinkier than I gave you credit for."

Because Tyler's apartment didn't scream kink. It screamed action-figure-fandom-museum-curator.

On one wall, black lacquered bookshelves stretched from ceiling to floor, the action figures on each shelf still in their plastic and cardboard containers. Perfectly spaced. Even rows. Nothing even a millimeter out of place. On the opposite wall, a locked glass case with built-in lighting housed plastic-sheathed comic books.

On a third, a workstation remarkably similar to the one I'd seen at the Oxbow Group office took up most of the available real estate. Three screens. Two keyboards.

There were no couches.

No TV.

No end tables and nightstands. No rugs or lamps.

No homey touches.

"Not big on the decorating, are you?"

"Why buy furniture I'll never use? I eat here, I sleep here, I game here. The end."

I pushed my hair behind my ears and snugged the latex down over them.

"Okay. What next?"

Tyler walked over to the coat closet and withdrew a hanger, unzipping a cover and putting it on a separate hanger before bringing what he'd just uncovered over to me.

I blinked.

I stared.

A costume. Consisting of what looked to be a leather bikini with decorative brass scrollwork and buckles. Attached to the top of the bikini, some kind of shoulder pads that looked like what an elven football player might wear. On the bottom, flaps of leather attached to the sides and back of the leather bottoms made a short, open-fronted miniskirt.

"Couldn't I just blow you?"

"Wearing this?" he asked, looking like he might actually be weighing this as an option.

"Instead of this."

"Definitely not." He shook his head emphatically. "I already promised the guys—"

"Guys? What guys? I didn't agree to any kind of kinky group sex thing."

"Is everything always about sex with you?"

"No," I said. Not technically a lie.

Sometimes it was about food.

Tyler hung the outfit on a hook affixed to the inside of the closet door and began dragging out folding chairs two at a time, taking them to the living room to unfold them.

"Some of the guys from my LARP group are coming over for a dress rehearsal, and I promised them Princess NightSpear would be here to offer her blessings."

"Like rub-a-dub-dub, thanks-for-the-grub kind of blessings?"

He handed me two printed pages in plastic sheet protectors. "Like a Midreign Imperial Quest blessing."

"You want me to put on that costume and read this blessing once all your friends are here? That's it?"

"Yes," he said. "That's it."

I sighed. "Where's your bathroom?"

"Down the hall on the left. Don't touch anything."

It's always kind of refreshing when people believe saying that is sufficient motivation to ensure you won't do it.

I closed and locked the door, leaping back when I caught sight of myself in the mirror.

I'd forgotten about the ears.

They looked like something that might belong on the love child of a gremlin and Barney the dinosaur. I took them off and set them on the counter so I could get my shirt off over my head. I stepped out of my skirt, letting it puddle at my feet and unhooked my bra, hanging it over the towel rack.

After several tries, I managed to get the costume on and was mildly surprised at how well it fit.

I wasn't sure which was the more troublesome thought. That Tyler just happened to have a dark elf costume my exact size lying around, or that he had accurately calculated my size on sight?

I leaned in to the mirror to reattach the ears, and noticed it was one of those old-fashioned medicine cabinet combos.

Reaching down, I tore off a couple of squares of toilet paper and put them between my fingers and the latch of the mirror door.

The contents were just as orderly as the rest of the home.

Neat stack of spare toothbrushes. Boxes of unopened soap.

And medications.

Many, many medications.

Garden-variety SSRIs like Prozac and Zoloft. ADHD standards like Adderall and Ritalin. Decent downers like Xanax and Valium.

And antipsychotics.

Clozapine. Risperidone.

Without touching, I checked the last-fill dates.

All within the last month.

"Are you almost ready?" Tyler's voice was close enough for his face to be wedged against the doorjamb.

I jumped, nearly yanking the entire medicine cabinet off the wall. Swearing under my breath as my pulse pounded in my ears, I closed it as gently as I could, hoping the telltale click wasn't as thunderous as it sounded to me.

"Almost," I called back. "Just putting my ears on."

"There's spirit gum on the counter for you if they won't stick. And the purple pancake makeup should work for any exposed skin."

I yanked open the door quick enough to startle him. "Purple pan-cake makeup?"

"Well, yes. You can't have purple ears and the rest of your skin pasty."

Pasty. Like it would have killed him to say *pale*.

I picked up what looked like an oversized pat of watercolor. Next to it, a large sponge. "You really expect me to paint my whole body with this?"

"Of course not," he said, bringing me momentary relief. "I'll do the parts you can't reach."

"This is going to cost you extra," I said.

"How extra?" He folded his arms across his chest, the shrewd bargainer's expression returning to his face.

"I want the security images from every single camera you have access to on Union Street both ten minutes before and ten minutes after the image of my mother. Five-second intervals."

"You're literally talking about tens of thousands of images."

"Well," I sighed. "If you can't do it . . ."

The direct challenge to the ego. Obvious, yes. But effective.

"I didn't say I *couldn't* do it. But for a file that large that requires that much interaction in the system, I think I should get a little more than purple paint."

"Look, the sex is not happening."

"When will you get it through your head that I don't want to have sex with you?"

I paused, managing one of those rare moments when I didn't open my mouth. There was something behind that denial. Something he wouldn't say and wouldn't have to say if I kept giving him things to disagree with.

"I just want you to tell the guys that I did."

"You want me to lie?" I had already begun to weigh my recent vow against the potential benefits I might gain by making this one exception.

"Only if you can manage to be convincing," he said. "Is this something you're capable of?"

I smiled as I stuck my hand out for him to shake. "Mr. Dixon, I'm your girl."

Ten minutes and several remoistenings of the sponge later, most of me was about the color of an anemic lilac.

"You sure you don't want to paint my boobs?" I said, glancing down at my cleavage, the last place we'd yet to address. "I'll throw those in, free of charge."

"In terms of volume, you could charge more for your ass."

"Are you saying I have a disproportionately large ass?" Just when I was beginning to develop the sprouts of goodwill toward him.

"*I'm* not saying anything. Gottfried Leibniz is."

"Well, bring him over and I'll dick-punch him too."

"That would be difficult, considering he's dead."

"I don't follow."

"He's the *true* inventor of calculus. Despite those relentless Isaac Newton fanboys who claim the contrary."

I picked my feet up off the floor and pretended to scuff something off the soles of my shoes. "Damn, but it's getting awfully nerdy in here."

Tyler's mouth flattened into an unamused line. "My point was, my statements are based on a mathematical assessment of the volume of your body parts."

"I'll take *Things a Serial Killer Might Say* for a thousand, Alex." I glanced unbidden at the medicine chest, remembering its varied contents. Why isn't there any good way to ask someone *why* they're on antipsychotic medications?

"Statistically speaking, any serial killers are also a good deal more intelligent than the average population."

"You're not helping your case," I said, sponging purple paint on my cleavage.

"Who says I'm making one?" Tyler stood back to admire his handiwork, his mouth turning down at the corners. "Your face isn't quite right, but it will have to do."

"*Your* face isn't quite right," I muttered under my breath.

"I'll change and meet you in the living room. Don't touch anything. And put this under you before you sit down." He handed me a purple towel before disappearing farther down the hall into a room I assumed was his bedroom. He hadn't offered a tour, and I didn't ask.

I'm the first to admit that it shouldn't have worked, Tyler's costume.

And yet, when he came swaggering toward me all decked out in a leather vest, breaches, a rough cloth peasant shirt, and a quiver of arrows strapped to his back, I felt a strange flutter north of my knees but south of my stomach.

If I forgot who he was and how much I disliked him, I could *almost* see him as a completely antisocial and unpleasant Legolas.

"Here," he said, unbuckling the intricately appointed leather pouch at his waist. He pulled out a long silver chain, the jeweled silver pendant at its end winking in the overhead canned lighting. "Put this on."

"It's going to need to be unfastened to go over my ears." I held up my hands, clad in the intricate leather gloves that had come as part of the costume.

"Turn around."

After a beat of hesitation, I did as instructed.

"What is it, exactly?" I asked, lifting the hair off my neck.

"It's the Tears of Ysthelion. It dispels all sorrow and offers protection to the wearer."

I picked up the amulet and held it to the light as Tyler worked to fasten the clasp. "Too bad it doesn't really work."

"Its powers are dependent upon the faith of the wearer," he said, releasing the chain against my neck with the barest touch of his fingertips.

The glittering stone slid down between my breasts.

We both looked at it for a strange, protracted second until the silence was shattered by a knock at the door.

Perhaps *a* knock isn't right.

A succession of knocks in a pattern as complicated and specific as Morse code might be more accurate.

Their prearranged signal. This, I knew without having to be told.

"The guys," Tyler said. "They're here. Go down the hall to the bathroom. I'll bring you out when it's time."

"Joy."

In the bathroom, I sat myself down on the closed lid of the toilet. Not just because it was the only available horizontal surface, but because it had no vantage point to the mirror. A girl can only catch so many unintended glimpses of herself in the getup of a purple she-elf before she begins to question her life choices.

I pulled my phone out of my leather bustier, listening to the muffled voices on the other side of the bathroom door.

No messages.

No calls.

Not from Valentine. Or Shepard. Or Shook. Or Melanie.

And if I was being honest with myself, that was what tweaked me the most about this evening. Not the ears or body paint, or even the leather tit-sling.

It was that I'd had to bow out of the offer of dinner from Shook, knowing this would leave him and Melanie at a table for two.

My brain, ever the helpful engine, began churning out images at the rate of a movie projector.

Melanie would be stunning by candlelight.

It would thread her hair with strands of glowing gold. Cast roses into her cheeks. Sparkle in her sapphire eyes.

They'd lean across the table over matching menus. Wine loosening their muscles along with their inhibitions.

The flirty glances over shared appetizers.

Her indulgent moan as she brought the first forkful of dessert to her mouth. The singsongy seductive way she'd say, "You have *got* to taste this, sugar," before holding out a bite to him on her own fork.

His lips closing over it as her foot slid up his muscled calf—

"Let's go."

For the second time that evening, my heart trampolined into my throat as I shot up from the toilet and flung open the bathroom door.

"Do you always have to be so fucking abrupt?" I grabbed the bottom edge of the leather top, shifting it to hoist the ladies aloft in preparation.

Tyler blinked three quick times in succession as his head twitched to the right.

I might have been complimenting myself to think it had something to do with the sudden onslaught of boobage.

"You're Princess NightSpear now," he said, not quite looking at me. "And Princess NightSpear doesn't use human profanity."

"Oh for fuck's—"

"Shhhht!" he hissed. "No profanity. You have your lines?"

I picked up the plastic-covered papers and limply waved them at him.

"Good." And then, to my utter surprise and confusion, he held out his arm.

Like a prom date. Or a father ready to escort his daughter down the aisle.

Neither of which I'd ever had.

I threaded my arm through his, noting how odd it felt to be this near to him. Smelling the leather and scrupulously clean scent of him.

And I'll be damned if my heart didn't start to pound as we made our way down the hall toward the living room entryway.

When we reached it, we stopped.

A collective gasp, then. Four men stood, immediately sinking down to one knee, heads bowed.

"What the f—fairy dust am I supposed to do now?" I whispered to Tyler through the side of my mouth.

Tyler withdrew a dagger from his belt and handed it to me along with a scrap of paper. "Go around the room, touch the dagger to both shoulders. Call them by name and tell them they are permitted to rise."

"But I don't know their names."

He had the look again. The exasperated look that told me I wasn't keeping up.

"The paper."

I glanced down at the paper in my hand. On it, Tyler had drawn an eerily precise replica of the circle, labeling each chair according to the man who occupied it and his respective title.

Only, I must not have looked at the names too closely, because when I got to the first chair, I had to stifle a burp of laughter after I'd done the dagger-touching thing but before I invited him to rise. "Mighty . . . PoonHammer? Are you fucking kidding me?"

This lapse in decorum prompted an angry little hiss from the character at his right, a black-cloaked wizard-looking dude with hair the color of an orange rind, pale eyelashes, and wire-rimmed glasses. "Princess NightSpear is a Dark Elf of the Gargoth Age. Her vocabulary doesn't include human profanities. Also, the Shiv of Eldenon must touch the left shoulder first, then the right."

I glanced at my paper, learning that the speaker was Lord Gnarth SilverShaper. Beneath his name, Tyler had written in small, but painfully neat script, "Guild Master."

"My apologies," I said. "You may rise, Mighty PoonHammer."

"Thank you, my lady." He took my hand and bent over it as if to bestow a kiss.

I felt something warm and wet against my knuckles and yanked my hand away. I glanced down at my hand where a streak of skin showed through the purple.

"Did you just lick me?"

"That's a sign of respect among my order," PoonHammer said, head still bowed.

Tyler jerked his head to indicate that I should keep going.

I sighed and moved on to the next, and to the next, until I had greeted them all, one by one.

Mighty PoonHammer, level-one Barbarian. Heavy, brawny, and beardy.

Lord Gnarth SilverShaper, Guild Master and level-one Wizard. The gingeriest ginger who ever gingered.

SmallPants, level-three Monk. Pale-haired, lanky, and with an Adam's apple that could take an eye out.

FullMetalPickle, level-two Archer. Eager, Asian, and prone to adjusting his junk.

And last but not least, Tyler, level-four Champion, whose battle tag, I shit you not, was KongDong.

Statistics my aubergine ass.

The costumes varied as widely as the names, with certain similarities shared across the board. Tunics seemed to be the order of the day.

Tyler—or should I say KongDong—cleared his throat. "Princess NightSpear will now give her blessing to our endeavor."

"Not yet, she won't." Gnarth's face flushed an alarming shade of Stroke Red. "Everyone knows that according to the *Dor Un Avathar*, gatherings will be conducted as follows. *First* comes the reporting of specific quests and missions; then, at the end of the gathering, blessings may be given. KongDong will report on his covert mission to the Duchy of the Iron Mountains."

The name rang little bells in my mind.

The Duchy of the Iron Mountains was based in Denver as Tyler had informed me earlier this afternoon.

"When were you in Denver?" I said, turning to Tyler.

"Any contributions to the conversation must be made in the language of the realm," Gnarth said.

I took a deep breath, as much to tamp down my urge to throat-punch Gnarth as to find words that sounded vaguely appropriate. "Upon what eve did your mission to the Duchy of the Iron Mountains commence?"

Tyler was silent a moment as if trying to remember.

"It was Saturday last," volunteered SmallPants with a shy smile. "Was it not?"

"It was," agreed FullMetalPickle.

Last Saturday.

Tyler Dixon had been in Denver last Saturday.

The day I found Lucas Logan Bell dead in my bed.

I swallowed the small planet in my throat and tried to keep my face neutral. "And may Princess NightSpear ask why Champion KongDong paid a visit to the Duchy of the Iron Mountains on this recent occasion?"

PoonHammer sat forward in his chair, eager as a puppy to know something important. "To assassinate Lucas Logan Bell, of course."

"All players must be addressed by their battle tags!" Gnarth pounded a freckled fist on the side table next to him.

Tyler winced. Not, I guessed, because of the noise it made, but because someone had touched his stuff.

"How is it your Duchy came to be acquainted with Lord BoneSmuggler?" I asked.

"On the forums, of course. Lord BoneSmuggler recently gave grievous insult to the Kingdom of the Northern Lights. So KongDong was deployed to assassinate him in order to restore our good name," Gnarth said.

"And how, exactly, would he be assassinated?"

"By striking him with a lethal blow." Gnarth lifted a pale eyebrow at me. "Why? How do they do it in your Kingdom?"

I blinked at him, struck dumb by the casual manner in which they spoke of ending a life.

"The Princess is distressed," SmallPants said, reaching both hands out in the general direction of my purple tits. "Perhaps she would allow me to comfort her with a healing spell."

"Hands off me, troll!" I said, slapping him away.

"She knows what I am!" SmallPants turned to FullMetalPickle and gave him a haughty nod. "And *you* said my costume was too vague."

"Silence!" Gnarth stood, lifting his staff like it was a megaphone. "KongDong, was your mission successful or no?"

"I was victorious," Tyler said.

A cheer rose up from the group, and I could no longer keep my seat.

"What the fuck is wrong with you people?"

"As I believe I explained before, Princess NightSpear is—"

"Princess NightSpear is about damn sick of your shit." I pointed at Gnarth, who had flushed to the color of a fevered beet. "And she's just used up her very last magical give-a-fuck. We're talking about this now and in whatever fucking language I choose to use. You got it, Gandalf?"

The Guild Master's mouth tightened like it was his face, rather than the dice pouch strapped to his belt, that had the drawstring.

"The Princess is in a lusty humor this evening," PoonHammer whispered to SmallPants, adding a husky, "I am most pleased," while stroking his Brillo beard.

"Talk," I said, hands on leather-clad hips, staring at Tyler. "Starting with the part where the man you flew across actual states to assassinate ended up dead in my bed."

FullMetalPickle's jaw dropped, displaying a lump of partially chewed pretzel between his molars. "Wait a minute. Lord BoneSmuggler isn't, like, dead IRL, right?"

"Wrong," I said. "In real life, he was found very dead and very naked in my bed."

"To die in Princess NightSpear's bed," SmallPants sighed. "An honor indeed."

"I only assassinated him," Tyler said. "I didn't kill him."

It was a credit to the costume-clad humans around me that it had taken me this long to catch on. So careful were their words, so thorough their rituals, that for a moment I had forgotten this was all just a game.

"So this assassination. This is some kind of LARP thing?" I asked.

Tyler blinked at me, his arms crossed over his leather vest. "You're just now picking up on that?"

"Well, forgive the fuck out of me, *KongDong*. Some of us have social lives that don't involve foam daggers and perpetual virginity. Not that there's anything wrong with that," I hastily added upon seeing SmallPants's lower lip wobble.

"I don't know if solo Netflix marathons and wine guzzling can technically be considered a social life," Tyler said.

I bit back the caustic reply in favor of preventing the conversation from devolving further. "So, fill me in on this *assassination*. When did it take place?"

"About 1:30 p.m."

I tried to resurrect what I remembered about the facts gathered from the autopsy. Estimated time of death was early afternoon, but not so specific that I couldn't have conceivably done it before or after my nail appointment.

I'd walked through that afternoon a thousand times in the long stretches alone in my cell, reviewing the things I knew.

I knew my apartment had been empty when I'd left it.

I knew I had armed the state-of-the-art security system Shepard had newly seen installed.

But I also knew even state-of-the-art security systems could be hacked.

Hacked by people like Tyler.

My stomach felt like a cold, tight ball lodged under my ribs.

"And what happened after you assassinated him?" I asked.

"I flew home," Tyler said.

He offered no justifications. No further explanations or denials.

Gnarth stood, gathering his leather man-bag and staff from the back of the chair.

"Where are you going?" PoonHammer asked.

"Send a raven when you're serious about the craft. Until then, I travel through the aether." He waved a hand and backed out of the room, slamming the front door behind him.

"Don't pay too much attention to Gnarth," PoonHammer said, leaning toward me. "Between you and me, he's a total *flurb*."

I felt my face crumple into a quizzical expression. "He's a what?"

"You know. A guy who only shows up for the *role-playing*," he said under his breath.

"And what do you show up for?" I asked, not quite familiar with the nuances of this social currency.

"Me?" PoonHammer tugged on his beard. "I'm your typical ditch monkey stick jock."

"He means he's all about the combat itself," SmallPants explained. "The weapons. The damage they can cause."

"So is it true what they say?" FullMetalPickle asked, his small dark eyes shifting sideways craftily. "About BoneSmuggler's . . . sword?"

"And then some," I said, looking over to catch Tyler's eye. "But it's nothing when compared to KongDong's *weapon*."

"You had congress with Princess NightSpear?" SmallPants's question was directed at Tyler but accompanied by an expression of such wonder, you'd have thought a unicorn had just pranced out of the kitchen.

"Oh yes," I said, answering for him. "Just this evening before you arrived. Four times in a row. We might have managed a fifth, but by that point, I scarcely had the strength to don my ceremonial attire."

PoonHammer, SmallPants, and FullMetalPickle stared open-mouthed at Tyler, who flushed red to the roots of his neatly parted hair.

"Will you pardon me, gentlemen? I think I need to find something to drink. Multiple orgasms make me thirsty." I made a show of walking bowlegged toward the kitchen.

A deal's a deal, potential murderer or no.

I brushed past Tyler on the way to the kitchen, raising an eyebrow at him in silent question as soon as I was out of the others' line of sight.

Acceptable?

He nodded.

He'd understood that nonverbal sign at least.

When everyone had a chance to reconvene, I read my blessing and the customary farewell as the players departed one by one.

"Well," I said when Tyler and I were again alone in his apartment. "I think I'll take a shower, change, and hit the road."

"No," Tyler said. "No shower. Not here."

"You can't be serious."

"Why not?"

"I look like the nerdier cousin of Barney the dinosaur!"

"Actually, you don't," he said. "Barney was more of a reddish purple."

I huffed off to the bathroom, at least determined to change back into normal clothes before I left.

Tyler was already seated at his workstation and seemed surprised to see me when I returned less than ten seconds later.

"Um . . . Where are my clothes? They're not in the bathroom."

"Where in the bathroom were they?"

"In a pile on the floor."

Tyler shrugged, a kind of "that's what you get for being a slob" gesture. "One of the guys probably took them by mistake."

"My bra? One of the guys took *my bra* by mistake?"

"Okay, *that* they probably took because they'd never actually seen one up close." Tyler's hands had commenced their dance, independent but oddly synchronized as they moved over two separate keyboards.

"You're seriously going to make me leave here in this outfit."

"Seriously."

It was back. That urge to drive his face into his keyboard until his teeth scattered like Chiclets across the desktop.

"You can leave now," he said.

I stood there, anger driving my heartbeat into my ears, blood burning new pathways in my cheeks.

"You know something? At least I *know* I'm an asshole. I don't try to hide behind my diagnoses."

I left him there, in the small orderly kingdom in which he made perfect sense.

On my way down the stairs in front of his apartment, I stopped, looking back at the window. Slices of Tyler's face showed through the blinds, the blue light from the monitors making an ice sculpture of him.

I knew it to be a human tendency, to put on a mask of propriety to hide the most undesirable parts of ourselves from the people around us. Some deep part of me knew and had known for a long time that this was precisely what my lying had been about. To build a personality others found acceptable.

Misanthropic though I am, I felt that pull. That need to bring myself into line with polite society's minimal expectations like Thou Shalt Not Kill a Bitch.

But watching Tyler's face unobserved, I knew something different. I knew Tyler felt nothing.

Chapter Ten

Empirical fact: the universe is a dick.

Okay, maybe not a dick. But definitely like that annoying relative you have who's always staying at your house and leaving their dirty socks on the coffee table, never flushing the toilet, and eating all the ice cream before you can have any.

Super fun for them.

Not so fun for you.

This is how I had come to understand my relationship with the universe in general, and all it took was a single word for me to know that it was about to have its fun at my expense.

"Jane?"

My name echoed off the unyielding surfaces of our Seattle hotel's lobby, echoes breeding like rabbits for anyone who cared enough to listen.

I stopped.

I sighed.

I'd done so well up to this point.

I'd made it all the way back to the hotel without many comments.

My Uber driver had assumed it was a cosplay thing. People on the street had largely ignored me. I'd even made my way across the sleek gray hotel lobby, slinking like a cartoon character between columns and concealing myself behind potted trees.

And I was almost home free by the elevators, key card already out of my leather bra in preparation, when someone called out to me.

No, not just someone.

Sam Shook.

My options were (a) run like hell—risky and likely to end in my running face-first into a door or wall; or (b) pretend I hadn't heard him—immature and potentially socially damaging.

"Jane."

His voice was closer now. *He* was closer.

The trick to getting away with anything is to act like you did it on purpose, Janey. Whatever you believe, they will too.

The illusive *they*.

Anyone who wasn't *us*.

When I was a young girl, I believed the word had been made up just to describe my mother and me. Two people. Two letters. An entire world contained within.

I squared my shoulders, though it was a mostly feckless venture beneath the winging leather shoulder pads attached to my medieval warrior bra. Pasting a confident grin on my purple face, I turned to Shook.

He actually took a step backward as if the full force of my attire had pushed him off balance. "This is quite the outfit," he said.

"I'm—"

"Princess NightSpear, of course." He raised his glass to me, bowing in mock-salute.

"*You* LARP?"

"No. Certainly not. But I have friends who do."

This is something I had never thought about. Shook's friends. Shook's life outside work. He belonged so completely to the terrain of the law firm in my mind that I half expected him to tuck himself into a cupboard every night and appear there magically the following morning.

"I was just having a drink," he said. "Will you join me?"

I.

Not *we.*

Which implied no Melanie.

Suddenly, a drink didn't sound like a bad idea at all.

"Even though I'm dressed like this?" I asked, more a concession than refusal.

"Especially because you are dressed like this." A conspiratorial smile lit up his face. "The bartender was just telling me that there's a convention of video game programmers in the hotel. I suspect you might very well make someone's entire week."

And then, for the second time in one night, I was offered an arm.

"You'll get purple on your—"

Shook was grinning to shame the devil.

It didn't take me long to realize why.

He was already wearing a purple shirt. Because Sam was the kind of guy who could rock a motherfucking pastel.

In a world where alpha males ruled the bed and the streets, this was a part of that beta male charm often overlooked and frequently discounted. The kind of quiet confidence that didn't announce itself with broken tables and slammed doors.

And obscure texts where *you* was abbreviated to *u.*

Shook squired me to side-by-side leather-backed barstools with a perfectly unobstructed view of the lobby.

I had a momentary shot of intestine-cramping panic when I imagined Shook watching me sneak all the way from the revolving doors to the elevators.

It was a long journey for a woman dressed like a purple elf princess to make incognito.

"Well, good evening." The bartender gave me a wide genuine smile. "And may I say, it's an honor serving you, Princess NightSpear."

I glanced at Shook, who seemed pleased at the attention. "Does everyone know this shit but me?"

"Live action role-play is an exceedingly popular pursuit."

"Huh."

"And what would the Princess like to drink?" the bartender asked solicitously.

"Dirty martini," I said.

"Gin or vodka?"

"Vodka. And before you ask, my only request is that it not have been strained through a hippie's sock."

The bartender favored me with a knowing smile. "I think we can manage that." He took himself off to make the drink while Shook sipped at his own.

Looking at the rosiness of his cheeks, I wondered if it wasn't his first.

"Did uh . . . did Melanie not want to join you for a drink?"

In terms of segues, it was about as subtle as a blunder bus. It would force him to tell me that either he hadn't invited her, or that he had and she'd refused.

"We parted ways after dinner. She mentioned that she needed to catch up on email. I went back up to my room and did the same."

I felt the perpetual crease that would most likely require Botox one day appear in the center of my forehead. How very unlike Melanie this was.

"And how was dinner?" I asked. Translation: *Did she give you a handy under the table?*

"Good." Shook took another sip of his drink, giving me his profile, aquiline nose and all. Translation: *Maybe.*

"Did you eat here at the hotel?" Translation: *Should I be picturing that handy happening beneath a white tablecloth?*

"We did, yes."

Ugh. I *so* would have preferred to imagine Melanie giving people handies under a sticky bar littered with peanut-shell shards.

"That's nice. I imagine that gave you some time to talk about the case."

"If I didn't know better, I might think I was being cross-examined." Shook's smile was mild. Unaccusatory.

"What?" I laughed. "No. Just making conversation."

The bartender returned, sliding my drink over to me on a gold-embossed cocktail napkin. I nodded my thanks and took a healthy slug of the briny liquid.

"You were missed in the meetings this afternoon," Shook said.

In terms of censure, it was about as gentle as smackdowns come.

"I'm sorry about that."

"Did you find out anything of use?"

"Maybe," I said.

"And may your mentor ask what it was that caused you to depart so quickly?"

"Tyler, mostly."

Shook nodded sagely over his drink. Bourbon, I decided. The lingering tawny sweetness would appeal to him the same way he appealed to me. "He was particularly unpleasant to you during the meetings. I've spoken with Curt about it."

Gratitude warmed the space behind the leather cups of my bra. That Shook had noticed this, and further, taken the trouble to talk to another human about it struck me as particularly considerate after the recent gathering I'd attended.

"It wasn't that. I mean, yes, he was a total shitshark, and I appreciate you talking to Curt about it, but that wasn't why I left."

"Why, then?"

"I'm afraid I can't tell you specifics. Not without compromising a potential source of information."

"I understand," he said.

Did he?

"Do you?" I wasn't nearly drunk enough to ask this question in earnest, nor he to answer it, but there it was.

"My mother wanted me to be a yoga teacher," Shook said. "Did I ever tell you that?" Backlit bottles threw incandescent sparks like fairy lights into his eyes.

"You didn't."

He took another sip of his drink, rattled the wet ice around the bottom of the glass. "She owned a studio in Chennai."

Owned.

Past tense.

As I had recently learned, past tense is never good where mothers are concerned.

"I grew up near an ashram. Learning the art. The practice. She said I had a gift."

I didn't doubt it. Shook had many.

"What did your mother want you to be?" Shook asked.

Better he had asked how I would arrange the particulars of my mother's funeral. Because to introduce the ways she had shaped me was to introduce the woman herself. The woman who had gone missing from my life.

"Myself," I said.

As much as her own chosen path of private investigation had informed the advice she'd so freely offered, she had never so much as nudged me in any vocational direction.

What you do doesn't matter, Janey. It's who you are.

This particular gem she had dispensed over cinnamon toast when I was yet but a nugget, getting ready to begin the fifth grade. I could still feel the gritty sweetness of it between my teeth.

What should I be when I grow up, Mommy? I had asked this question to her back.

It seemed I was always seeing her that way. With her back to me. Her coffee-colored hair spilling down her shoulder blades as she moved from task to task. Packing my lunch. Cleaning the counter. Cleaning her gun.

You should be you, she had said.

But what does that even mean?

It means that who you should be when you grow up is who you already are.

And who's that?

Kind. Smart. Maybe a little mouthy. Her laugh was the most beautiful sound in the world. Rich and throaty. *In fact, I don't envy whoever has to take you on in a verbal tussle.*

A pattern that had proved to be true throughout my schooling.

"*Mummyji* said teaching yoga was my dharma. My purpose." Shook pulled me back into the present. "But I wanted the money. The prestige. We had a terrible fight. She died of a stroke a week later. I never got the chance to apologize."

"I'm so sorry," I said. I looked at my own hand hovering over his back, wanting to offer him some sort of conciliatory touch. But in the end, it seemed too ridiculous. My comforting him while I looked like this. *Princess NightSpear grieves for your loss.*

"So am I," he said. "But this is what I meant when I said I understand. I would give anything to have my mother back, Jane. Even for five minutes. For the chance to tell her that she was right."

"Right about what, exactly?"

He sagged over the creamy granite bar, his knees resting against the corrugated metal tiles that decorated its front. "I should have been a yoga teacher, Jane. This case has made that abundantly clear to me."

"Why do you say that?"

"Did you not see it? Sitting there in that room? Could you not feel it? The ceaseless wrangling over who came up with what first and who should get the money for it? I'm so sick of this kind of conversation. So tired of being the mouthpiece for men with money."

"And whose mouthpiece are you now?" I asked.

His dark intelligent eyes contemplated my face with far more seriousness than it deserved, current configuration considered. "Do you not know?"

"I don't. I've never met the owners of BitSled."

"Oh, but you have." Shook's eyelids lowered to half-mast. That mischievous dimple appearing in his cheek. He was going to tell me something I wasn't supposed to know, if I could manage not to fuck it up in the next five seconds.

"Valentine," Shook said. "Always Valentine."

"Valentine? Valentine *owns* BitSled?"

"Where else would a technology shop that size get the resources to take on a company like Oxbow Group?"

"I knew he was invested in BitSled, but I had no idea he was funding the lawsuit for the patent rights."

"How did you know he was invested in BitSled?" Shook asked. "I did not think this was information he usually volunteered."

"It isn't."

Shook raised a dark eyebrow at me in invitation. He wanted the rest of this story.

And since he had parted with information I most likely wasn't supposed to have, I gave it to him.

"I saw him this afternoon. He mentioned that tech was one of his many investments."

"And how did this topic come up?"

Shook's manner was so unassuming, his presence so disarming that it was easy to forget that he was Dawes's go-to litigator. His lawyer's brain capable of taking my words, picking them apart, following them all the way back to their source faster than I could remember to dissemble it.

"He tried to poach Tyler," I said.

Shook sat up straighter on his stool, his face going all serious. "How do you know this?"

"Tyler told me."

"This is unbearable." Shook's long fingers dove into the unruly crop of his hair, blue-black beneath the pendant lighting. "How am I supposed to represent someone's interests when they refuse to give the necessary information?"

"I *know*, right?" I said, excited to have someone who might, at last, understand my frustration. "Also, that's not all I found out from Tyler."

"What do you mean? What else do you know?"

"Tyler knew Lucas Logan Bell. Directly."

"What? How?"

"They were both part of this LARPing thing. And I guess at one point, Bell had insulted the kingdom Tyler was part of, and Tyler was dispatched to Denver to assassinate him." I bracketed *assassinate* with double bunny ears so he'd dig that I wasn't talking about actual death.

"He admitted this?"

"Freely. But LARP assassinations are more about public humiliation than they are about actual dying." I explained this like I hadn't just learned it an hour before.

"But even so, if we can prove Tyler was in Denver during the time period that Bell was murdered, that is enough to establish reasonable doubt. His motive is far more compelling than yours."

"Precisely what I was thinking," I said. "It's a start, anyway."

Shook squeezed my hands in his. A warm, affectionate gesture that made my stomach do a backflip.

"Has anyone ever told you that you have a remarkable brain, Jane Avery?" His hands were still sandwiched around mine. His mouth near and smiling.

"Not especially often," I admitted. People were generally more concerned with how smart my mouth was rather than the brain behind it.

"This reminds me." Shook poked a finger in the air like he was bumping the bubble of a thought. "I have something for you in my room. Let me get the check and we can go grab it."

My heart fluttered at the base of my throat.

Something for me. In Shook's room.

There would have been a time when I would have said that I knew Shook well enough to guarantee he wouldn't try anything funny. But from my present position, I couldn't quite assure myself that was the case.

"For me?" I asked.

"Yes. It won't take but a moment to grab it." He signaled for the check, which the bartender brought over with a strange, secret smile. Shook opened the small leather folder and stared at it quizzically. "But there's nothing on here," he said.

"There's no charge to you, sir," the bartender said. "I just appreciate all your help."

"You are most welcome, my friend." Shook took a twenty out of his billfold and left it in the leather folder. A rather generous tip.

We rose, and I dropped my napkin over the purple streaks the back of my thighs had left on the chair. So maybe it wasn't 100 percent pure, undiluted assholery that had caused Tyler to insist I sit on a towel while at his house.

"What was that all about?" I asked as soon as we were out of earshot.

"All what?"

"The bartender." My pointy ear invaded my peripheral vision as I tipped my head back toward the bar. "What kind of help was he thanking you for?"

"It's a little side project," Shook said. "Not something I like to talk about at work."

"Because?" I punched the little button with the arrow pointing up.

"Because I don't want Gary to feel like there's a conflict of interest."

I had always loved the way Shook pronounced Gary Dawes's first name even if I didn't exactly love the man it belonged to. That gentle tongue-tip caress that turned the *r* into a soft *d*.

"What kind of side project?" I asked. *Scandal right under my nose, you say? Sign me up.*

"I connect people in need of pro bono legal advice with lawyers looking to donate their time. It just so happens that our bartender is in the middle of a probate dispute with his father's much-younger widow."

I was tempted to rip open his shirt, not because of any lingering kink on my end—at least, not *entirely* because of any lingering kink on my end—but because I suspected there might be a red Superman *S* emblazoned across his chest.

My stomach flipped as the elevator made its sudden ascension, as much because of gravity as because now we were actually on our way to Shook's room.

I couldn't see him making a pass.

Truth be told, I don't even know if the idea of him making a pass bothered me all that much.

It was that I didn't know how I would react if he did.

The elevator dinged, and the doors opened up on the floor two below ours.

The men standing in front of the elevator greeted me with open-mouthed surprise a split second before dropping down to one knee.

"Your highness!" the shorter of the two cried.

"You've got to be fucking kidding me." I folded my arms across my purple boobs as my face slowly turned a color close to magenta.

"This is such an unexpected honor!" his taller friend said. "Please, bestow upon us your blessings."

The elevator doors commenced to beeping, the sensors displeased by the solid lumps of nerd that prevented them from closing. Passersby began to stop and stare.

"Get up," I growled through clenched teeth. "Do you hear me? Get. Up."

"We may not rise until the Princess has honored us with the Shiv of Sardil," the shorter of the pair said.

"I'm going to honor your teeth with my foot if you don't get up right this second."

I glanced over at Shook, who was making a strange sound somewhere between a hiss and a snort. His perfect white teeth dimpled his lower lip. His chest silently shaking as moisture leaked out the corners of his eyes.

"This is *not* funny," I said.

He nodded hastily, all agreement with his eyes and stifled laughter with his mouth. "But perhaps you ought to humor them if we ever wish to get to our floor."

"Oh, for God's sake," I sighed.

I walked over and slapped each of them on one shoulder, then on the other. "Rise WhatsHisFace. And also RandomDude. Blessings be upon you and all that happy horseshit."

The pair shared a sideways glance, then slowly rose, looking hesitant the entire time.

They boarded the elevator at last, casting reverent glances back at me as the elevator rose two more levels and Shook and I exited.

"Goddess go with you, Princess NightSpear."

"Yeah, yeah," I called back over my shoulder.

We stopped in front of Shook's room, on the opposite end of the hall from mine. He patted down his pockets for the plastic key card.

"Well, that was embarrassing," I said.

Maybe lie.

Almost lie.

The naked truth: adoration does not entirely suck.

"You handled it remarkably well." He pulled the thin plastic card out of his suit pocket and slid it into the reader.

We did a sort of awkward dance then. Shook opening the door, beginning to walk through it, stopping, offering to let me walk through first. Me, stopping, then starting, then stopping again as we both made false starts.

Finally, laughing, we walked through together.

And right into the barrel of a gun.

Chapter Eleven

My life has always followed certain patterns.

I always choose the wrong shoes.

I spend an inordinate amount of time hiding behind plants.

And whenever anyone is sent to kill me, they always come in twos. Never three. Never one.

Always two.

"Is there something in the bad guy bylaws that states they can only ever travel in pairs?" I asked.

"Greetings from RedWolf." The henchdude sitting in the chair by the hotel desk tugged on the creases of his black slacks, folding one knee over the other. His legs were skinny beneath a belly gone soft. I didn't recognize his voice. Or his face, the sallow shade that indicated long-term liver problems. But the particular cadence of the name he'd mentioned rang the cherries.

I felt an epic eye roll coming on.

As far as battle tags, it was a good sight better than SmallPants or KongDong, but still. I'd had about e-goddamned-nuff of this shit for one night.

"For God's sake. I don't even really do LARP, okay? I just dressed up in this outfit to help out a friend. I don't care if you're friends with RedWolf or Beefalo Soldier or anyone else for that matter."

"We're not here for you." The one with the gun had hair slicked back from a shining pate, a round whiskey-bloomed nose, and the shoulders of a chicken. "We're here for him."

I followed the extension of his arm to where the pistol—a .38, I noted—was pointed straight between Shook's eyes. The exact location where Lucas Logan Bell had been shot.

Shook himself looked unusually calm. Arms raised to shoulder level, bent at the elbow, palms facing forward in a gesture of surrender. His gaze was steady. His breathing regular and even.

"Go ahead," Shook said. "Shoot me."

"Sam," I hissed. "What are you doing?"

"I practice nonviolence," he said, as much to me as to them. "My life is not worth the conflict that fighting would require. So if you are going to shoot me, then shoot me. You would only free me to my next incarnation."

I tried and failed to read his face. Was this a ploy? Some sort of intellectual Rambo shit, perhaps? Or was Shook seriously just going to stand there and let these men kill both of us?

For all its benefits, and they were many, this is where the allure of the beta male ran straight out of railroad track.

I couldn't decide what *I* was going to do until I knew what *he* was going to do.

I had no overwhelming desire to kick asses and take names, but I also knew a little about self-defense.

And by a little, I mean everything my mother could possibly teach me.

Always use an assailant's momentum against them, Janey.

Suddenly, I was five years old again, standing in the center of the tattered living room area rug. Mom had pushed all the furniture to the sides of the room, baring a broad space in the center for what she called "bad guy playtime." In these games, Mom was always the bad guy. Crouching low and furrowing her brow in a nefarious manner.

What's momentum? I had asked, licking a sticky spot of maple syrup from the blade of my hand. We'd had my favorite dinner: breakfast.

It's the force something has when it's moving. Like when I lunge for you, you want to try and shove me off balance in the same way I'm going. Make sense?

I nodded, dark pigtails tickling my earlobes.

Good. Now, next time I reach for you, I want you to grab my hands, pull as hard as you can, and jump out of the way. Got it?

Got it.

But I hadn't gotten it. Not the first time, or the second, or the third, or the fourth.

By the fifth time, I had broken into frustrated tears.

Mom squatted down in front of me, taking my smaller hands in her larger ones. Hers had always been warm and dry; mine, perpetually cold and clammy.

She'd tucked the knuckle of her index finger under my chin, gentle pressure to bring my gaze in line with hers. Eyes the same hue as her own staring back at her through red-rimmed lids.

I don't want to try anymore, I'd said through hiccuping sobs.

When you want to stop trying is when the real fight begins, Janey.

She'd wiped the tears from my face with the hem of her threadbare Rolling Stones T-shirt, given my chin a squeeze, and said *again.*

That time, I'd gotten it.

And every time after.

"And what about you?" sitting henchdude asked. "Do you practice nonviolence?"

I nodded slowly, shyly, and said, "Nope."

Three movements.

This is all that was required to turn the barrel of a gun toward the person pointing it at you.

1. Nondominant hand grabs the barrel, yanks it fast toward whichever direction is farthest away from your vital organs.
2. Dominant hand comes down hard and fast to the assailant's wrist, breaking the grip.
3. Nondominant hand pushes barrel back toward the assailant while dominant hand retrieves the butt of the gun until *shazam*.

The gun is now pointing at the person who was pointing it at you.

This is what my mother would have done, anyway.

Me, I operated a little differently.

Instead of merely reversing the grip, I brought the butt end down hard on the henchdude's skull.

Incapacitation is like nature's friendliest coma.

I preferred the odds of one on one, seeing as Shook didn't seem all that inclined to provide assistance of the physical variety.

When I had the larger henchdude dropped into a pile at my feet, I pointed the gun at his partner, who'd only had time to half rise from the chair, his mouth miming words that never materialized.

In my peripheral vision, Shook wore a similar expression of shock. He'd never seen me "in action" so to speak.

"Jane," he said. "That was most impressive. Where did you learn to do such things?"

"You know how your mother taught you yoga?" I asked, cocking the gun.

Shook nodded.

"Mine taught me how to greet gun-toting dick weasels."

The quick double beep of a key card being inserted in the slot served as the prologue to the door imploding inward hard enough to leave a dent at handle level in the opposing wall.

And then there was no doorway at all because a man was filling it. All of it.

My reptilian brain had already begun to memorize the negative spaces created by his shoulders, his narrow hips, his powerful legs.

Shepard.

It was his gun, not his eyes, that seemed to glance around, acquainting itself with everyone in the room. Henchdude. Me. Shook. Double take back to me.

"Don't say it," I said preemptively.

He came up beside me, stealthy as a panther, aiming his gun where I aimed mine. A strange show of trust. I felt the warmth of his body radiating on my bare purple arm.

"Don't say what?" he asked.

"The thing you were going to say."

"How do you know what I was going to say?"

"I don't," I said. "But whatever it is, I know I wouldn't like it."

"And how do you know that?"

"Because I don't like most of the words that come out of your mouth."

"This your boyfriend or something?" Henchdude asked.

Shepard and I had one of those weird word collisions common to a campy 1980s sitcom. We both said *no* at precisely the same moment and with enough emphasis to sound overly insistent.

"You should let me shoot him." Shepard's trigger finger twitched. "Your gun doesn't have a silencer."

"Dude," I said. "Stow the murder boner. There will be no killing."

"You shouldn't aim your gun at anyone you're not willing to kill."

"I didn't say I wasn't willing to kill him. It's just that I don't want him dead right this second."

"It is a pleasure to see you again, Mr. Shepard." Whether Shook said this to remind us he was in the room, or to stop the rapid devolution of my and Shepard's conversation into verbal ping-pong, I didn't know.

He and Shepard exchanged a cursory nod. Their acquaintance had been brief and strange, beginning when Shepard had showed up at the law office under the guise of my boyfriend and proceeded to tongue-wrestle my tonsils in front of God, Judy, and the legions of evil spirits who attend her.

"Your arrival was most fortuitous." Shook folded his arms, then unfolded them. Shifted from foot to foot. Cleared his throat. I found his inability to decide what to do with his body when he was the only one without a gun (or without a gun trained on him) somehow endearing. "How was it that you knew we might be in need of assistance?"

"Because you're with Jane," Shepard said. "And anyone with Jane will generally need assistance sooner or later."

"What the hell gives you the right to say that?" I wanted to fold my arms but remembered that tucking a loaded gun under my arm was maybe not the best idea.

"Experience," he said.

"Name one person who has needed help because of something I did."

"Officer Bixby."

Shit.

"That was an isolated incident."

"No incident is an isolated incident with you."

"I think the point you're missing here is that this gun, the one in my hand right now? This was aimed at my face. *I* disarmed him," I said, nudging the crumpled pile of bad guy at my feet. "So far, the only assistance you're providing is taking up the available oxygen in this room."

"Really?" Shepard said.

"Really."

"So you don't need my help?"

"Nope."

Shepard clicked the safety on his gun and dropped it down to his side. "All right, Rambo. What's your next move?"

"Easy," I said. "I'm going to ask this guy stuff."

"And he's going to tell you stuff *why* exactly?"

"Because I have a gun pointed at his head."

"And that's going to be enough to motivate him, you think?"

"Yes."

"Hey, guy," Shepard said. "You going to tell her stuff?"

"Nope," Henchdude replied. "I'll die first."

"What now?"

Now, I briefly considered acquainting the butt of my stolen gun with the back of Shepard's head and running like hell, hoping the trauma might just relieve him of any memory beginning with seeing me in costume. That was a thing, right? Temporary memory loss associated with blunt force trauma?

I bet shit like this never happened to Sam Spade.

"Who said you're going to die?" I lowered the sight of the pistol from between his eyebrows to between his knees. "The way I see it, you're either going to tell me who RedWolf is, or I'm going to turn your dick into a party popper."

The assassin's knees clenched together swift and sharp. "Whatever you can come up with would be nothing compared to what RedWolf would do to me if he found out I told you anything."

I smiled. "So RedWolf's a *he* is he?"

"Shit," the henchdude said.

"So now I know he's a he, and that *he* wants Shook dead. Which leads me to believe he's associated with Oxbow Group in some way."

"Why would you assume this?" Shook asked.

"Why else would someone want you dead? The intellectual property rights for the 3-D microchip printing technology are worth billions. And you have the only existing copy of BitSled's code repository. What else would they be searching the room for?"

Shook glanced around the room. "It does not appear to be searched to me."

"Exactly," I said. "Everything is perfect. There's not a pillow out of place."

Shook's smooth brow creased at the center. "I'm afraid I don't understand."

"Don't feel too bad." Shepard patted him on the shoulder with the non-gun-bearing hand. "Happens to me all the time when I'm around her."

I shot him a look with only slightly less force than a bullet would have left the gun in my hand.

That's the mistake most people make, Janey. Not leaving things too messy. The human eye is programmed for imperfection.

"You mentioned that you came up to the room after dinner. There would have been some signs of your having sat on the bed. Or in a chair."

"That remarkable brain of yours again." Shook had the best nonsmile smile I'd ever seen.

I turned back to the man in the chair, noting with pleasure the oily sheen of sweat that had bloomed on his upper lip. "I'll ask you one last time. Who is RedWolf?"

The assassin clamped his lips together and turned his face over his shoulder like a pouting toddler.

"All right," I sighed, cocking the gun's hammer.

"No!" Shook, Shepard, and the henchdude shouted in unison.

"I suppose you both have a better idea?"

"How about you tell me what you want to know and leave me alone with this guy for a little while." Shepard rolled his neck, releasing a series of hollow pops and shrugged his shoulders like he was loosening up to get after a punching bag. If he hadn't had a gun in his hands, I was pretty certain he would have cracked his knuckles.

"I'm afraid that won't be possible," Shook said.

"Why is that?" I asked.

"Because while you two were arguing, I sent a text to Melanie asking her to call the police." Shook pulled the phone from his front pants pocket and held it up demonstratively.

"You had Melanie call the police?" I asked. "Are you mad?"

"This seemed like a reasonable thing to do when a gunman shows up in a hotel room and threatens your life."

Actually, it had been the Melanie part I objected to most, but this worked too.

"You were going to let this guy shoot you, and *now* you decide to get reasonable?" My voice had ratcheted up a couple of octaves and was quickly approaching something like shrieky. I pressed a finger to my forehead where the vein had begun to pulse above my eye. "You know what? Fuck this. No way am I hanging around to give a statement to the cops. I'm fucking purple and wearing a leather bikini."

"And also charged with a homicide in another state," Shepard added.

"Thanks for that reminder, Captain Assbadger," I said. "I'll let you two figure out which one of you wants to lie."

"The more accounts we have to corroborate what happened, the more likely it is they will believe it was the truth." Clever of Shook to use his courtroom voice. That authoritative but infinitely reasonable tone capable of having juries convict *themselves* if that was what he'd asked.

And had I been a more reasonable person, it might have worked.

"Which part of the truth is that?" I asked, looking at Shook. "The part where I disarmed the assailant threatening your life?" My gaze toggled to Shepard. "Or the part where, after watching the hotel through a military-issued scope, you broke into a room with an unregistered weapon that's not legal to be concealed in the state of Washington?"

Shook and Shepard glanced at each other.

"On second thought, you do perhaps appear a little tired," Shook said.

"Maybe you ought to go lie down for a while," Shepard added.

"That's what I thought." I stepped over the man at my feet, who had begun to groan. "Take care of that, would you?" I said to Shepard.

As soon as I turned my back to slip into the bathroom, I heard a grunt and a gasp, and the henchman was silent once more.

I walked into the suite's bathroom, retrieved a washcloth from the neatly folded stack next to the sink, and began wiping the gun down. After I'd given it a thorough polish, I walked back into the room, squatted down next to the unconscious thug and picked up his meaty palm, pressing his fingertips onto the parts of the gun he had touched while it was aimed at me.

"Congratulations on disarming your assailant," I said, placing the gun on the floor at Shook's feet. "You'll probably want to keep this away from him. My guess is he isn't going to be overly chipper when he wakes up."

Shook gingerly picked the gun up the way you would an animal that might bite. I thought I heard Shepard snort.

"You two have a lovely evening." I gave them a half-hearted salute and marched out the door toward my own room.

———

One hour, three showers, and a veritable army of purple-tinged cotton swabs later, I stood bathrobed and towel-haired, contemplating the exorbitantly expensive contents of the minibar when there was a knock at the door.

This is never a good thing at 11:37 p.m. on a Monday.

And especially considering the kind of Monday I'd had.

Sticking a modestly priced twenty-dollar Snickers into the freezer for later consumption, I shuffled over to the door and peeked through the keyhole.

Fucknuckles.

Melanie. Fucking. Beidermeyer.

Because this day hadn't been quite shitty enough.

I unlocked the dead bolt but left the security latch engaged, opening the door just wide enough to peep through the crack, evoking a voice I hoped was sleep-fogged and bleary.

"Hey, Melanie. What's up?"

"Oh, good, you're still up. I brought you something." Melanie held up a colorful paper gift bag plumed with several artfully fluffed wads of tissue paper.

I gazed at it through eyes made slitty from too much scrubbing and inherent distrust of blondes bearing gifts. "Why?"

"I just thought you might could use a couple things since you had to catch the plane in such a hurry this morning." A threadbare Texas twang had crept back into Melanie's dialect along with the grammatical anomaly.

"And you thought I might be able to use them at 11:30 at night?"

She looked down at her feet, clad in black slip-ons with pink stitching that matched the detailing on her velour loungewear.

"Well, I stopped by earlier, but you weren't here. And I tried to call, but I didn't seem to be able to get you."

My self-righteousness was squelched by a feeble pang of guilt as I had somewhat of an automatic reject policy when Melanie's name happened to flash on the phone's caller ID. This was usually followed by my hissing and making the sign of the cross.

"Anyway," she said, picking at a spot of chipped paint on the door-frame, "I saw you leaving Shook's room not too long ago and thought now might be a better time."

She'd slid the innuendo in so cleverly that I almost didn't twig it at first.

I saw you leaving Shook's room.

I shifted my weight from one foot to the other, arms crossed over my chest. "So, you were watching the hall?"

"Goodness, no." She gave me her patented disarming laugh. "I was fetching myself some ice, and I just happened to see you leaving. So, I figured maybe now was a better time to bring *this* by."

This was the gift bag.

It was too big to fit through the crack, which meant only one thing.

I would have to open the door.

Crafty bitch.

I unlatched the security bar and opened the door just wide enough to pull the bag through.

"Well, thanks a bunch." I opened my mouth for a dramatic yawn. "I'm sure you're just as exhausted as I am."

"Not really," Melanie said.

We stood there considering each other like two street fighters. Only instead of gang colors and knives, we wore terry cloth and velour. Me armed with pure iron will. Her, with her brilliantly crafted tactical gift bag.

I heaved a beleaguered sigh that said all the things I couldn't. "Would you like to come in?" I offered, stepping aside.

"Sure," she said. "Awful nice of you to ask."

I closed and latched the door after her. "Have a seat." I indicated the corner opposite the bed where a hideously printed chair and its equally unprepossessing lamp friend pretended to be a cozy reading nook.

She wandered in and plopped down not in the chair, but on the bed. The same bed I had been looking forward to crawling into only minutes earlier before my dream had been so cruelly wrenched from me.

I sat down across from her, folding my robe carefully around my knees to avoid flashing a second human in one day.

Melanie hugged her knees, golden curls tumbling around her shoulders in the lamplight. But then, Melanie looked good in every light.

The bitch.

"This is just like a sleepover," she said.

I shrugged. "I wouldn't know."

Melanie stared at me aghast. "You . . . never had a sleepover?"

"My mom wasn't a big fan of people staying at our house." *Houses.* Also, it took too long to undo all her booby traps and hide all the firearms.

"And you never went to stay at other friends' houses?"

"Not really."

The truth, but not the whole truth.

The whole truth: friends were a resource that cost more than they were worth.

"Well, that's just sad." Melanie even *frowned* pretty.

I shrugged again instead of saying *so is having parents who murdered two people just so they could avoid having their pharmaceuticals company go bust.*

"Aren't you gonna open it?" Melanie glanced at the gift bag, which I'd set on the bed between us.

"Now?"

I always hated opening gifts in front of the givers. I'd never been especially good about making my face do what it was expected to in real time. People tended to get all butthurt when you were unable to shower them in the kind of unstinting praise they were due as a result of their selfless generosity.

"Of course now." She laughed in the kind, patient way you would when someone makes a blunder while trying to teach someone the more obscure customs of your culture.

I reached over and captured the bag by the handles, dragging it toward me on the bed.

Melanie bounced like an excited spaniel while I pulled out wads of tissues. Stacked in the overwide bag were several white clothing boxes.

She'd been shopping.

Why is it I suddenly had the feeling that I knew exactly how the Trojans felt when they saw the snout of a large wooden horse rolling toward their gates?

One by one, I opened the boxes.

The first one bore a set of silky pajamas.

The second, a sleek black pencil skirt and a couple of matching blouses.

The third, several pairs of silky panties and matching bras.

Below the last was a zippered case of brand-new toiletries: toothbrushes, soap, deodorant, et cetera.

How remarkably fucking thoughtful.

I needed all these things. Desperately. But that didn't stop me from being resentful at having to be grateful to Melanie for bringing them.

Sidenote: honest self-examination can suck a hairy ballsack.

"How did you know my size?" I asked, holding up the skirt.

She waved a hand at me. "Easy. I just looked for one I would wear and then bought a couple sizes bigger."

My eye twitched.

This.

This right here was the reason I found letting bygones be bygones so difficult where Melanie was concerned. Was she simply stating an empirical fact? Or was this a subversive comment about her own diminutive proportions in relationship to mine?

I wasn't sure I could handle the answer to this question, exhausted and raw as I was.

"Speaking of outfits." Melanie cleared her throat delicately. "That was quite the getup you were wearing in the lobby." She leaned forward on the bed, all conversational curiosity and girly grins.

And so it began.

This gentle back-and-forth wrestling match of Melanie making sure I knew she had witnessed something that would cause me abject humiliation. And me making sure she knew I didn't give a ripe shit what she knew.

I smiled right back at her. "Yep."

She waited for me to continue.

I didn't.

"What was it for?"

"A favor," I said.

Her smile slipped from its moorings for a split second. "For Shook?"

And God, how I wanted to lie. Make up some elaborate account of elicit role-playing and purple-smeared sexy times.

"Nope."

Melanie pushed herself up from the bed. As much, I suspected, to mask her frustration with my abbreviated answers as to feign disinterest in their contents. "So, what were you two talking about anyhow?" She ran a hand across the nearby credenza, toying with the remotes.

"When?"

"Tonight. Shook sure looked interested in what you had to say."

Red flags popped up like spring tulips.

"I thought you only saw me leaving his room?"

"Oh, I was just coming home from picking out your present, and I happened to see you two at the bar." She cast a casual smile at me over her shoulder. "You looked like you were talking about something pretty intently. I didn't want to interrupt."

The hell she didn't.

If there was one thing Melanie Fucking Beidermeyer didn't seem to mind, it was interrupting my life in new and inventive ways. Witness: the bag on my bed.

"He was just catching me up on what I missed this afternoon." I gave her a smile as vague as hers was frosty. "Why? What did you think we were talking about?"

"Oh, I don't know. I thought maybe . . . maybe you two were discussing the partnership opening."

Ah.

Pay dirt at last.

"You mean the one created by Kristin Flickner's death?"

Somehow I felt the need to remind her of this, if not the fact that it was her own mother who had caused it. Just as I didn't point out that whether she liked it or not, her stealing information from Kristin's case files had in some way contributed to her untimely demise, however unwitting.

"Well, it did leave an opening," Melanie said. "I thought maybe Shook might have mentioned to you who might be up for it."

"I sure as hell don't think it would be one of us." I unwrapped the towel on my head, finger-combing dark tangles out of my face. "There are associates who have been there a heck of a lot longer than we have."

"Seniority isn't the only consideration." Her lips parted in the easy smile that always left me wondering if she brushed her teeth with Vaseline.

It was moments like this when it occurred to me that, guided by some sense of misguided pity and stupidity, *I* had been the one who made sure Dawes never knew about Melanie's having stolen the case files.

If it hadn't been for me and my very own efforts, I wouldn't even be sharing Shook with Melanie.

No good deed and all that.

The tightness in my throat turned to bitter bile and I saw it all. The real reason she had gone shopping for clothes for me.

"Oh my God," I said. "You think Shook is pouring me the pork, don't you?"

"What? No." Her face vacillated between surprise and carefully arranged dismay. "It's just that you two seem to be awfully chummy."

"Shook is my *mentor*."

"He's also not so bad to look at." Her eyes went a little sly and slutty. "I know I'd date him if given half a chance."

"And did you get one?" I asked. "Your half a chance?"

"Of course not," she insisted.

"Is that why you got Gary Dawes to assign you to Shook? Because you thought maybe you'd have a better chance at the partnership if you just cozied up to him?"

"No. I would never—"

"Not everyone resorts to sucking dick to get ahead, Melanie."

The old anger had risen up in me like molten lava, burning up my throat, drawing a fine red haze to the edges of my vision.

As is so often the case, I regretted my words the second they were out of my mouth. The smile couldn't have disappeared from her face quicker if I had knocked it off with a hockey stick.

Tears glazed her eyes.

"You would think that," she said.

She turned on her slipper and stomped out in a huff, my hotel room door swinging closed behind her, heavy as an epitaph.

Chapter Twelve

My phone rang before dawn.

Like the archaeologist I dreamed of being as a girl, I excavated myself from layer after layer of a self-styled blanket cocoon and blinked at the strange gray netherworld of the hotel room.

I saw the name on the display, groaned, and answered it with a sleep-smeared voice and my face muffled by the pillow.

"I'd ask what you were wearing, but by the sound of your voice, I'm wagering it's long and made of flannel." Valentine, on the other hand, had the kind of mannered calm that suggested he might have been awake long enough to shower, shave, go for a run, and drink some sort of green smoothie with lots of flax.

In short, totally un-Valentine-like.

"And from the sound of yours, I'd say you're wearing an asshat."

"Shepard tells me you had a rather interesting night."

"Shepard and I define *interesting* in very different ways," I said, the last word hijacked by a yawn.

"And what would you call an evening of narrowly avoiding being shot by an unidentified gunman while dressed as a purple warrior elf princess?"

"A Monday."

"I never figured you for a LARPer."

"That's because I'm not."

"But you were dressed as Princess NightSpear?"

"You know who Princess NightSpear is?"

"Everyone knows who Princess NightSpear is."

"Well, apparently I'm not everyone."

"This, I would not argue with."

"And is that why you called me at the buttcrack of dawn, if not to argue? To mock me for dressing up as a purple elf?"

"No. Mocking you for dressing up as a purple elf is just an added bonus."

"I can just *feel* you wanting to get to your point," I said. "Don't fight it."

"I actually called to answer one of your questions."

Shock popped one of my eyes open. The other was still firmly committed to contemplating the back of my eyelid. "Why the hell would you do that?"

"Because I have some very important work to do today, and that work would go better if I didn't have to worry about you showing up in the middle of it and making my life a veritable hell."

"As honored as I am by your faith in me, I feel that's somewhat overstating my talents."

"You underestimate yourself."

"Mighty kind of you to say." I rolled over onto my back, making a snow angel beneath the clean sheets, relishing the feeling on my freshly shaved legs. "What kind of work is it you'll be doing today?"

"I know you'll find this a deeply shocking revelation, but there are, in fact, things that are none of your damn business."

"I'm a constituent of the universe, Valentine. The affairs of all creatures great and small deserve my care and consideration."

"It's the creature named Tyler I called to discuss."

My other eye popped open, both sides of my brain sufficiently interested in the conversation to commit at last. "What about him?"

"Yesterday, you asked me why I was trying to poach Tyler. The answer I gave you isn't entirely true."

"I'm shocked," I said. *"Shocked."*

"The reason I was trying to poach Tyler is because BitSled was about to lose Lucas Logan Bell."

I waited for this to feel significant. But then, the feels weren't exactly a strong point of mine at *fuck this* o'clock in the morning. "How did you know that?"

"Because he handed in his two weeks' notice a week before he was murdered."

I sat up straight in bed. "What? Why didn't you mention this earlier?"

"I didn't think it was necessarily relevant."

"For future reference, everything, and I do mean every *fucking* thing you know about any man who is found dead in my bed is relevant."

"Noted," Valentine said. "Of course, BitSled management went apeshit trying to convince him not to leave the company. The CEO called me, frantic, to ask if we could offer him a bonus to stay on."

"Why frantic?"

"Because when HR looked into Bell's personnel file, they discovered that he'd never been asked to sign a nondisclosure or a noncompete."

"How is that even possible?"

"You have to understand. BitSled is a small shop, and Bell was one of their longest- standing employees. He'd worked his way up from tech support and had pretty much flown under the radar the whole time. When they were originally hired to take on the 3-D microchip printing project, no one ever imagined that they'd be the company to finally solve it."

"I guess not." I leaned back against the wooden rectangle that served as a hotel headboard and smoothed a hand over my hair, which was sticking up every which way like the feathers of a startled chicken. "I don't suppose they knew where he'd accepted a new position."

Silence. Whatever Valentine was going to tell me next, it was something he wasn't supposed to know. "I might," he said.

"I'm all ears."

"Bell had accepted an offer of employment at Oxbow Group."

"But Oxbow Group already had a principal engineer," I said. "What would they do with another?"

"It just so happened that Oxbow Group was getting rid of their principal engineer."

"Tyler? Why?"

"Word on the street was that the management felt like he was especially difficult to work with and that the project might move faster if someone more solicitous was involved."

Sadly, I had no trouble at all imagining this conversation.

"Of course, we wouldn't have been that lucky with Tyler. I know damn well he'd signed a noncompete, but those run out eventually."

I scrubbed my face with my hand, convinced it was entirely too early for conversations of this magnitude. "So, the reason you were going to poach Tyler is because Oxbow Group had already poached Lucas Logan Bell?"

"Yes," Valentine said. "That's correct."

"And do you think that's why he was killed? Because someone didn't want him to go to work for Oxbow Group?"

"That's one theory," Valentine said.

"Got any others?" I sandwiched the phone between my ear and shoulder as I reached up over my head, stretching my arms over to one side, then the other.

"You shot him because he wasn't able to satisfy you sexually."

"Ha," I said. "And according to this theory, I also arranged for the failed attempt on Shook's life last night for the same reason?"

"I had considered the idea."

"Mark my words, Valentine. *If* I ever allowed Shook into my bed, I suspect he'd have no trouble whatsoever on that score. Those yogis are into tantric sex, after all."

Valentine snorted. "Tantric sex."

"What's the matter? Don't have the sexual stamina to withstand blowing a nut as long as it takes to establish a spiritual connection?"

"It's not stamina I lack," Valentine said.

"A soul?" I suggested.

"That's an entirely different debate."

I flopped back down on the bed like a shot bird, the small burst of information-induced energy I'd felt having quickly evaporated. Quick mental math informed me that the distance between the coffee maker and me was somewhere between ten feet and seventy thousand miles.

"Not that I haven't enjoyed the shit out of this chat, but words are still coming out of your face, and I haven't had coffee. Let's bottom line this shit. You're really telling me all this because you don't want me to come hunt you down today?"

"That, and I thought perhaps you might be able to do a little reconnaissance while you're on location at Oxbow Group."

"Are you suggesting I go digging for information that may or may not be related to the case that I am currently involved with?"

"I'm not suggesting anything. Just putting the information out there and suggesting you do whatever feels appropriate with it."

"Right. Because that's just the kind of guy you are."

"Considerate as fuck. That's me."

I peeled back the covers and kicked my feet over the side of the bed, stretching up onto my tiptoes and inhaling deeply. "That reminds me," I said in the mottled language of yawns. "Ever heard of the name RedWolf?"

Silence seeped out of the phone and expanded in my ear. "Where did you hear that name?"

"One of the goons who showed up in the hotel room last night to come after Shook said that RedWolf had sent them. Seeing as you seem to know everything about everyone, I thought I'd ask."

A pause.

A *meaningful* pause.

"Sounds like one of those battle tags. Are you sure it wasn't some LARPer who sent them?"

"LARP assassinations involve public humiliation," I explained. "Not guns. And anyway, they were after Shook. Not me."

"Sounds like someone really doesn't want this lawsuit to move forward," Valentine said.

"That was my thought as well. First Lucas Logan Bell, now Shook."

"Did they seem to want anything other than to kill him?" There was a rumble in the background. An engine starting. In my mind's eye, I imagined Valentine in the back of a limousine now, surrounded by leather and chrome.

"Like what?"

"Like the copy of the BitSled repository Shook has in his possession?"

"Tell me what it is you're doing today and maybe I'll answer that," I said.

"I can't," Valentine said.

"And why not?"

"Because it's of a personal nature."

Something cold uncurled in my stomach, spreading a darkness like tar through my middle. "I thought the whole reason you were out here was to look for my mother."

"It is, primarily, but other matters have arisen that I must deal with as urgently as possible."

"You do realize that I'd be a lot less curious if you just tell me what it is. And the less curious I am, the less chance there is I'll find the need to show up and say hello."

"Aren't you and the Tantric Wonder taking depositions today?"

"Shook is flexible." I debated on a follow-up comment but decided it was better to let Valentine infer whatever he wanted from that.

Which reminded me. Shook had never actually gotten a chance to give me whatever it was he'd brought me up to his room for last night. I made a mental note to ask him when I saw him.

"What were you doing up in Shook's room?"

"Reverse cowgirl, the Triple Lindy, a little light ball-gargling. You know, the usual."

The whispering sound that came through the speakers suggested Valentine may or may not be doing some deep breathing. If I listened hard enough, I could almost *hear* his jaw clenching. "Are you deliberately trying to provoke me?"

"I don't have to try," I said. "It's raw, natural talent." I grudgingly gathered up the small bag of toiletries Melanie had provided me and padded into the bathroom with them. "Anyway, why would that provoke you?"

A flurry of sounds bloomed in the background. A car door opening. Closing. The low, deep rumble of Valentine's voice as he spoke to someone with the receiver covered. "I have to go," he said. "I'll be in touch."

"You were wrong, by the way," I said quickly before he could hang up.

"About what?"

"I'm not wearing *anything*." And then, because I am a terrible, terrible person, I disconnected the phone and set it by the sink. Normally, this was the kind of thing I would have said just to fuck with Valentine, but in this case, it happened to be true.

After Melanie's abrupt departure last night, I hadn't wanted to put on the clothes that she bought me, settling instead for crashing in my bathrobe, which had come undone during the night. I'd woken up naked as a jaybird and fairly well rested, all things considered.

My cell phone buzzed. I picked it up, smugly certain it would be a rejoinder from Valentine.

A text message from Shepard.

Nice birthmark.

I snatched a towel from the rack and closed the blinds. What served as plenty of cover against human eyes in the high-rise across the street was no match for Shepard's scope.

Where are you?

Everywhere, came his immediate reply.

Ugh. I hated it when he was in vague dramatic vigilante mode.

How did it go with the cops last night? Translation: *Did my name come up?*

Fine.

And then, Open ur blinds back up. Can't protect what I can't see.

Fuck all the way off, I texted back.

With the towel firmly wrapped around me, I penguin-walked back out to the sitting room and grabbed the gift bag from Melanie. As much as I didn't want to wear the clothes she'd provided me, it was that or put on the same thing I'd worn the day before, and I'd had quite enough of Princess NightSpear, *thankyouverymuch*. Closing the bathroom door behind me, I slipped into the silky panties and bra, followed by the pencil skirt and one of the blouses.

I then mined the toiletries bag for toothpaste and a toothbrush and was surprised to find a smaller bag inside it. Unzipping it, I felt yet another pang of guilt.

Melanie had not only brought me pajamas and name-brand duds, she'd provided me with makeup. Foundation that matched my skin exactly. An eye shadow palette designed for blue eyes. Mascara, eyeliner, and several complementary shades of lipstick.

I considered the various items.

My efforts on this score were usually half-assed at best, but I had to admit to a certain level of curiosity.

I'd watched my mom put on makeup as a child, but usually it had been the kind that transformed her not into a more glamorous version of herself, but a frighteningly accurate rendering of someone else. Whoever she needed to be to get what she wanted. The little old lady eavesdropping on an important conversation. The harried minivan mom who could drive right past security.

On this particular morning, the idea of being *not* myself appealed to me more than I wanted to admit.

I spackled my face with a liberal application of the various products provided, examining myself this way and that when I was finished. Not altogether bad, I was forced to admit. To the nearsighted cube monkeys at Oxbow Group, I might even pass for female.

I found a plastic dry-cleaning bag in the closet and balled Tyler's elf costume into it, knowing by instinct how much he'd prefer to get it back folded. Petty revenge, perhaps, for making me wear it back to the hotel, but it made me feel better anyway.

As if some part of him sensed the insult in progress, Tyler chose that precise moment to text me.

I have the pictures. Meet me outside the building.

Chapter Thirteen

It was the kind of morning that only happened in cities near the sea.

Clouds conspiring in the sky overhead, promising rain they had no intention of delivering. The air thick with the scent of salt and soft with humidity that my skin greedily drank in after its years at a mile above sea level.

Melanie, Shook, and I had walked in a pack from our hotel to Oxbow Group. Melanie and I on either side of the gentleman in question, neither of us willing to give up our proximity to him even if it meant shoulder-checking the occasional pedestrian or narrowly dodging one of Seattle's many cyclists.

Shook made no mention of the previous evening's events. A display of discretion I would have gladly volunteered to bear his beautiful brown-eyed children for . . . if I didn't harbor an inherent distaste for very small people prone to sharing their bodily fluids without invitation.

This lack of conversation had provided the perfect opportunity for Melanie, who pointed out how lovely I looked in the clothes she'd bought so Shook would have ample opportunity to notice her generosity, and I'd have ample opportunity to thank her for them.

And I had.

And had.

And had.

When we reached the building, I spotted Tyler in the small stone courtyard outside. He raised a hand in greeting, which I decided to take as the Tyler equivalent of a full-body hug.

"I'll be right behind you," I said to Shook.

People who had spent less time contemplating the perfection of his face in three-hour-long, tedious meetings might not have noticed the subtle shift in his features. A lightning-fast slip from good-natured humor to tight-lipped hesitance.

I could guess at its source.

Yesterday, a disappearing act in the middle of a meeting. Today, potential tardiness. My overachiever's shine had long since worn off, and I had become as dull as I was unreliable as of late. "I promise, I'll only be a minute."

"See you soon, then." Shook offered up a chagrin-flavored smile and opened the door for Melanie, who glanced back over her shoulder at me before swinging into the building ahead of him.

I sat down next to Tyler, who looked scrubbed and shiny. Hair precisely parted. Eyes still boyishly puffed from sleep. The marble bench we shared still clung to the previous night's chill.

"I heard that sitting on cold things gives you hemorrhoids," I said, sterling conversationalist that I am.

"That hasn't been scientifically proven as fact."

"Of course, I've also heard that sitting on cold things is good for *soothing* hemorrhoids."

"I don't have hemorrhoids."

Because I am a pillar of good taste and discretion, I resisted the obvious comparison about their both being a wicked pain in the ass.

You're welcome.

"Why do you not strike me as the kind of guy who would willingly choose the great outdoors as a meeting place?" I asked.

The small clogged fountain in the courtyard's center colored in the silence with an anemic gurgle. It sounded more like the sounds you hear in a urinal (trust me, you don't want to know how I know) than a soothing water feature.

"Too many cameras inside the building."

He would know.

Tyler, who was not generally a facer of people as far as I could tell, turned to face me. His narrowed eyes traveled the terrain of my face, stopping at the parts I'd made colorful with Melanie's makeup. "You look different."

"Thanks," I said.

"I didn't say *better*."

I had walked right into that one.

"It's too early for this shit." I stood up, ready to walk away when Tyler caught me by the wrist.

We both stared at it for a second. He had willingly touched me.

Had purposefully put his hand on my skin. He dropped it as if he'd grabbed a branding iron instead of my arm.

"I have the file," he said, digging around in the kangaroo pocket of the same hoodie he'd worn the day before. Truly, I wouldn't have been shocked at all to discover that, like the stories I'd heard about Einstein growing up, Tyler had a closet stocked with multiple pairs of the same jeans. Same T-shirts. Same tattered shoes.

It would be motivated by his impatience with this kind of needless daily choice. A monkish dedication to the few textures he found bearable.

He held the small black stick out to me on the strange road map of his open palm.

"Thanks bunches," I said, tucking the drive into the new bra that was slowly and surely crushing my rib cage.

"No!" Tyler shouted, nearly causing me to fall backward off the bench when he reached in and grabbed it back out.

Of my bra.

With his hand.

And we're not talking one of those quick dips into the top of the cleavage. We're talking side-boob, corner pocket, full-on manual excavation. As in, if Tyler hadn't already mentally calculated my cup size by assessing Lefty's volume in his palm, I'd eat a lunch box full of gerbils.

"No, no, *no*," he scolded. "This is a Kingston DataTraveler Ultimate GT USB 3.0 with a two-terabyte storage capacity. Do you have any idea how corrosive the natural salts in your skin are?" He held it away from me with cupped hands like it was a newborn animal in need of protection.

"And do you have any idea how corrosive my elbow could be to your face? You do *not* just go reaching into people's bras, you dillhole! Not okay."

"Neither is putting a flash drive in your bra."

"Fine. I'll put it in my laptop bag." I held out my open palm, the other still clapped to the neckline of my blouse.

Tyler handed it over gently.

"While we're trading things." I picked up the bag of clothing I'd stashed beneath the bench and thrust it at him. "Here," I said. "Burn these."

He opened it and peeked inside, distaste creasing his brow. "I sent you home with a hanger."

"Did you? I must have forgotten that sometime *after* I ran into my boss while dressed as a purple elf but *before* a couple guys pulled a gun on me."

Okay, so they had technically pulled the gun on Shook, but it had happened damn close *to* me.

"And were they the ones who stole the hanger?" he asked.

I gaped at him.

"Did you not just hear the part where I was held at gunpoint?"

He shrugged. "I didn't see how it was relevant to my question."

I stood up, slinging the bag containing my loaner laptop over my shoulder. "You know, this kind of thing is *exactly* why they were going to fire you."

"Fire me? What are you talking about?" Tyler's face grazed as close to a human emotion as I had yet seen it. I'd name this one disbelief, if pressed.

"That's why Valentine was trying to poach you, okay? Because Lucas Logan Bell had handed in his two weeks' notice, and Valentine heard you were getting the ax."

"That's impossible," he said. "I'm the best at what I do. Curt would never be able to find a replacement."

"He already had," I said.

I could see the exact moment when all the facts aligned in his mind. Tyler's face went blank. And not the kind of blank that came from not being able to see and mimic facial expressions. The kind that comes from shock powerful enough to temporarily relieve your muscles of all memory of how to function.

I knew, because I'd felt it before.

The day my mother had disappeared and many times since.

Disbelief was a short walk. Anger shorter still.

Tyler couldn't manage either of these. Instead, his face was going through the kind of contortions common to hilarity or grief. The corners of his mouth jerking into what might be a smile or a grimace.

He pitched forward over his knees and started to rock. "This doesn't make any sense. This doesn't make any sense." He repeated these words to himself over and over like a mantra.

Many had been the movies I'd seen where someone under extreme duress made similar motions. I'd done it myself sarcastically on occasion. I'd even looked it up once out of curiosity, strangely heartbroken at the explanation I'd found. It was the body's way of simulating the sensation of being rocked by a mother, triggering the natural release of endorphins. A tragic form of self-comfort.

And yet none of this had prepared me for witnessing another human in such distress that this was their body's preferred coping mechanism.

"I'm sorry," I said. "I shouldn't have told you like that. That was a dick move on my part." I placed a hand between his shoulder blades, only to have him shy away from my touch like a cat.

"Don't," he said.

People were glancing our way as they walked into the building. I offered up my best *everything's fine and this is totally normal* smile as I did my best to block their view.

"How would Valentine know what the management of Oxbow Group was going to do?" Tyler asked. "I thought he was associated with BitSled."

Good question.

One I hadn't thought to ask.

"I don't know," I said.

"Bell did this," Tyler said. "I know he did. He's been trying to sabotage me for years."

"That's a little drastic, don't you think?" A noncommittal statement. Testing the waters.

"They're always watching," he said. "Waiting for their chance."

The capital *T* in *they're* and *their* was implied by his pronunciation. *Paranoia.*

As much as I hated myself for the thought, my mind strayed back to the array of pill bottles in his medicine chest. The kind of drugs that might be prescribed for someone who was delusional or perhaps just the tiniest bit schizophrenic.

"*Who's* waiting for their chance?"

"The people who want to see me fail. Just because I'm different. Just because I'm not like *them*. You wouldn't understand what it's like. Having someone who constantly humiliates you both personally and professionally. Someone who's undermining and subverting you at every turn. Someone who steals every opportunity presented to you and finds a way to make you look bad while they do it."

"Actually," I said, "I just might."

His rocking had slowed slightly as he talked, the words seeming to drain off some of whatever poison was fueling it. "We graduated from the same class at MIT."

This revelation set me back a little. "So you lied when you said that you met him through the LARP community?"

"I didn't lie. I just didn't tell you the whole truth."

No, dear reader, the irony is not lost on me.

"So your reasons for *assassinating* him weren't entirely based on the LARP world?"

"Not entirely," Tyler admitted.

"The guys don't know that, do they?"

"And they never will." His voice went cold as he said it, his face serious and his whole body suddenly eerily motionless.

"We should get inside," I said, possessed by a sudden longing to be where there were people. Not just people, if I was being honest. *Witnesses.* "The dev meeting will be starting soon."

Tyler remained silent until we were in the elevator on our way up.

"You know what to do with the file?" he asked without looking at me.

I considered his profile, noting for the first time the way his hairline reached for the edge of his eyebrow just above where his sideburn descended. And just above that, a strange pale scar traversing the closely cropped coffee-colored terrain of his hair.

Head injury?

Brain surgery?

"I know what *not* to do with it," I said, glancing down toward the neckline of my shirt.

"I meant, do you know how to use it?"

"I'm sure I'll be able to figure it out." No telling how long it might take me, though.

"I didn't just give you the images you asked for," he said. "I pulled down all the images from that location beginning the morning of the day your mother's picture was captured there all the way through this morning."

He glanced my way in much the same fashion as Melanie had every time she mentioned that she was oh so glad that the outfit *she* had picked out fit me so well.

I took a deep breath, ready to offer up yet one more thank-you.

"Thanks," I said. "That was very generous of you."

"I didn't do it for your benefit," Tyler said. "It was easier not to isolate them."

I mentally kicked myself in the ass so hard I could taste shoe leather. When, *when* would I learn never to make assumptions based on Tyler's face?

"The file is huge, so I indexed it like a database." He rocked back on his heels, fidgeted with the drawstrings dangling from the eyelets on the hood of his sweater.

I resisted the urge to take his hand and press it firmly to his side. Urge him to be still.

"I know that should mean something to me," I said.

He did his soul sigh thing again, his eyes falling closed as he rested the back of his head against the brushed metal wall of the elevator.

On an elemental level, I knew his doing this was most likely a sensory thing, elevators being somewhat overwhelming in that capacity. But he somehow still managed to make it look as if he had to block out my stupidity in order to respond.

"I associated the names of known entities like your mother and Valentine with their facial features so you can search the results that way. The rest, you're going to have to process manually. I tried to make the user interface as simple as possible since I knew you'd be the one using it."

I promise you, physical violence is not my first and only reaction to provocation. But something about Tyler's lean form made assault so infinitely easy to imagine. This time, it was grabbing him by the ears and introducing his face to the elevator railing.

Repeatedly.

Instead, I forced a smile onto my face. "I'll get this back to you as soon as I scan through it."

"Keep it."

The elevator doors opened, and Tyler barreled out without waiting for me. I stayed a few steps behind him, observing his shuffling, pigeon-footed gate at close proximity. As much as I hated to admit it, there was something mildly endearing about the completely unselfconscious way he moved.

Everyone was waiting for us in the same conference room where yesterday's meeting had unfolded. I quickly took one of the two available chairs, farther from Shook and closer to Agent Smith (as I had begun to think of him) than I would have liked. Curt Allen and his developers had all taken their same seats at the table. All but Tyler, whose seat was currently occupied by none other than Melanie Fucking Beidermeyer.

Instinctively, I knew he wouldn't take kindly to this and quietly thrilled to the prospect of his booting her out.

I wasn't disappointed.

"Good morning, Tyler Dixon." Melanie rolled his name over her tongue like a maraschino cherry, batting her eyelashes up at him for good measure.

"You're in my seat," he said.

Odd how I didn't mind Tyler's terseness at all when it wasn't pointed at me.

"There's another seat right there, sugar." Melanie glanced at the chair adjacent to the bank of windows overlooking the courtyard where Tyler and I had had our not-so-pleasant chat.

"That seat can't lean back against the wall, and I need to lean back against the wall."

I found the look of disbelief on Melanie's face intensely satisfying. I could verily *see* the question forming in her eyes.

Was this really happening *to her*?

"Well, my apologies." She stood, gathering her things. "I didn't realize people were so *particular*," she said, managing to make the word sound like an insult in the way only someone who never says *fuck you, fuckball* can.

"Good morning, everyone," Shook said with his typical graceful nonchalance once she was reseated. "As we decided in yesterday's meeting, today Mr. Smith will begin reviewing the repository with Mr. Dixon. This plan is still acceptable to everyone?"

"Actually, I was thinking." Curt Allen looked paler today, his hair rumpled and his chin and throat frosted with grayish shadow. "Maybe it would be better if *I* went over the codebase with you. As the chief technology officer, I might have some insights about the project that Tyler doesn't. What do you think, Tyler?"

Tyler didn't answer. Only rocked back in his chair again and again. The rhythmic thump of the wooden armrests created a tattoo on the wall behind him not unlike a headboard banging against the wall mid-epic-bones-jumping.

Which *shouldn't* have made me warm in strange places, but . . . there you go.

Curt cleared his throat, his eyes sliding to the side of his bifocal lenses. "Tyler?"

"Is this bothering you?" Tyler asked without stopping.

It was as much a challenge as I had ever heard, and that was fucking saying something considering I'd shared space with more than one homicidal human in the past few months.

Curt, gentle soul that he was, didn't answer.

"I am not opposed to this plan," Shook said. "Would that be acceptable to you, Mr. Smith?"

"I have no objections," Smith said.

"Splendid." Shook flipped over the top page of his yellow legal pad where he had scratched out some notes. "Now, as to the matter of the repository, were you able to find out if you have any copies from before the instance of rebasing?"

A sly little whinny from the end of the table reminded us all of the reason this had happed.

"We reviewed our records and determined that there were no copies made," Curt said. "We were not yet at a point in the project when that would have made sense."

"You are certain?" Shook pressed. "Because that would most definitely help us prove that there were no undue similarities between Oxbow Group and BitSled's code before it was manually rebased—"

My phone chimed loudly, vibrating against the table, which earned me a mildly censorious look from Shook, who had stopped midsentence.

Sorry, I mouthed, quickly silencing it as I glanced at the screen.

A text from Shepard. It annoyed the ever-loving fuck out of me that the mere presence of his name on the display was enough to make a strange tingly thing happen at the tips of my fingers.

What did U do to Valentine?

I didn't know which bothered me more. That he was accusing me of something, or that we were apparently back to the abhorrent abbreviations.

What do you mean, what did I do to him?

He's missing.

My left armpit had begun to sweat. Lefty being something like my body's check-engine light indicating that shit was about to go sideways. Define missing, I texted back.

I showed up at the designated meeting point this morning at the appointed time, and he was AWOL.

When were you supposed to meet him?

30 mins ago.

Maybe he's just running late. I quickly glanced down at my lap while I typed, doing my best to be as covert as possible about texting during the middle of a meeting. I talked to him just an hour ago. He said he had some private business to take care of today.

Negative. Something is wrong.

The complimentary hotel coffee I had swilled had magically turned into a small but agile badger, enthusiastically clawing my stomach lining to shreds.

While Shook began outlining in detail the discovery plan we would follow for gathering pertinent information related to the lawsuit, I cracked open the loaner laptop, stung by an idea.

There were three things I knew about Valentine with absolute certainty.

First, he had once upon a time been a talented breaking-and-entering artist given immunity by the feds for testifying against one of their most wanted.

Second, he was a man of particular taste in women, cars, and whiskey.

And third, he was a creature of habit who detested surprises and uncontrolled variation.

Money didn't buy spontaneity, and in the time I'd been acquainted with him, Valentine had predictably moved on a greased track from his high-rise loft to his high-rise office to his favorite gin joint at the Denver Country Club. If he insisted on returning to the same places again and again in Denver, there was a chance he'd do the same in Seattle. And if he'd done that, there was a chance that there might be new images of him from this morning.

I reached into the laptop bag and retrieved the flash drive, plugging it into the USB port. Opening the folder icon that appeared on the desktop, I saw it contained only two files. The first was titled NyxWare and the second, Princess NightSpear's Midreign Quest Blessing. That snarky sack of shark-wank *would* leave it on there just to fuck with me. I double-clicked on NyxWare and watched while it loaded.

"Where did you get that flash drive?"

The whispered question had come from the table neighbor on my left, a gray-goateed wire-rimmed-glasses-wearing systems administrator named Terry.

The expression on his face was somewhere between awe and abject longing.

"It was a gift," I whispered back.

Technically, not a lie.

"I've always wanted one of these." He reached out and petted it reverently with the tip of one finger. "I've never seen one in person."

"Why don't you get one?" I gave him my best *please stop talking to me* smile.

"Fifteen hundred dollars for a flash drive?" He snorted under his breath. "My wife would kill me. So would Curt, for that matter."

I felt my eyes go as round as doorknobs.

Tyler had *given* me a flash drive worth $1,500?

I glanced up from the laptop, trying to catch his eye, but he was staring blankly at the tabletop, light-years away.

True to form, NyxWare's user interface was painfully simple. A black box with a button at the bottom for the image archives and a small search rectangle at the top.

I typed Valentine's name and clicked the small magnifying glass to the right side of the box.

The page loaded with the oldest images first. Beneath each one was a time and date stamp with the location of the camera the image had come from. I scrolled through all the ones I had seen yesterday, came to the end of the list, and froze.

One new image from this morning.

I didn't have to look at the location. I already recognized it. A wooden bench on a street corner two blocks up from Ivar's Acres of Clams.

The camera was overhead, slightly to Valentine's right, but near enough to capture his face in three-quarters view. I'd had occasion to observe Valentine both up close and at significant distances. His posture as he sat on the bench was similar to the Valentine who often appeared in the back of his limo. Alert but relaxed, easy. Freshly pressed in his tailored shirt and slacks.

The man he was sharing the bench with, not so much.

He was small and thin, his eyes concealed behind sunglasses. His prominent cheekbones shadowed with grime. His face scabbed over with a patchy goatee, his clothes baggy and rumpled. He held a cardboard-sleeved coffee cup in one hand, the other slanted across his mouth. He was bent forward at such an odd angle that for a moment, I thought he might be vomiting.

Without the benefit of sound and motion, recognition came more slowly.

No. He wasn't gagging. He was laughing.

Something about the way his hand fell across his mouth. The angle of the shoulders . . .

I went deaf.

My ears swarmed with a strange high-pitched buzzing. My face numb and tingling.

The man wasn't a man at all.

It was my mother.

Chapter Fourteen

Everyone was looking at me.

I had a vague auditory memory of sound.

Had I said something? Made some sound of shock or dismay?

"Weren't you telling me about that just last night, Jane?" Melanie asked, her lake-blue eyes fastening onto mine. "How you were having trouble getting the initial disclosures to print in the hotel business center?"

My initial confusion quickly gave way to sphincter-puckering panic.

Shit.

The initial disclosures.

I was supposed to print out the initial disclosure documents for Shook to review with the development team, then with Oxbow Group's lawyers.

I'd completely forgotten.

"You can print them here," Curt offered. "You'll just need to connect to the Wi-Fi."

My face was hot. My fingers, cold. I couldn't think. I couldn't breathe.

"Which network?" With shaking hands, I opened the laptop's wireless Internet settings.

"Gloryhole," Terry said.

"Password?"

"Fucked if I know."

I looked up from the laptop. "Excuse me?"

"That's the password," Terry said. "Fucked if I know. No spaces. Capital *F*, shift-one for *I*."

"Right. Let me go print these off and I'll be right back."

I picked up my laptop and phone and scurried out of the conference room and down the hall on wobbly legs, dialing Valentine's number as I walked.

It went directly to voice mail.

"Son of a bitch."

Life is full of moments like these. Times when nothing is the same, and yet everything has to be. Your entire world can be effectively destroyed, and yet the water bill still needs paying. The garbage, taken to the curb.

I pulled up the documents and sent them to the printer, which reluctantly cranked to life, beeping angrily as it began to warm up.

I rested my head against the scratchy industrial fabric of the cubicle wall, overwhelmed by emotions tumbling over each other like waves. Anger, fear, embarrassment, denial, betrayal, hurt.

My mother. And Valentine. Sharing a bench.

She was laughing. *Laughing.*

Not a single time since she disappeared had I laughed like that.

And Valentine. How could he know where she was, sit down next to her, and *not* tell me?

"Jane."

My shoulders sank in time with my heart.

I took a deep breath and pasted an embarrassed smile on my face before turning around to face Shook. "I am so, so sorry," I said. "This won't happen again, I promise."

"Jane, you know how much I admire you." Shook reached out a hand and put it on my shoulder.

And to my horror, my nose began to sting. My throat tightened.

No, I bid my treacherous body. *You will not cry. Not here. Not in front of him.*

"I know you are amply capable of assisting with this case. But when you're so distracted—"

And just then, my phone pinged with another message from Shepard as if to illustrate Shook's point.

We need to find him. Now.

"I know," I said. "It's just—"

"Your mother," he said. "Not to mention your recent legal difficulties."

A rather kind way of saying *being charged with murder,* I thought.

"I would be the same in your situation. Which is why I feel it might be best to focus your efforts on that for the time being. Dawes will know nothing. Melanie has agreed to take on the responsibilities I had assigned to you. We can do what needs to be done here."

Melanie.

"No," I insisted, dashing tears away from my face with the back of my hand. "I can do this. I know I can."

"It has never been your competence I questioned," Shook said.

I picked up the pile of documents, still warm from the printer, and handed them over. For once, I had nothing to say.

"Why don't you go back to the hotel?" Shook suggested. "Get some rest. We can see about getting you a flight back to Denver when I'm done for the day."

I only nodded, staying silent as I walked toward the door. Some internal timer had already begun the countdown, precious seconds ticking away until I broke into horrible, ragged, double-inhale sobs.

I had made it down the elevator, across the lobby, and out to the sidewalk when a sleek black Hyundai screeched to a stop in front of me. The passenger-side window rolled down, revealing Shepard's face framed in the car's black leather interior.

"Get in," he said.

But I didn't get in.

Not immediately, anyway.

Shepard and I didn't have good car karma.

The last time we'd shared one, I'd decorated his lap with my stomach contents. An event neither of us had fond memories of, I expect. Me, because vomiting on people isn't necessarily a preferred pastime. And him, because it preceded my handcuffing him to the shower.

Which I still maintain was his fault.

I'm pretty sure Shepard's driving is the metaphor used by bats out of hell when they're inclined to complain about reckless motion.

"Get in," he repeated.

Still, I hesitated. "What are you doing here?"

"I could ask you the same thing. You were supposed to be at the dev meeting."

"How did you know I wouldn't be?" I suspected I already knew the answer, but I wanted to hear him say it all the same.

"I was watching you," he said.

I looked at him then. *Really* looked at him.

The sandy hair he usually kept closely cropped had started to sprout longer twists and whorls. His cheeks and jaw were sanded by toffee-colored stubble. His hazel eyes were almost blue in the windshield's reflection but ringed with dark circles.

It seemed like no one I knew was sleeping much as of late.

"You do know that this isn't the kind of thing you should be readily admitting, yes?"

He shrugged behind the steering wheel. "The truth is the truth."

If only my own philosophies on the matter could be so simplistic and self-assured.

"You coming or not?" he asked.

Cars were piling up behind him, honking their displeasure.

I made the sign of the cross and slid into the passenger's seat, into air intensely populated with his scent.

Deodorant did something magical with his skin, and Shepard wore a lot of it.

He'd served a couple of tours of duty in places where temperatures stayed in the three-digit range for months on end and had never fully surrendered the habit of swiping it over far more than just his armpits, or so I had come to believe.

Just as he'd never surrendered the idea of wearing a uniform, though the one he lived in these days wasn't strictly army issue.

Black T-shirt, worn jeans, and military tattoos.

Perhaps because we were neither pursuing nor evading capture, nor were we chatting with the police about a dead body that happened to be in our immediate vicinity, my eyes lingered over the various shapes and shades of ink.

An elegant black banner in a horseshoe shape peeked from beneath the sleeve of his T-shirt on the part of Shepard's arm where his mounded deltoid gave way to the elevated planes of his triceps. The feathery fletching of a pair of arrows crossed at the top, the grip of a sword in the space between them. On the bottom of the scrollwork was printed *DE OPPRESSO LIBER*. Grave, no-nonsense script in all caps.

My monkish fascination with Latin terms during my law school tenure demystified this for me.

To free the oppressed.

Dangling beneath this insignia in shockingly accurate trompe l'oeil gray scale hung a pair of dog tags.

The names engraved on them weren't his.

"You didn't answer my question," he said.

I wrested my gaze from his arm and stared at the road ahead. "Which one was that?"

"I asked you why you weren't working. I thought you were doing depositions today."

"I thought I was too."

I hoped the dejection in my tone related to this minor work-related issue might cover for the true source of my dismay.

All this time, I had thought the second I knew where my mother was, I'd fly into her arms or she into mine. And now, I was afraid. Afraid to call out an address and to tell Shepard to go there. Afraid of what we might find if I did.

Shepard gave me a sidelong glance.

"Hey," he said. "You okay?"

As soon as he said it, I knew I was in trouble.

He could have asked me any other question on earth and it would have ended differently. Without fail, I could always keep my shit together right up until someone asked me if I was okay.

And just like that, my face dropped into my hands and I was sobbing.

I mean *wailing*.

Hideous, horrible, backbreaking, double-breath-gulping, tears-shooting-horizontally-out-the-corners-of-my-eyes hysterics.

Stereotypes in movies had me worried that a man like Shepard might just throw himself out of a moving vehicle in order not to be next to a woman caught in a fit of ugly-crying.

Shepard said nothing.

Instead, he quietly steered the vehicle over to the side of the road, put it in park, and turned off the engine.

Then he did the thing that shocked me most of all.

He reached across the armrest, unbuckled my seat belt, and gathered me to him.

Not being a hugger myself, these kinds of impromptu embraces had only ever ended badly for me. My bony shoulder in someone's windpipe or my head butting their teeth together with a clack.

So, imagine my surprise when Shepard tucked me against his chest without incident. My cheek pressed against the plane of his chest, his heartbeat like a steady, binaural drum in my ear. My arms sandwiched between us. Head tucked neatly under his chin. His arms around me. One between my shoulder blades, the other at the small of my back.

Every point of contact both unyielding and strangely familiar.

For me, the daughter of a single mother, comfort had always been indelibly associated with softness. The smoothness of my mother's skin. The feminine scent of her lotion and shampoo.

Never in my life had a man held me while I cried.

And cry I did.

My tears soaking through the fabric of his T-shirt. My shuddering breaths the only thing creating space between us.

He made no comforting sounds. No shushing or soothing.

He just let me stay like this until every single tear had gone out of me and the sobs had dwindled to sniffles.

Our faces stayed close for a brief moment. I could taste the air he exhaled along with the salt from my tears, feel it cooling the tracks on my cheeks. His hazel gaze stayed fixed on my lips, swollen from my blubbering.

Less than a centimeter of motion on either of our parts would have brought our mouths together.

Shepard backed away first.

Clearing his throat as he reached into his pants pocket and pulled out a handkerchief.

An actual white linen, hand-embroidered, monogrammed handkerchief.

I dabbed at my eyes, horrified when it came away covered in a grayish sludge. I flipped the visor down and consulted the mirror on its back, stifling my own scream.

It *would* be my luck that the one day I decided to lose my shit would be the same day I had ventured boldly into the world of liquid eyeliner.

I did the best I could to repair my face, wishing I would have thought to stash some of the cosmetics in my laptop bag for touch-ups.

"I'm sorry," I said.

"Don't apologize," he said. "Well, not for this, anyway. You can totally apologize for the rest of the asshole things you do."

I laughed in spite of myself.

"So." He leaned back in his seat and turned his torso to face me. "You going to tell me what's wrong?"

I looked at the damp crumpled square of fabric in my hand. "J. S., huh? What does the *J* stand for?"

"Don't change the subject."

God, I hated it when people knew me well enough to see that kind of thing coming.

"*Everything* is wrong, Shepard. Everything."

"Tell me," he said. "Start at the beginning."

So I told him.

I told him about the security camera photo of Valentine and my mother. About the rude things Tyler had said to me. About Shook sending me away.

"That motherfucker," Shepard growled through gritted teeth, his forearms bunching as his hands clenched into fists. "You want me to kill him?"

"Which one?" I asked, unsure which part of my story had elicited this response.

"All of them."

"No." I sniffled, dabbed at my nose. "But it's sweet of you to offer."

"Shook will live to regret that decision." Such was Shepard's talent for non-emoting that I couldn't exactly tell if that was conjecture or a threat.

"I don't blame him." I gazed through the windshield, looking at nothing. Envious and resentful of every smile I saw. "I *have* been distracted. And this case is really important to the firm. They can't afford to have me fucking it up."

"He'd be *lucky* to have you fuck it up." Shepard poked the leather dashboard with a stiff index finger for emphasis. "Your fucking things up is better than most people's best efforts."

I glanced down at my hands, touched by the strange compliment and taken aback by the fervency with which it had been offered.

"He didn't tell me," Shepard said.

"Pardon?"

"Valentine didn't tell me he was meeting with Alex this morning."

It was odd to hear Shepard refer to my mother by her first name. He had become such a regular fixture in my world that I had almost forgotten that my mother had known him first.

As had Valentine.

"I think that's why he gave me the wrong address." Shepard stared through the windshield, his face empty and blank. "He didn't want me to know."

"I thought he told you everything."

"Not when it comes to you."

The reasons for this could be many, and none of them pleased me.

"Where were they?" Shepard asked. "Valentine and your mom."

"Down by Waterfront Park. But it was an hour ago. They could be anywhere by now."

Shepard withdrew his phone from the utilitarian clip on his belt and entered a code on the password screen that he successfully prevented me from seeing.

I knew it wasn't *strictly* my business, but it never hurts to know stuff, am I right?

The center console screen of the Hyundai flashed to life, the sound of a phone ringing coming through the car's speakers.

"What's up, Junior?"

"You're on speakerphone," Shepard said.

"Does that mean I should tell your mom to keep it down?"

My tired mind connected a face with the voice, and my heart flooded with a little wave of happiness despite the shitstorm.

"D-Town!" I shouted.

Danny B., call sign D-Town, was a contact of Shepard's and the owner of my second favorite laugh in all the world. He was effusive, foul-mouthed, proudly Italian, and a thirty-year veteran of the private investigation game.

Between him and Shepard, it was a toss-up as to who had the more disturbing war stories.

"Calamity Jane! How the fuck are you?"

"I've been better, sir," I said, thankfully still sufficiently wrung out of tears that I didn't break into sobs once more.

"I'm awful sorry to hear that, darlin'. How can I help?"

"We need a phone trace," Shepard answered on my behalf.

We. Shepard had said it without any big production. Without qualification or hesitation. How I'd neglected to fully appreciate the simple pleasure of being part of a team. Having a partner in crime.

"That's a *cop* favor," D-Town said.

"I know," Shepard said.

"And if I have to call in a cop favor, then you know you're going to owe me one in return."

Part of me was surprised D-Town hadn't added a *Godfather*-esque *on the day my daughter is to be married* to the end of that statement.

"I know," Shepard repeated.

"Number?"

Shepard rattled off a series of digits.

A beat of silence and then, "You have got to be out of your god-damn mind. You want me to trace Valentine?"

"You have a problem with that?" Shepard asked, taking on some of the same swaggering challenge that D-Town evoked so effortlessly.

"Yeah, I got a problem with that. I know you remember what happened to the last guy who put a phone trace on Valentine without permission because *you* were the guy he sent to do it. Poor fucker still can't walk without a limp."

"He's not going to find out," Shepard said.

"And how do you know that?"

"Because I'm *also* the guy he has track that kind of shit."

D-Town's snort rasped through the phone's speakers. "Junior, you owe me fucking *huge*. We're talking Super Bowl tickets huge. We're talking . . ." D-Town paused, apparently waiting for further inspiration to suggest itself.

"Two blondes and a midget with a lube ladle huge?" I suggested.

Shepard gave me a dark look.

He had never much cared for my and Danny's smart-ass chemistry.

"Yeah!" D-Town agreed. "And maybe throw in a contortionist for good measure."

I smiled at the naked bravado of this last request. Danny B. was, as he'd told me, one of those rare happily married men who would sooner surrender a testicle than cross his wife.

"Are you going to do it or keep jawing about doing it?" Shepard asked.

"Hold your wad," D-Town said cheerfully. "Give me a minute."

The connection went dead, dropping Shepard and me into a tense silence.

"He can really do that?" I asked. "I thought the best they could do is tell you which cell phone towers someone's phone has pinged recently."

"And the cops would prefer to keep it that way."

"Ahh," I said.

"Most smartphones come standard with satellite-trackable location services," Shepard said.

"I'm surprised Valentine hasn't disabled that on his phone."

Shepard turned his torso to face me. "He has."

"Oh," I said. Then, *"Ohhhhhh."* The idea of this, that Shepard would willfully defy a direct order from Valentine by enabling the tracking again without his knowing filled me with a strange mix of wonder and dread. I mean, *I* did it all the time, but Valentine didn't sign my paychecks. "Mister, you must have some kind of brass balls."

"Sometimes the success of a mission requires tactical maneuvers that are in direct contradiction to the commander's orders."

"I can't see that being a particularly popular philosophy among the Army Special Forces."

"It wasn't." The void spiraled behind his eyes as he stared out into the distance.

Goose bumps danced from my scalp all the way down my arms.

I jumped when the car's speakers rang abruptly.

Shepard pressed the answer button, and D-Town's voice once again filled the car, chasing away the shadows that had begun to gather there.

"Have I mentioned that you owe me?" he said.

"Briefly. Coordinates?"

"Because I'm a good friend if not a stupid one, I already satellite mapped it for you. He's on a yacht just off of Bell Harbor Marina."

Shepard cranked the engine over, and we rocketed out into traffic with enough force to clamp my teeth down on the tip of my tongue. The tires screamed as we took a corner hard enough to send a puff of burnt rubber through the vents.

"Jesus. He's doing his *Fast and the Furious* thing again, isn't he?" D-Town asked.

I gripped the handle on the door while simultaneously pressing my feet onto invisible breaks. "Totally doing the thing."

"I'll let you guys get after it."

"Thanks, D-Town," I said.

"Hey, Calamity?"

"Yes, sir?"

"Stay safe, okay?"

There was enough fondness in his voice to bring a few more tears to my eyes.

I made no promises.

———

"So, do you mostly use that without the rifle parked under it?"

Shepard didn't answer.

He was frighteningly still. The scope glued to his face was long, black, full of buttons and dials, and most likely worth more than my human life.

He had aimed through the small space left unblocked by the visors he'd put in the car's windshield.

"I mean, it's just good to know what to envision for mental image purposes," I continued. "Not that I spend much time envisioning that kind of thing. But if I did—"

"*Gotcha.*"

And then, without warning, Shepard yanked his face away from the scope like it had turned to lava. Or spiders. Or spiders made of lava.

"What? What is it?" I resisted the urge to elbow him out of the way like pirates did in the movies when they were jostling over a spyglass.

The blood had drained from Shepard's face. "Mission aborted," he said, quickly snapping open the scope's case and dropping the expensive gadget in with far less care than I would have expected. "We're leaving."

"Not until you tell me what you saw."

When he looked at me, I could almost *see* the calculations happening behind his eyes. The odds that he would make it out of this situation with both his testicles intact if he tried to just leave anyway.

The odds were not in his favor.

He lifted the scope to its previous position, offering it up to me in wordless invitation.

I squinted one eye closed and pressed the other to the sight, still warm from his face. A few minor adjustments brought Valentine into focus.

I gasped.

"He's wearing a . . . a," I stuttered, scarcely able to believe my waking eyes. *"Hawaiian shirt?"*

"Look again," Shepard instructed.

I moved the scope downward, my gaze snaking along the eye-frying print down to the bistro table's edge.

I gasped again.

"*And* pleated khaki shorts!" I stifled a gag.

"Not the clothes. The company."

I swiveled the scope slightly to the right, taking in the other side of the table. Across from Valentine sat a woman in a sleeveless wrap dress of the same print as Valentine's shirt. The kind of woman I had come to know as his "type." Large breasts of such perfection in shape and size as to suggest surgical assistance. High cheekbones, full lips, overlarge anime eyes. Hair the hue of cherrywood furniture stain lifted from her bare shoulders in a well-timed sea breeze.

"What's so shocking about that? I mean, yeah, she's better-looking than your average whore, but I'm sure Valentine can afford her."

"She's not a whore," Shepard said. "She's his wife."

Chapter Fifteen

"Miranda?" I peered through the scope again.

I'd heard plenty about her as a consequence of Shook's role as Valentine's divorce attorney. How she had accused him of domestic violence. How she had refused Valentine's offer of half of everything in favor of trying to take him for every cent he was worth. How she drank the blood of virgins and tortured orphans for sport.

I'd *heard* plenty but had never actually *seen* her. The woman sitting across from Valentine didn't look capable of any of those things.

"What's she doing here?" I asked, keeping the scope trained on her.

"Aside from plotting a way to end humanity as we know it?" Shepard asked. "Your guess is as good as mine."

"I can't believe it," I said. "Big, bad Shepard afraid of a tiny, little woman."

"You're only saying that because you don't understand."

"So explain." I handed the scope back to him and folded my arms across my chest.

"It's not *Miranda* that's the problem. It's who *Valentine* is when he's around her."

"And who is that?"

Thoughtful wasn't exactly what I would call Shepard's default expression, but he did a decent job of it. "When Valentine's around *tiger swo*, he becomes *not*-Valentine."

"*Tiger swo?*"

He spelled it out letter by letter. "*T-G-R-S-W-O.*"

"Which stands for?"

"The Great Red She-Whore."

I indulged in an epic eye roll. "First of all, you've got to get with the times, dude. Sexual confidence is no longer considered a bad thing, and second, I'm not sure that *not*-Valentine wouldn't be an improvement."

"We're wasting time." Shepard grabbed my wrist, fervently squeezing it while his eyes widened. "Every minute we stay here is one more minute that we could be putting distance between them and us."

"Distance?" I scoffed. "I'm not going anywhere until I've talked to him."

"Negative," Shepard said. "I can't allow that."

"James Shepard—" I paused, waiting to see if he would correct me. It seemed like an opportune moment to try out some of the ideas I had about what the *J* in J. S. might stand for.

"Nope."

"*John* Shepard?"

"Afraid not."

"Jehoshaphat Shepard?"

"Now you're just being ridiculous."

"Well, whatever the fuck your name is, I'm getting on that boat." I slipped my wrist out of his hand and grabbed the door handle.

Shepard engaged the child locks.

"Really?" I said, turning back to him.

"Jane, you have no idea what you're up against. She is *evil*."

"Men love to say that about powerful women that they don't understand." I reached across him and disengaged the lock.

"Hold up." He dug around in the black duffel bag behind my seat and took out a small black velvet case.

"Why, Shepard!" I pressed my hand to my chest, feigning excitement. "This is so sudden! I don't know what to say."

"Very funny." Shepard popped it open with a flick of his finger to reveal a lapel pin in the shape of an airplane. "Take this with you."

"For luck?" I asked.

"For listening," he said. "It's a wire. Just in case something goes wrong."

I didn't bother asking what could go wrong because we both knew the answers to that were many and varied.

I dropped it into the pocket of my blouse and patted it.

"You might want to put it in your bra," Shepard suggested.

I took the pin out of my pocket and snuggled it down in the cup as instructed. "You think it would get better sound there?"

"No," he said, one corner of his mouth tugging up into a wicked grin.

I sighed and rolled my eyes, levering myself out of the car and slamming the door behind me.

"Wait!" Shepard called out of the open passenger-side window. "How are you planning on getting aboard?"

"You know me." I glanced back over my shoulder. "I'll figure something out."

Trouble is, I had precious little experience where sneaking onto boats was concerned, and the plans my brain was churning out had a distinctly pirate-y flair. You know the kind. Where the dashing hero—me, in this case—lays hold of a rope and swings gracefully aboard the enemy vessel—Valentine's yacht—while announcing her presence with a triumphant *Ha!*

Of course, this plan fell down right around the part where I reached for my rapier (which I didn't have) and romantically twisted my Errol Flynn–style mustache (which, shit, I would have waxed off anyway).

I had amended the vision to include tossing my hair haughtily instead when a gentleman in full boat-captain regalia came over and tapped me on the shoulder.

With his white uniform, white eyebrows, white mustache, and white goatee, he looked like he'd stepped right off a package of oatmeal or kid's cereal. Save for the sour expression on his face, distinctly unimpressed with the likes of me.

"Don't get your boxers in a bunch," I said. "I'll be moving along in just a minute."

"That isn't why I'm here, Miss." I detected the slight, clipped cadence of a British accent.

"No?"

"No. I am here because Mr. Valentine would like me to escort you onto the boat. He requests the pleasure of your company."

My intestines migrated an inch to the south. Valentine anticipating my arrival was decidedly *not* a good sign.

"I wouldn't be so quick to shovel bullshit in a white uniform like that," I said to cover up the sudden burst of panic flooding my chest.

"Pardon me, Miss?" His eyebrows, twin bushy caterpillars, ascended his forehead as he lifted his beaky nose.

"No way in hell did Valentine *request* the *pleasure of my company*."

"But he did, Miss. Those were his precise words."

"And I thought *I* was a liar." Nevertheless, I surrendered my spot behind the crab shack and stood to follow him. "Lead the way, Captain Crunch."

———

"Jane!" Valentine stood and threw his arms wide, closing the distance between us with three broad steps of his rubber-soled deck loafers. "I'm so . . . happy . . . to . . . see . . . you!" Each word was punctuated with a playful side-to-side rocking motion as he wrapped me in a bear hug, my arms pinned to my sides.

I leapt a foot back when he released me at last. "Who are you and what have you done with Valentine?"

He laughed broadly. "Oh, Jane. Always such a kidder. Come with me. I want to introduce you to my wife." He tugged me by the hand like a preschooler wrangling a parent over to the art wall to show off his latest drawing.

Miranda shucked off her cat-eye sunglasses with the grace of a 1960s Hollywood starlet when she saw us rounding the corner, her face splitting in a broad grin.

"Darling," Valentine announced. "Look who I brought to meet you."

So now she was *darling* and not the Wicked or Ex-Beast or She Who Must Not Be Named?

I didn't like this. I didn't like it one bit.

She breezed toward me, taking me by both hands like she was going to twirl me around.

"You must be Jane," she said, giving my hands a squeeze. "It's so wonderful to meet you at last."

"Me?" I could feel the almost canine expression of confusion on my own face. "Why?"

"Because I have you to thank for bringing us back together!"

"And what the everlasting fuck do you mean by that, pray tell?"

She released my hands, stepping to Valentine's side. Her arm snaked around his back, her manicured hand tucking itself in the front pocket of his shorts just as she leaned her head against his shoulder. "If it weren't for that unfortunate Lucas Logan Bell incident, then Archie would have never bailed you out. And if Archie hadn't bailed you out with money from our trust, we wouldn't have had to meet face-to-face to change the divorce settlement days before it was supposed to be finalized. And if we hadn't met face-to-face, we wouldn't have realized how much we missed each other." These last few words were distorted by her pooched lips as she leaned in and nuzzled Valentine Eskimo kiss–style.

"It wasn't an *incident.* A man was murdered."

"Of course." Miranda winked at me, conspiratorial and approving. "But between you and me, sometimes a woman's got to do what a woman's got to do, doesn't she?"

This wasn't a question.

It was a gauntlet.

And Miranda had thrown it directly at my feet.

She was telling me in no uncertain terms that she, too, wouldn't hesitate to cut a bitch if it came to it. And if that bitch happened to be me, all the better.

"Yes, she does," I agreed. "Just like a man has to do what a man has to do."

"As long as his wife approves. Am I right, honey?" Valentine's grin could have covered enough nachos to feed an army of football players.

"And did Miranda approve of you meeting with my mother this morning?"

Miranda's predatory smile briefly slipped from its moorings. "You didn't mention that you'd seen Alex so recently, darling."

I wanted to slap my mother's name off her lips.

Valentine waved a hand and planted a kiss on Miranda's cheek. "That's all in the past."

"It was an hour ago!" Seething rage boiled up from my stomach. "An hour ago you fucking sat next to the woman I've been looking for for almost a month, and you didn't tell me a damn thing. You *knew*. You knew where she was. You knew how much it hurt me not to know. How sick and stressed and insane it's made me, and you said. Fucking. *Nothing*."

I heard someone clear a throat over my shoulder. I turned to see that Captain Crunch had returned with a tray of cocktails. Well, two cocktails and a glass of water.

You could have knocked me over with a feather when, after handing one of the cocktails to Miranda, he turned and offered the second to me.

I shook my head no and only then did he present it to Valentine.

Valentine waved him off enthusiastically, taking up the glass of water. "None of the hard stuff for me. Miranda and I have agreed it was time I quit drinking, didn't we, darling?"

I grabbed Valentine by both lapels of his polyester shirt and shook him.

"What the fuck is wrong with you? What did she do to you? Please, Valentine, if you're in there, give me a sign!"

For a split second, I thought I saw a spark of recognition on his face, but it was doused as quickly as it had arrived.

"Please," I pleaded. "Please. Tell me where my mother is. I just need to see her. I just need to know she's okay."

For all the years I'd spent lying, the truth still felt strange on my tongue. Strange to know that I wanted this even more than I wanted to ask my mother the questions that had piled up in her absence. Why she could talk to Valentine, and not to me. Why she could tell him her plans. Why she didn't miss me the way I missed her.

"That's something I always loved about Archie," Miranda purred, curling a finger in a dark lock of hair at the nape of his neck. "He's always had a weakness for unfortunates. Poor, pathetic women with daddy issues who don't have resources of their own. Clinging to him for safety and support."

A brass bell rang somewhere within the bowels of the boat.

Valentine's eyes brightened like a kid who's just been handed a brand-new bike for his birthday. "You know what that means!"

"Conga time!" he and Miranda shouted in unison.

Valentine brought one hand to the opposite elbow, his other hand high, index finger pointed toward the sky. He began a rhythmical little shuffle back and forth, singing "Ya-da-da-da-dah . . . hey!" as he danced over to Captain Crunch. Much to the older man's dismay, Valentine relieved him of his tray before guiding his hands to Valentine's hips, the next link in the chain he was trying to build. They picked up the bartender, followed by a waitress and one of the cabin staff, before shuffling off in a train around the corner of the deck.

I looked Miranda directly in the eye. "I don't know what you did to him," I said, my voice quivering as pure sweet adrenaline surged through me. "But rest assured, I'm going to undo it. You and your magic pussy are going down hard."

Miranda laughed gaily, taking a sip of her cocktail before sending a little wave toward Valentine, who had paused to blow her a kiss from the other side of the deck. "Silly girl. You don't even know what you don't know." She leaned in close, her lips next to my ear. "Greetings from RedWolf."

Chapter Sixteen

Coming off the boat, I knew three things.

Valentine was seriously unhinged.

I wanted to punch Miranda in the taco.

And if I didn't get some food in my face soon, I was in infinite danger of inciting a small-scale riot.

Shepard and I stopped by a fish-and-chips stand, where I ordered the biggest basket they had, drowning both the fries and the cod in a small tidal wave of malt vinegar before greedily attacking it with my face.

Shepard ordered only a water, downed the beverage in three large gulps, and shot the plastic cup at a nearby trash can, suggesting that we walk while I ate. He cited a need for cardiovascular exercise after so long buttoned down in the car, but mostly I thought it was a solid alternative to his needing to break something.

So we walked.

As I quickly learned, one didn't so much walk down the sidewalk *with* Shepard as walk down the sidewalk *near* Shepard, who tended to inspire a mass exodus of pedestrians to anywhere that wasn't in his direct path.

"Tell me again where my five-hundred-dollar covert listening device is?" he asked.

"In the yacht's stateroom," I said. Only, around a mouthful of battered fish it sounded more like *"Mim the yop's stay oom."*

"And how did it get there, exactly?"

I held out my hand for the fresh-squeezed lemonade that Shepard had offered to carry, because I needed one hand to hold my newspaper cone of fish and the other to stuff it enthusiastically down my throat.

After a healthy swallow, I answered him somewhat more intelligibly. "I put it there on my way out."

"And why did you do that?"

"Because the stateroom doors open onto the deck, and the device records sounds in up to a thirty-foot diameter. I thought it would be our best chance of catching something."

"I meant, why did you leave my five-hundred-dollar listening device on Valentine's *fucking* boat?"

I took a deep breath.

"Because either Miranda *is* RedWolf or is working for RedWolf, and RedWolf is the one who sent goons to kill Shook, and Shook has the only existing copy of a codebase for the 3-D printing technology worth about four billion dollars, and I had this crazy idea that she might say something we would find useful." I took another bite of fish.

"You do realize this is two bugs you've cost me," Shepard said.

"Not technically true," I said, taking another slurp of the lemonade before handing it back to him. "The other thing I ruined was an earpiece. The bug itself remained perfectly intact."

"But you never returned it."

"I was mad at you. That happened just after I learned that you'd been lying to me about working for Valentine."

"*I'd* been lying? You really want to play this game?"

"Maybe I do. I never got the chance to ask you about the ex-wife you conveniently forgot to mention. Or her lover who was inconveniently shot in the head."

"At least he wasn't found dead in my bed."

"Details, details. Point is, in all the conversations we had, you never once mentioned that you had been married. Or divorced."

"And are discussions of previous marital status acceptable for a purely professional relationship?"

Touché.

Lord love a duck, how I hate having my own words thrown back at me. I had been the one to insist that our relationship remain purely professional, after all. And now, it was up to me to nudge it in the opposite direction if I wanted to know more.

The ball(s) remained firmly in my court.

I found blessed distraction in the form of fish and french fries, taking a bite and hastening my stride.

"Do you even know what that shit does to your body?" Shepard asked.

"You mean besides releasing life-enhancing dopamine?"

"There are ways of releasing dopamine that don't involve clogging the fuck out of your arteries with saturated fat."

"I like to think of them as wrapped in a cozy blanket of lard-love." I pretended to snuggle a fry to my cheek before popping it into my mouth.

"Don't think I didn't notice that you deliberately ignored my question."

"I didn't ignore it. I simply chose not to respond because I felt reopening that conversation isn't an effective use of our time."

"Tell me you've never thought about it."

"Thought about what?" My tone was breezy; my thoughts, less so.

"You. Me. *Us*," he said.

Why was it I had thought swearing off lying was a good idea?

"I also think about what Mr. Clean would look like naked. That doesn't mean I would bang an animation whose very existence is derived from the female psyche's latent desire to have a bald, buff man-slave assist them with the household chores."

Now the Brawny guy, on the other hand . . .

"Mr. Clean isn't standing here offering you orgasms." Shepard stopped in the center of the wide sidewalk, foot traffic moving around him like river currents around a boulder.

"That may be the strangest sentence anyone has ever spoken to me." I tried to resume my pace, hoping Shepard would follow suit, but he only reached out and caught my wrist, drawing me back to stand opposite him.

"Look at me," he said.

Which for me meant looking *up*.

So much of our time had been spent sitting in cars that it was easy for me to forget the near one-foot height differential that existed when we were standing.

"Shepard—"

"Just hear me out. We're both free of romantic attachments. I'm pretty sure we're both disease-free. We've already seen each other naked."

"Because you were watching me through a scope!"

"And that's better than you having handcuffed me to a shower *how*?"

All right, so he had a point.

"It's not that I don't appreciate the offer, because I totally do."

His jaw flexed. "But?"

"But we still have to work together, and I don't care who you are or how good your intentions might be. Sex always complicates the shit out of things."

He pushed a stray lock of hair out of my eyes. "What if I like it complicated?"

"You like it *now*," I said. "But you wouldn't like it when it starts arguing about whose turn it is to take out the trash and to pick your goddamn socks up already."

"That's not the kind of arrangement I'm talking about."

"I know," I said. "I've had the kind of arrangements you're talking about before. I know how they end."

"Who says it has to end?" The question was playful despite the resigned sadness in his eyes.

"I have a better idea," I said.

"What's that?"

"Close your eyes and open your mouth."

He narrowed his eyes at me. "How likely would you be to trust me if I made the same request?"

"Oh, come on. Don't be such a baby."

He met me halfway, complying with the mouth opening but not the eye closing. More than likely an unwillingness to render himself blind to potential threats than any innate desire to be difficult.

I broke off a piece of battered fish from the bottom of the paper cone where it was still warm and crispy, sliding it between his lips.

He chewed thoughtfully, never taking his eyes off me.

And in that moment, he looked so innocent, so painfully boyish that despite everything I had said, it took every ounce of my severely limited restraint not to go on tiptoe and collect the scattered grains of salt clinging to his lower lip with my tongue.

I swallowed the well of saliva that had gathered at the base of my throat. "Tell me that's not just as good as sex."

He swallowed and stole a sip of my lemonade for good measure. "You've been having the wrong kind of sex."

Shepard's phone chimed. He unclipped it from the holster on his belt and uttered a vivid oath.

I tried—and failed—to peek over his shoulder. "What?"

"Automatic notification from the listening device. The voice recognition audio is picking up sound."

We both turned on the spot and hustled back to the car. A strange exercise wherein I took two and a half steps for his every one.

Once inside, Shepard turned the car on so the Bluetooth sound system could pick up the audio coming from his phone.

"You want to hear it from the beginning?" he asked. "Or stay in real time?"

"Real time," I said. "We can always go back if we need to."

He turned on the radio, and the vehicle was suddenly filled with the sound of Miranda's throaty purr.

Shepard made the sign of the cross.

Without knowing exactly why, I pulled out my own phone and set it to record.

"Oh, *Miranda*." Valentine's moan was deep and languorous. The kind that came with a full-body shiver. "You have no idea how I've wanted this."

"And you have no idea how I've wanted your *mmmph*." What the remainder of her reply had been muffled by, I didn't really want to think about.

"Jesus Christ," Shepard said, turning the volume dial all the way down. "I can't listen to this."

"They could be talking about how much they've wanted to sit down and discuss RedWolf's nefarious plans," I said, turning it back up. "You don't know."

"Your mouth," Valentine gasped. "I should have it bronzed."

Shepard raised an eyebrow at me and turned the sound down once again.

"Maybe she's eating dinner and he's grateful that she has such an appreciative palate," I said, turning it back up.

"Oh, she's eating all right," Shepard said.

"You want this?" Miranda's question was full of lurid suggestion.

"Yes," Valentine moaned. "God, yes."

"See?" I said, knowing that my already-paper-thin argument was quickly dissolving away. "She's just offering him the rest of her baked potato."

"Baked potato." Shepard snorted. "Is that what you call yours?"

"Tell me one teeny, tiny thing and it's all yours." Miranda's voice had gone all breathy and soft.

"Anything," Valentine rasped.

A few squishy sounds followed by a rude, wet pop.

"And what was that sound?" Shepard asked. I had the feeling he was actually beginning to enjoy this game.

"That was Miranda uncorking the wine."

"Yeah," Shepard said. "With her mouth."

"Tell me you'll say yes." Miranda's last word was punctuated with a hollow knock not unlike the one made by Tyler's chair as it bumped against the wall. It was followed by a second, then a third at ever-quickening intervals.

The sound Valentine made was barely recognizable as human, let alone credible as an answer in the affirmative. Then there was nothing but the rhythmic bumping interrupted only by the occasional grunt from Valentine.

Shepard shifted in the driver's seat. Clearing his throat as he tugged on his pants leg. Somehow, both the driver- and passenger-side windows had fogged over.

"RedWolf . . . wants you . . . back," Miranda said in time with the bumping noises.

Back.

Back?

A thousand little insects crawled across my face with prickly little legs. Their cousins swarmed my brain with facts and revelations.

Valentine had worked for RedWolf.

"He's even willing to forgive you for testifying against him."

It was around this word, *testifying*, that the memory hinged.

Valentine had told me a story once.

About a young man good at sneaking into places he wasn't supposed to be and the criminal mastermind who had made use of this talent.

Fragments of the conversation floated back to me now.

A criminal mastermind who had a reputation for making people disappear.

Even with the offer of immunity, only one person was willing to turn state's evidence and testify against him.

Valentine.

But the one thing Valentine had really wanted, the feds were unable to deliver.

Safety from the network of associates he had betrayed.

They found him every single time.

He'd learned to be creative about how to protect himself.

My mother had sought him out for that same protection.

The criminal mastermind Valentine had testified against as a young man was RedWolf.

And RedWolf had found Valentine once again.

"What does he . . . want?" It was Valentine who was panting now.

"You *know* what he wants." All the syrupy sweetness had evaporated from Miranda's voice. What showed through was closer to the tone she had used with me. Ruthless. Mercenary. Manipulative. "The missing copy of the BitSled codebase."

"I don't . . . have it."

"But you know who does." Miranda didn't so much say this as growl it. In my mind's eye, she had a handful of Valentine's hair, clutching it to mingle pleasure and pain as she rode him. "And you know where to find her."

Her.

My throat closed over. My lungs ached. I couldn't move. Couldn't breathe.

I didn't need to hear Valentine's muttered promise or the name that followed to know who Miranda was talking about.

I already knew. I knew it the way you know even before opening your eyes whether it's day or night.

The *her* who had a copy of the missing BitSled codebase was my mother.

Chapter Seventeen

We sat in the ringing silence that followed the final crescendo of Miranda and Valentine's coupling.

I pulled the folding sunshade away from the windshield on my side of the car, possessed of a sudden urge to see the sky.

Still gray. Still endless. Like this day.

"Did you know?" I asked the question to Shepard without turning to look at him, wanting the answer but not his expression.

"Jane—"

"When you let me stand there and question the guys sent to kill Shook, did you already know who RedWolf was?"

"No one knows *who* RedWolf is. No one who works for him has ever seen him in person."

"But you knew Valentine had worked for him? Or are you speaking from personal experience?"

"Listen to me—"

"Did. You. Know?"

"Yes, I knew Valentine had once worked for RedWolf, but I swear to you, I do not now nor have I ever worked for him. Valentine only told me what I needed to know in order to protect him."

"What about Miranda?"

"What about her?"

"Did you know that she's working for RedWolf?"

"No," he said. "And if Valentine knew, he sure as fuck never mentioned it to me."

"And did Valentine happen to *mention* to you that my mother had in her possession a copy of a codebase that could determine the outcome of a four-billion-dollar lawsuit?"

Shepard said nothing, which somehow said everything.

Hot limbic anger shot through my system, filling my blood with a rage so big my body didn't feel large enough to contain it.

"I see. This whole time while I've been searching for her, you and Valentine knew *exactly* why she's been in hiding and neither one of you said one fucking word to me about it."

"It was for your protection."

I heaved a disgusted sigh and opened the car door. "I've had enough of your *protection*."

"Where are you going?" Shepard called after me.

"Anywhere," I said.

———

Alone in my sleek but sparse hotel room, I picked up one of the mini-bottles of gin and jumped it two squares on the impromptu chessboard I'd made by drawing squares on the lid of a pizza box. "King me!" I said to myself.

"Don't mind if I do," I also answered, unscrewing the gin's tiny lid and bringing it to my mouth.

A shrill and unwelcome sound penetrated my pleasant liquid-limbed haze.

My phone was ringing.

I glanced down at the screen and let my head fall back on the hotel room's giant fluffy pillow.

I'd been waiting for a call, but not this one.

Melanie Fucking Beidermeyer.

"Why do you hate me?" I asked the universe at large.

Had I been even slightly less buzzed, I probably would have ignored it. Hell, I'd ignored five of her calls already this evening. But as it was, I was just sauced enough to feel invincible and self-righteous.

"Hello, Melanie."

"Jane! Thank goodness!" Her words came through the speaker in a syrupy-sweet rush. The Melanie who lived in my mind dramatically put a hand to her chest. "I've been trying to reach you all day."

"Really? Why's that?" I suspected I knew why, but some part of me wanted to hear her say it.

"I thought you might be upset with me."

Even now, lit like a torch, my mother's advice still wandered through my head. *Practice silence, Janey. It's amazing the things people will tell you just to fill it.*

"For what?"

"For . . . for what happened with Shook."

"Why would that upset me?" See *Black's Law Dictionary* under *leading question.*

"I just didn't want you thinking that I was trying to take your place. We just know how much you've had on your mind lately, and we thought maybe it might be best if you didn't have to deal with this case on top of it."

As if deliberately bringing up her victory wasn't enough, now she was *we*-ing all over me.

"Of course not. Shook has to do what's best for the case."

"Jane, are you okay?"

"Why wouldn't I be okay? I mean, my mother has been missing for almost a month, I've basically been laid off, and, oh yes, let's not forget, I've been charged with a fucking *murder*." My giggle sounded insane even to me.

"Where are you? I think maybe I should come over."

My phone beeped, informing me I had another call coming in. I held it away from my face. Glanced at the name.

"Gee, Melanie, as much as I'd love to chat, I have a call on the other line."

"Jane—"

"Bye-bye now." I clicked over to the incoming call. "What do you have for me?"

"You're drunk," Tyler said.

"I would have said moderately lubed. But I'm pretty sure I could make drunk happen without too much effort." I unscrewed the weensy cap on the bottle of Beam that had been serving as a pawn and let the liquid fire slide down my throat.

I'd been sober as a judge, clammy, and shaking when I called him only an hour earlier to broker yet another favor in exchange for information, but the booze had helped remedy the fallout from that conversation considerably.

"I don't have the information you wanted," he said. "But I know where to get it."

"I'm listening," I said.

"I don't know if you're going to want it."

"Why wouldn't I want it?"

"You would owe another favor."

I lifted the chessboard to snag a piece of the crust I'd left behind. "What would it be this time?" I asked, chewing my doughy cud. "Dressing up like a Gorgon and doing the dance of the seven veils?"

"I don't know what the favor would be because it wouldn't be to *me* that the favor would be owed."

A worm of fear swam through the small lake of booze and pizza in my belly.

"Who, then?"

"Gnarth."

My head thumped on the headboard behind me as I contemplated the ceiling in lieu of the universe's infinite celestial realms. "Okay, but seriously. Why do you hate me?"

"What was that?" Tyler asked.

"Nothing. Tell Gnarth yes. We can discuss the terms once he has the information."

"You're sure?"

"I'm sure."

Tyler disconnected without saying goodbye only to call back five minutes later.

"You have something to write with?"

I grabbed the hotel-issued pen and pad of paper.

"Go ahead."

———

There are two ways to keep yourself from being killed.

Make sure no one knows where you are, or everyone does.

This bit of advice had come not from my mother, but Valentine.

I had opted for the latter, choosing a busy restaurant near Waterfront Park for the meeting I had arranged with one piece of information given to me by Gnarth SilverShaper, level-one Wizard and level-four cellular technician.

Miranda Valentine's cell phone number.

I'd arrived half an hour early and chosen a table for two in the corner, sitting with my back to the wall where I had a view of the main entrance and emergency exits—a nugget of advice that had come to me courtesy of Shepard.

Miranda arrived precisely on time, bypassing the maître d' with a haughty wave when she spotted me. All eyes moved to her body, wrapped in a snug sheath the dusty green of pine needles, a color setting off crimson flames in her hair. Even pushing forty, Miranda Valentine had the kind of beauty that would reduce admirers to warm puddles on the floor.

I stood to greet her.

She kissed me on both cheeks like a long-awaited friend.

"Jane. I was so *delighted* to receive your invitation."

But she didn't look delighted. She looked . . . hungry. The smile revealing even white teeth with unusually sharp incisors didn't quite reach her eyes, which gleamed with the naked avarice commonly associated with their color. She was rosy beneath the freckles that had cropped up since yesterday, signs of a leisurely afternoon spent on the deck.

"Thank you for agreeing to meet with me," I said. "After yesterday, it became clear to me who was the real power player in your relationship. I thought our conversation would be much more effective if we just sat down woman to woman."

The gold bangles on her wrists jingled as she brushed hair back from her face. "I appreciate your practicality."

"Speaking of practicality, I assume you have the information I requested?"

My plan was as simple as it was dangerous. Bluff my ass off in exchange for information.

The terms of the arrangement were simple.

If Miranda would use her voodoo pussy powers to find out from Valentine where my mother had been hiding, I would give her Shook's copy of the codebase. The trouble with this being that I didn't actually *have* Shook's copy of the codebase. What I had was a fake copy of a codebase given to me by Tyler.

Miranda reached into her voluminous Hermès shoulder bag and withdrew a white letter-size envelope. She set it on the table before her. "And you?"

With a flick of my wrist, I produced the flash drive from my sleeve with a magician's flourish.

"Before I hand it over, I have a question."

"What's that?" Miranda asked.

"If ol' RedWolf is rolling in the dough, why is it he wants the copy of this codebase so badly?"

Miranda stared at the flash drive, suddenly silent.

"You know what I think?" I continued. "I think it's because RedWolf has some of that dough sunk into Oxbow Group, and this codebase is going to prove that the technology belongs to BitSled. That would explain why he sent people after Shook as well. Am I getting warm?"

Her tight smile showed a few extra teeth. "They told me you were clever."

"They?"

"My associates."

"Ahh," I said. "You mean RedWolf's henchdudes?" I rested my elbows on the table and steepled my fingers. "Between you and me, you really ought to tell him to quit hiring cheap help. I get the feeling he can afford better."

"He can," she agreed. "Many times over."

"What *I* can't figure out is why exactly RedWolf would want Valentine to work for him again so desperately."

Now Miranda's face didn't just strain, it snapped. "How did you—"

"But my congratulations to you on some solid fuckery. I mean, you must be able to bend a metal bar down with that thing, the way he was spurting out answers."

"I'm so . . . *flattered* that you admire my work."

"Absolutely. I mean, women like me, we only have the cerebral approach. Using our wits, resourcefulness, and intelligence to get ahead." I opened my mouth to feign a yawn. "Not nearly as much fun."

Miranda raised the auburn arc of an eyebrow. "I trust your *wiles,* such as they are, worked successfully?"

"Sure did." I held up the flash drive. "Shall we?"

We exchanged them on the count of three.

Miranda sighed, seeming genuinely pleased. "You see how much easier this is when all those men aren't involved?"

"I couldn't agree more," I said, tucking the envelope into my pocket. "You have no idea how refreshing it is not to be asked for my panties in exchange for information."

Miranda nearly did a spit-take, choking on the ice water she'd been sipping. She dabbed at her mouth daintily with the linen napkin.

I was mildly impressed when it came away clean of lipstick.

I'd started to notice things like that.

Matte finish versus glossy. Density of pigmentation. Smear resistance.

Miranda took her time refolding the napkin, long red claws smoothing every crisp fold in the cloth. "My husband asked you for your panties?"

"He certainly did. Made me slip them off beneath the table right in the middle of a crowded restaurant. Damn shame too. They were my lucky Wonder Woman panties."

I wasn't sure which had gone paler. Miranda's knuckles, or her face. "You listen to me, you little slut. Whatever you had with my husband is over now, do you understand me?"

"But I didn't—"

"I know your type. I've been playing the game much longer than you have. You think you can claw your way into his bed and establish the same control over him in a month as I had after ten years of marriage?"

And as I sat there, looking at Miranda, another of my mother's oft-repeated adages found its way back to me.

Anger is a secondary emotion, Janey. Look behind it and you'll find fear every time.

When I looked at her, I saw it written plainly all over her face.

"Look, I totally get it," I said. "You're getting older. Your boobs aren't as perky as they used to be. Your skin isn't as tight. Your ass not as firm. But let me tell you something my mother always told me." I reached across the table and patted her hand. "The important thing to remember is to trade in the currency you own. You know, like when your beauty is fading, you can still rely on your sparkling personality—oops, I guess that doesn't work for you, does it? Well, there's always your warm heart—nope, you don't have that either. Surely, there's *something*." I pretended to think while Miranda quietly seethed.

Her mouth twisted in an ugly smile, her nostrils flaring as she panted with rage, her chest rising on ragged breaths. "Your mother had some very strong words for a woman who was no more than RedWolf's whore."

My chair was gone.

And the earth under it.

I was falling, falling though I hadn't moved an inch. My stomach a lead weight at the end of my throat. Cold moving through my chest like a sinking fog as a wave of nausea clawed at me. Rogue goose bumps infested my scalp and trickled down my neck and arms.

"You would say anything," I said. "You're so desperate to maintain control of your own pathetic little life that you would say anything to hurt me."

Now it was her turn to lean across the table, her voice lowering to a volume only we could hear. "Why don't you ask her yourself?" She paused, her face crumpling with artificial pity as she leaned back and brought a hand to her cheek. "Oh, that's right. You can't. Because Mommy left you without saying goodbye." Her fists rose to the corners of her eyes, miming rubbing tears out of her eyes while pooching out her lower lip.

The chair scraped back as I stood.

Words, ever my ally, had deserted me utterly.

Like a witch in a fairy tale, Miranda's cackling laughter chased me out into the street.

Chapter Eighteen

The rain finally came as night fell.

And everywhere I looked, the puddles collected ribbons of red.

Red, the traffic lights.

Red, the stop signs.

Red, the beacons blinking on the tops of skyscrapers.

Red for RedWolf.

I couldn't remember how long I'd been walking. The cozy couples leaning into each other over tables bathed in candlelight told me hours must have passed.

I'd been going nowhere. Walking in circles both mental and literal.

My mother.

My father.

RedWolf.

Valentine.

Miranda.

She could have been lying.

It had been my first thought and perhaps the most comforting. And by that feeling alone, I knew to discard it.

Lies bring temporary comfort. The truth makes terrible sense.

That brutal, feel-it-in-your-bones power of the absolute. Devoid of any of the delightful fancy that falsehoods had so often afforded me.

Memories piled up, sewing themselves together like the terrible squares in a quilt.

Our frequent moves.

My mother's insistence on teaching me how to defend myself.

Not because we'd been running from everyone, but because we'd been running from *someone*.

I had sometimes in my darker moments suspected that I had been the result of a one-night stand rather than a sperm bank. But never had it occurred to me that my biological father just might, in fact, be a sociopathic criminal mastermind capable of making people disappear.

At what point was I supposed to have come to that conclusion?

My mother wanting to keep the codebase out of RedWolf's hands made all the more sense.

She fucking *knew* him intimately.

And he knew her.

Would be able to anticipate her moves. Her missteps. Her mistakes.

Which explained why he had gotten to the scabby apartment in the abandoned flophouse where my mother had been hiding before I had.

After wandering the Seattle streets until my face stung and my feet ached, I'd returned to myself enough to use my phone to navigate to the address Miranda had provided in our brief but exceedingly unpleasant meeting earlier. But when I'd gotten to the building in Eastgate, I hadn't wanted to go in.

I had stood on the sidewalk, staring. Unwilling to believe that my mother had been living in a place like this, even temporarily.

An abandoned flophouse with a mural of brightly colored graffiti climbing the brick wall, half painted over by someone who had given up. There were signs of life outside. Beer cans and cigarette butts and banana peels black with age in the bushes. The kind of wild and weedy greenery that takes over when no one is there to tend to more pleasant-looking plants. A stark contrast to the parrot tulips outside my mother's lovely gingerbread cottage in downtown Littleton, Colorado.

Of course, it had taken seeing a list of Valentine's assets among the divorce paperwork in Shook's office days after her disappearance for me to figure out that the house my mother unabashedly loved had actually been owned by Valentine all along. Another protective measure to make tracing her an impossibility.

My heart ached with the memory of her coming in from the garden, a basket containing that day's pull dangling from her forearm. The way her hands smelled of rosemary when she squeezed the back of my neck and dropped a cherry tomato still warm from the sun in my open palm.

Had that really been our life once?

Could it ever be again?

Steeling myself, I crawled through a gap in the chain-link fence much the same way I'd let myself out of the trailer park in California.

A life in reverse.

I moved aside a splintering plywood plank that served as a back door and ducked inside, cell phone flashlight in one hand, a boot knife I'd borrowed from Shepard's glove compartment in the other.

I staggered back a step, overcome by the human smells polite society usually keeps at bay. Sebum and sweat. Old urine. The cloying sweetness of rotting food and worse.

Rustling in the dark. I swung my phone's flashlight beam at it only to catch something small and dark darting into a pile of rags.

I cleared my throat.

"So, uh, if anyone's in here, I'm not the police, and I have no burning desire to cut a bitch if I don't have to. But fair warning, if you fuck with me, I shank your ass faster than you can say colorectal exam. Umm . . . thank you."

No reply.

Only the sound of water dripping somewhere in the bowels of the house.

"All right, Jane," I said to myself by way of motivational speech. "Let's do this."

Tony Robbins I am not.

I picked my way among the rubble of food wrappers and discarded cans, past an old stained mattress littered with burnt-out spoons and discarded syringes.

"And here we have a cozy little nook for shooting up." The sound of my own voice failed to comfort me as I had hoped it might.

Taking care not to step on any needles, I walked over to the mattress and into the next room, where the faint outline of stairs loomed in the dark.

Shining my phone flashlight up them, I assured myself they were at least structurally sound, though they creaked in protest when I began my ascent. I had to step over several bags of trash on the landing before I reached the top.

A quick sweep revealed a hallway with four doors, two on either side.

"I'll take door number one, Bob." And somehow, imagining myself standing next to a benevolent game show host with amply tanned skin and a crest of white hair infused me with grudging bravado.

No sooner did I play my flashlight over the room's contents than I knew my mother had been there. The signs of her presence abounded even among the utter chaos resulting from a hasty search.

The air horn and trip wire on the inside of the door, for instance. The makings for one of her favorite booby traps. And there, at the window: fishing line and a keychain siren.

But the most predictable sign of all?

The sleeping bag lying there like a discarded cocoon.

The force of the memory rocked me back on my heels.

"Camping" in the trailer in Mojave. Coyote songs unspooling outside the window, the stars like notes in songs only they could read.

The sound of the zipper and Mom saying, "Always travel with one of these, Janey. Not only does it help hold in body heat, but no matter what kind of a shithole you're staying in, this provides a layer between you and the bedbugs."

She had tickled me then, fingers crawling up my back, making me shriek. I had crawled in first, then she next, fitting her larger body around my smaller one.

"Like peas in a pod, Janey."

My scalp tingled with the sensory memory of her fingers threading through my hair. Tugging gently in the way that always made goose bumps erupt down my arms.

I hadn't remembered dropping to my knees next to the old stained mattress, but there I was. My hands full of fabric, bringing the sleeping bag to my nose.

Tears hot down my cheeks then as the scent of her filled my lungs. Soap and softness, her skin.

I refused to exhale until my chest ached, not wanting to release any molecules of her that yet lingered in my lungs. Hating the realization that, in this horrible place, I was closer to her than I had been since the morning of my graduation.

What madness had driven her here?

I stood beneath the weight of that question, offering up my heart like a dowsing rod, willing myself to understand, and by understanding, to follow her scent like a bloodhound.

The quick blur of shadow moved across the doorframe in my peripheral vision.

I dropped the sleeping bag and snatched up the knife, whirling around to aim my flashlight at the door.

"Who's there?"

Not that I expected an answer.

Not that I could have heard it past the rushing of blood in my ears, the flashlight beam pulsing with my own heart's pounding.

My mouth metallic with fear, I quietly got to my feet, knees threatening to give out no sooner than I had them under me.

"Whoever the fuck you are, you better show yourself before I blow a hole in your ass straight through the wall."

A small, slim hand threaded around the doorjamb, followed by a disheveled head of tangled black hair. The girl held a hand in front of her eyes against the flashlight's beam.

"Miss Alex?" Her reedy voice full of trepidation. "Is that you?"

"No," I said, lowering the light. "I'm not Miss Alex."

"You sound like her."

My heart leapt at the possibilities indicated by this statement. This girl had heard my mother speak.

"Who is Miss Alex?" I asked. "How do you know her?"

The girl leaned against the doorframe, hugging herself through several layers of tattered sweaters. Her legs matchstick thin in her dirty jeans. "She showed up a couple weeks ago. I was . . . living here with someone."

Beneath their hooded lids, her coffee-colored eyes skated to the side, a gesture that spoke volumes.

That *someone* had been a man. A much older man.

I noted the yellow-green bruise fading on her neck. A matching badge on one of her high, prominent cheekbones.

She was older than I had originally guessed. Closer to a petite sixteen than a healthy thirteen or fourteen.

My mother would have shown up, seen it all in an instant.

And threatened to relieve *someone* of his balls if he didn't beat it posthaste.

"What's your name?" I asked.

"Mary."

"It's nice to meet you, Mary," I said. "My name is Jane."

Her eyes brightened within the waxy olive mask of her face. "Are you her daughter?"

"She told you about me?"

Mary nodded. "She's been staying here. She brings me food. We talk nights when I can't sleep."

A wave of hot irrational jealousy clutched at my heart. Jealousy for this poor girl whose only crime had been to speak to the woman I'd been searching for. "What did she tell you about me?"

"She said she missed you a whole lot. She said you were the smartest, kindest, bravest woman in the whole world."

I blinked away a sudden sheen from my eyes.

Fucking mold dust.

"When was the last time you saw her?" I asked.

"This morning. She said she'd be back later today, but then these guys showed up and—"

"Were there two of them?"

"How did you know?"

"Just a guess," I said. "What happened then?"

"I hid in the attic. Then they left and you came, and I thought you were Miss Alex."

"Did the men say anything?"

Mary shrugged, thin shoulders jerking toward her ears. "I didn't hear all of it, but I think they were looking for something."

The codebase.

RedWolf's men.

RedWolf. A phantom name for the man they represented.

My father.

"Why are you here all alone, Mary? Don't you have anywhere to go?"

Another hasty shrug. "My dad ran off when I was still a baby. My mom OD'd a couple years back."

"I'm sorry to hear that."

"What about you?" she asked. "How come you're here? Your mom said you have some fancy lawyer job in a big city somewhere."

I deeply hoped the present tense was still applicable.

"I was in town for work," I said. "I thought maybe I'd say hello." The words were like razors, scraping my throat raw.

Mary sat down on an old chair whose guts had fallen out in clumps on the floor below it, excavated by mice. She pulled her knees into her chest. "I can tell her you came by."

I partially parked one butt cheek on the nearby dresser, bringing myself closer to Mary's level.

"You can't stay here, Mary. Now that they know my mom has been here, those men will be back."

Her face hardened, mouth setting in a determined line I knew all too well. "And where else am I supposed to go?"

"Why don't you come with me? We'll get you something to eat, and then we can do a little research. They have programs—"

"*No.*" Mary's face had gone from fearful to feral just that quickly. "No foster homes."

"But that's the reason systems like that exist. Because—"

"Those people don't give a shit!" she spat with bitterness surprising for one so young. "They don't give a shit how many homes you get bounced to or whether or not the other foster kids might be sticking their hands down your pants at night. All they ever do is send you somewhere else. I learned a long time ago that the only person I can trust is myself."

No wonder Mary and my mom had gotten along famously.

I squatted down in front of her. Rested my hands on the tops of her beat-up sneakers. "Listen, Mary. I know you're tough and you've learned to take care of yourself. And part of doing that is knowing when to let other people help you." I reached into my bra and pulled out a twenty-dollar bill and a business card. "Here's some money for food and a card with my phone number on it. You can call me. I just need you to promise me one thing."

"What?" The naked suspicion in her voice crushed my heart like a tin can.

"Find somewhere else to stay."

"I'll try," she said.

"Good girl." I squeezed the sides of her sneakers and got to my feet.

Back out on the street, I pulled sweet lungfuls of the night air into my body, banishing the musty hell of the building.

I knew what it was like.

To have my mother, then not have her.

I strode forward in the primal dark, this part of the city where streetlights had gone out and city maintenance couldn't be bothered to mind. A brisk block brought me to a depressing strip mall. Squat gray boxy offices where desperate people sought services they didn't want to need. Payday advances. Pawnshops.

Bail bondsman.

And just like that, I was back under the desert sky, the night of my mother's arrest. My ten-year-old face bathed in blinking neon as the marquee lit and dimmed time and again.

"E-Z Bail Bonds." A slogan had been added beneath in hand-painted letters: "Get out before the soap drops!"

A bell jingled overhead as I had pushed open the front door. Across a small sea of industrial gray carpet sat a lone office desk. The man behind it wore a short-sleeved white dress shirt and a *Star Wars* necktie. His head was bald save for a wreath of brown curls above his ears and a small island right up top that reminded me of the fluff of whipped cream that always came on top of Jell-O at school lunch.

He looked up from the noodles he was noisily slurping from a Tupperware container, chopsticks pinched in one hand.

"Well, hi there," he said, lips glossy with sauce. "Can I help you?"

"I'm supposed to bring you this." This was the part where, according to plan B, I would hold out the envelope. But I'd spent so long rehearsing the words while working up the nerve to come in that I had forgotten to actually pull the envelope in question out of my backpack.

"Bring me what?" He lifted another tangle of noodles to his mouth.

"Just a sec." I quickly shrugged the straps off my back and set the backpack in one of the chairs opposite his desk. Only the envelope wasn't immediately visible when I unzipped the pouch. My face burned as I began pulling out all my various effects and setting them on the desk.

My pellet gun and plastic handcuffs—in case shit went sideways. Juice boxes—in the event I got thirsty. Strawberry lip gloss and spearmint gum—because they made me feel sophisticated and confident. Crackers and cheese—which I'd already dipped into on my long walk from the trailer park. And finally, a hat and scarf—brought not as protection against the desert evening chill, but because my mother had always admonished the importance of carrying on my person at least two accessories capable of changing my appearance.

At last, I seized upon the envelope and slid it across the desk.

The man—Russell Dorton as I learned from the gold-plated tag on his desk—set down his chopsticks and picked it up. He gutted the envelope with one quick slash of his letter opener, slid on a pair of reading glasses, and read.

To this day, I don't know what my mother had written on that trifolded sheet of stationery.

I only knew that whatever it was made Russell's root beer–colored eyes lift to me over the rims of his reading glasses. He rubbed a rough palm over a stubbly jaw as his bushy brown eyebrows drew together at the center of a forehead pocked by acne scars.

"You're Alex Avery's daughter?" he asked.

I nodded.

What began as mild dismay turned into alarm when he had tucked the paper into his pocket, stood up, and walked over to a brass coatrack.

The sport coat he shrugged into could have been a hunting trophy from an expedition where ugly plaid couches had been the quarry.

"Where are you going?" I asked.

"To get your mom." He took a fat ring of keys from his top desk drawer and walked to the office's wire-reinforced glass door, turning to me after he hit the lights. "You coming?"

If shoving objects into a backpack had been an Olympic sport, I could have been the youngest medalist in history.

The night had been so quiet, I could hear the lonely echoes of shoes on the sidewalk.

They had been Russell Dorton's then.

They were someone else's now.

I'd been so firmly planted inside my own head that I wasn't sure how long I'd been hearing them.

I glanced back over my shoulder.

Half a block behind me, a dark figure walked with his head down, face in shadow, shoulders hunched against the steady drizzle. I didn't know how long he'd been there. Whether there had been distance and if he'd been closing it.

Part of me wanted to stop. Turn around. Invite a confrontation. Eager for the opportunity to inflict upon an assailant my every disappointment and rage.

Instead, I quickened my pace.

And the man behind me quickened his.

My head swam with an adrenaline-laced rush of blood. Fight or flight.

As much as my humor inclined me toward the former, I knew damn well my body was far from peak fighting form.

The numbness in my fingers and toes, my limbs stiff and aching. Breath shortened by lingering shock and cold.

Flight, then.

I ran.

I ran like I had run when I was ten years old, focusing all my energy on the bus stop one block up where a bus hunkered down at the curb. The last passenger was boarding, the doors already beginning to close when I slapped its side with the flat of my hand.

"Wait!"

The air breaks hissed as the doors opened up once again and I scrambled on, dumping the fare into the appropriate slot. When the bus trundled into motion without anyone flinging themselves aboard behind me, I let loose the breath I'd been holding and slumped into the nearest available seat. Panting and out of breath, I once again resolved to up my cardio game if my life ever returned to something at least approximating normal.

Unlikely.

I glanced out the window beside me, searching the night for the man who had been following me.

The chill that stole up my arms had nothing to do with my soaked clothing.

There, standing in the golden cone of the streetlight.

Watching.

Only when the driver steered the bus's bulk around a corner did I realize that, in my haste, I hadn't bothered to decide exactly where I would be fleeing *to*.

I didn't want to go back to the hotel, where I'd only face questions from Shook that I was more than ill prepared for. Also, he might try to make me fly back to Denver, and no way was I going back there. District Attorney Wiggins would have to extradite my ass in addition to kissing it as far as I was concerned.

I had no idea where Shepard had gone, and if he was following me, he'd managed to hide himself pretty damn well.

Hell could freeze over before I'd set foot back on the love boat. One look at me, and Miranda would know just what she'd successfully wrought.

"Excuse me." Leaning toward the seat in front of mine, I tapped the shoulder of a woman with amazing ash-gray dreadlocks gathered into a birdcage-sized bundle on the top of her head. "Can you tell me which bus this is?"

"This is the 241. Eastgate to Bellevue."

And as soon as I heard the stops, I knew where I could go.

Chapter Nineteen

On the heels of a harried mother with two urchins in tow, I slipped
through the main entrance to Tyler's apartment building. Once inside,
I made my way to his door.

I rang.

I knocked.

I waited.

Okay, *waited* might be a little generous. But some length of time
measurable to man passed before I pounded on the door again.

"Open up!" I shouted. "And don't bother trying to pretend you're
not there. I can literally *feel* you looking at me through the peephole."

There was a clicking of locks and the door opened a crack, the chain
still engaged.

Much the same way I had opened the hotel room door to Melanie.

Again, the irony: not lost on me.

Tyler's face appeared in the narrow opening. "Whatever you're sell-
ing, I don't want any."

"Was that an attempt at humor, or do you honestly think I'm here
to talk to you about home security or pest control? I can never tell with
you."

"Neither," he said. "A polite dismissal."

"Don't try polite." I hugged myself to keep from shivering. "Polite
isn't your thing."

"Okay, then. What are you doing here?"

"Better," I said. "At the moment? Dripping onto the terrible industrial carpet of your hallway."

"I could bring you a towel."

"Tyler. I'm cold, I'm wet, and I have nowhere else to go. Can I please come in?"

He slammed the door in my face.

Then opened it again, without the chain.

"Stay," Tyler said, pointing to the small patch of tile that served as the entryway.

I stepped out of my flats and peeled off my sodden cardigan, shedding as many wet layers as I could while remaining somewhat modest.

Tyler returned moments later with the same purple towel I had sat on during the LARP gathering. Another detail that testified to his overarching sense of order.

I lifted it to my face, patted my cheeks dry, then squeezed my dripping ropes of hair. As I did so, I couldn't help but notice the towel's fresh scent and fluffy texture. Which led me to only one solid conclusion.

This towel had been laundered and fabric-softened since the last time I had made its acquaintance.

Score one point for the beta male.

"Take off your clothes."

From the darkness of the terry cloth towel tent over my head, I peeked out at Tyler.

"Excuse me?"

"You're making a puddle." Tyler pointed to the small estuary gathering beneath my bare feet.

"Taking off my clothes at your house didn't end well for me last time."

"Just take off your clothes and I'll put them in the dryer."

"All right." The afternoon's events had caused something reckless and wild to take root deep within me. Flowering in the darkness

218

between my heart and my stomach. I shrugged off the towel and let it fall to the floor. Without warning, I reached down and pulled my camisole over my head before Tyler had the presence of mind to turn away. And because I'm a terrible, terrible person (have I mentioned this?), I lobbed it at his head.

His hand shot out and caught it with alarming dexterity considering he wasn't actually looking at the target. Apparently, spatial relationships were annexed to the part of his genius that extended to databases and perving on security cameras.

I stood there in nothing but my bra, skirt, and panties, hands on hips in a direct challenge. "So you're comfortable reaching into my bra and grabbing my boob, but not okay with looking at it?"

He didn't take the bait.

"Incidental contact as a result of retrieving the flash drive. The skirt." He beckoned with an upturned palm. "Hand it over."

I unzipped my skirt and stepped out of it, feeling something like savage pleasure as I remembered the "Dry-Clean Only" tag on the inside of the waistband. Take that, Melanie Fucking Beidermeyer.

Then, on a whim, I unhooked the bra and slung it at him. The panties, clammy though they were, were a bridge too far even for me.

Tyler disappeared for a moment, the familiar domestic sound of a dryer door opening and closing the only break in the silence.

I retrieved my discarded towel and made a wraparound shift of it, securing it beneath my armpits. Not exactly haute couture, but it beat the shit out of tripping around Tyler's apartment bare-ass naked. He hadn't offered the use of some of his own clothing, and I hadn't asked, not wanting to push my luck.

Not that luck and I were on speaking terms anyhow.

I bit down hard on my lower lip, which had begun a treacherous wobble.

Hadn't I been valedictorian of my law school class?

Hadn't I been an overachiever, full of promise and sass?

How was it possible that I now stood here stripped, both literally and figuratively, without even the clothes on my back? Employment prospects uncertain as my parentage. My life, everything I thought myself to be, no better than the lies I'd so willingly spun around me?

Distant rustlings hinted at Tyler's presence elsewhere in the apartment.

I quickly dashed the tears from my eyes, sniffed the gathering snot ball from my nose, and, rather than stand there with my metaphorical thumb up my bum, tiptoed into the kitchen.

For I had found that, much like medicine cabinets, refrigerator contents often yielded far more information about a person's habits and habitats than most basic background checks. And let's be honest, I was searching for any sign that there might be another human more fucked up than I.

Opening the fridge, I quickly scanned its contents, piqued but not surprised by what I found.

All the food had been separated into sections not organized by date or age, but by *texture.* Or so I surmised by the words written on various shelves in a painstakingly careful dry-erase marker script. A *crunchy* section for containers of sugar snap peas and celery. A *creamy* area for small pots of yogurt and sour cream. A *chewy* section for things like bagels and dried fruit. And perhaps most charming of all, a *misc.* section for things like bacon and eggs that didn't fit neatly into any of the other established categories.

"Enjoying yourself?"

I jumped and spun around to find Tyler standing behind the breakfast bar, watching me.

I cleared my throat and readjusted my towel. "I was just looking for something to drink."

"You won't find it in there," he said as if this were the most obvious information in the world.

"Time for some grocery shopping?"

He walked around the corner and opened the pantry door, revealing neatly organized shelves of water bottles, craft brews, and enough Mountain Dew Code Red to last until the Rapture.

"You drink your beer warm?"

"I have a sensory aversion to cold beverages." He took two beers from the shelf and popped their tops off with a bottle opener magnet attached to the fridge. After handing one to me, he put the magnet back precisely where it had been before, parallel with the handle to the freezer door and square with the door.

I took a sip of my beer, warm and tasting of roasted grain. Not what I was used to, but not half-bad. Beggars can't be choosers and all that.

We leaned against kitchen counters opposite each other, sipping our beer and pretending the silence wasn't awkward. Or rather, I pretended. Tyler didn't appear to notice.

After an extended period during which I tracked the progress of Tyler's sips down separate parts of his esophagus purely by sound, he finally spoke.

"You're sick?" he asked.

Trying to map Tyler's words to the thoughts behind them felt like observing a colony of prairie dogs. For every one you saw, there were thousands scuttling beneath the surface. Some sleeping. Some sniffing. Some quietly humping in the corners to make still more little prairie dogs. "I'm sorry?"

"You left early yesterday and didn't come to the meetings today. Shook said you weren't feeling well."

Ahh. This was Tyler doing small talk.

Though we had spoken the night before to set up the information exchange with Gnarth, Tyler and I hadn't discussed any particulars of my having disappeared from the dev meeting.

"Not exactly," I said. "He suggested it might be best if I took a few days of administrative leave so I could focus my attention elsewhere."

Tyler exhaled short and sharp. "Looks like we're both on the chopping block."

"Maybe so," I admitted.

Another round of noisy, protracted swallows.

Any other human would have asked me what was wrong. What series of events had ended with my sipping warm beer in his kitchen in nothing but a towel.

In this way, we were a perfect pair. Me, not wanting to talk about what had happened and him not knowing or caring enough to ask.

The silence was interrupted by strange chirping coming from the pocket of Tyler's button-up shirt. The sort of *pew-pew-pew* sounds that commonly followed someone being ordered to set the phasers to stun.

He reached into his pocket and pulled out his cell phone, swiping his thumb across the screen before uttering, "What is it?" into the receiver.

As silly as it is to say, there was a small strange comfort in realizing I wasn't the only one who routinely received such nongreetings and crusty responses. That it wasn't just me, personally.

"Yes."

"No."

"Why?"

"Fine."

"We'll be there."

I choked on a mouthful of beer-flavored foam. Had he just said *we'll* be there?

Tyler slid the phone back into his pocket and looked in the direction approximating my face. "Gnarth just called in his favor."

"What does he want?" I asked between coughing up bits of hops-flavored curds.

"He wants you to come with us to trivia night."

"Trivia night." If I had been thinking a simple repetition of the words would be enough to force them to sound less horrifying, I had been terribly, terribly wrong.

"Every Wednesday the local taproom does a trivia night where teams compete against each other to win free beer and a bunch of bullshit prizes."

"And Gnarth wants me there *why?*"

Tyler's lids lowered, his eyes slipping from one side to the other as if confirming there was no one around who could overhear our conversation. "He has it on good authority that one of the double-score rounds will be focused on legal trivia. Gnarth has an in with the quizmaster."

Quizmasters . . . guild masters . . . damned if my life wasn't as warm with a metric fuck-ton of sex appeal as of late.

I narrowed my eyes at him. "How the hell did Gnarth even know I went to law school? I'm pretty sure Princess NightSpear wasn't permitted to mention anything from her life in the *mortal realms.*"

Tyler seemed remarkably interested in his own socks all of a sudden. "It might have come up when I was calling him to ask for the favor on your behalf."

"I see. And how did he know I was here tonight?"

"He didn't. He asked me to get you to come to trivia night. It just so happens that you made my job easier by showing up here uninvited."

"You just had to find a way to work that in, didn't you?"

"It's the truth, isn't it?"

On this point, I didn't feel at all equipped to debate.

"When does this delightful gathering commence?" Resignation, pure and simple.

"Half an hour," Tyler said.

"Lovely." I chugged what remained of the beer, turning my face away to make an unladylike noise against the back of my hand as I padded past him. "On that note, I guess I should check my clothes."

"No." Tyler all but arm-barred me to prevent me from leaving the kitchen. "I'll do it."

Two instances of willing physical contact in one day. This was getting downright creepy.

"What's the big deal?" I asked. "Do you keep your severed heads next to the fabric softener or something?"

"I . . . I just don't like people touching things."

"Ahh, but that's where you're wrong. Those clothes are *my* things."

"In *my* dryer."

Normally, I could have kept this sort of hairsplitting debate going for a good hour on the legal justifications for property ownership alone. But the simple words *legal trivia* had introduced a pinprick of light into the miasma of gloom hanging about me.

"How about this?" I asked. "You open the dryer, and I'll take out the clothes."

This solution appeared to be acceptable to him.

I followed him through the kitchen to the laundry closet where he opened the folding wooden slat doors, then the dryer.

I reached in and grabbed the clothes—slightly damp, but far more serviceable. Warm as I hugged them to my toweled chest.

"Let me just change, then I'll be ready to go."

Tyler was at his desk when I emerged, triple monitor display glowing before him.

I would have sworn one of them displayed what looked to be a musical score, but he promptly closed down the window when I cleared my throat.

He swung himself around in the seat and paused, a strange look on his face.

I'd done my best to finger-comb my hair away from my face, securing it in a thick short side-braid that lay against the curve of my neck, the end brushing my collarbone. My face bare of all but the most rudimentary smudges of mascara on my lashes. Lips gnawed naked of lipstick.

I waited for the insult to come.

It didn't.

"Ready?" he asked.

"Ready," I said. "Let's go make some know-it-alls eat a bag of dicks."

Chapter Twenty

The Glass Half Empty Taproom had the kind of dimly lit oaken ambiance of a Jazz Age bar. If jazz had been invented by hipsters.

Among the men there were many a waxed handlebar mustache paired with suspenders and ironic T-shirts, covered by brand-new cardigans pretending to be vintage. Their female companions managed to look both brainy and hard with blunt Bettie Page bangs and black-framed glasses floating above lip and nose piercings that caught the electric candlelight in little sparks. Conversations at the various tables were hushed and low, punctuated by the kind of laughter designed to let others know that something terribly clever has just been said. An inside joke about Proust, let's say.

We entered on a whoosh of warm air, the scent of wet asphalt clinging to us as we threaded our way through the tables to a booth containing Gnarth and an assorted complement of faces I did not recognize.

We slid onto the booth bench across from him, its one occupant scootching over to make room for us.

"You're late." Gnarth looked up from the small but vividly illustrated booklet before him. The pencil in his freckled fingers carefully lettering something onto the first line of every page in small, meticulous script.

"The quiz hasn't even started yet," Tyler said.

Gnarth sniffed in Tyler's direction, small and abnormally round nostrils delicately dilating. "I smell beer. Have you been drinking?"

"I only had half a beer—"

"We agreed there would be *no* drinking on trivia nights. We must be at peak mental capacity," Gnarth scolded.

"Dude," I said. "You want me to get you a block of ice to hug so you can cool your tits? Even after half a beer, I'm pretty sure Tyler's mental capacity is about double the rest of these shrubs, and it doesn't look like they're holding back." I glanced at the next table over, where the proliferation and variety of glasses suggested an assortment of craft beers. And this was to say nothing of the shot glasses full of poison-green liquor I suspected to be absinthe, favored tipple of tortured fin de siècle artists such as van Gogh and Toulouse-Lautrec. Or so I had learned in my college art history classes.

Trivia, bitchez!

I could have warmed my still-clammy hands by Tyler's burning cheeks. He looked at his lap and picked at one of his already-bloodied cuticles.

Gnarth puffed like a dyspeptic duck, feathers clearly ruffled by my comments.

"So whatcha writing there, Gnarth?"

"Here, I am *not* Lord Gnarth SilverShaper."

"No?"

"No. Battle tags are only to be used in the LARP realms. In the mortal realms, we have only our human powers and will be addressed by only our human names."

It required monumental effort to suppress my eye roll. Had I let it fly, I wasn't entirely sure I'd ever be able to retrieve my irises from the back of my skull. "And your human name is?"

"Greg."

"Are you sure I couldn't just call you Gregnarth? You've got to admit, it has a certain ring to it."

Greg gave me a look to suggest that if he *could* have melted my face with lasers at that very moment, he'd have done it.

"All right, then," I said. "Whatcha writing?"

"Our team name," Greg said without looking up.

"Which is?"

"The Agatha Quizties," Tyler said somewhat grudgingly.

Warmth spilled down my shoulders. I couldn't quite call it providence, but in contrast to everything else happening in my life at present, I was willing to deem it a good sign at the very least.

"It just so happens that my middle name is Marple."

"Good for you." Greg had returned to his scribbling. "You want a cookie?"

"I might have to shoot your friend," I said to Tyler. "Like, in the head."

After that revelation I noted the alarmed expressions on the faces of the table's other occupants.

"My apologies. I usually at least introduce myself before I commence with the death threats." I reached across the table and offered my hand to Greg's benchmate—a slim brunette with wide-set eyes and skin as pale and smooth as the underside of a fish. "Since it appears no one is making formal introductions, I'm Jane."

"Dagney. Pronounced like Daphne, but with a *g*." She blinked at me through wire-rimmed spectacles not unlike the ones sported by Greg himself.

"Pleasure to make your acquaintance, Dagney." I leaned around Tyler and repeated the gesture with the man-bun-sporting gentleman sharing our bench. "Jane," I said, giving his hand a squeeze.

"James." And he was as much of a James as I was a Jane. That is to say, nothing outwardly remarkable until we dispensed with the pleasantries and commenced with the battle.

In battle, James of the Marvel superhero T-shirt and blue eyes as mellow as his disposition proved to be a stone-cold killer.

I recognized the look in his eye when, after round one, the quiz-master announced the winner of the first bonus beer.

Which went to the quiz team named—I shit you not—Stephen Hawking's School of Dance.

"What kind of name is that, anyway?" James sipped at his water as disdainfully as any man bun could, looking at my beer with as much longing as Greg did with disgust.

"What would you do if you had won the beer, anyway?" I asked.

"Keep the ticket, of course." Greg looked at me as if this was the most obvious answer in the entire world. "It's not the beer that matters. It's knowing that you're right that matters."

"Uh-huh," I said, taking another sip of my beer.

Greg pushed his glasses up the bridge of his nose, pale lashes judiciously dusting the thick lenses. "Perhaps you shouldn't be indulging when we've yet to reach the legal trivia round."

I almost wished I had glasses so I could willfully push them *down* the bridge of my nose.

"You said the bonus rounds are three and eight. At the rate this evening is moving, I'll be sober as a judge for either."

As if on cue, our waitress chose that moment to stop by, bearing aloft an empty tray in hand. "Can I bring anyone anything?" she asked.

"I'll have a Shiner Bock," Tyler half said, half mumbled.

Greg's audible gasp had me biting down on my lower lip for fear of inwardly cheering for Tyler's show of independence.

She returned scarcely a minute later with the suds.

I held my own beer aloft, inviting the kiss of glasses.

"Tyler Dixon," I said. "You're a rebel."

The smallest shadow at one corner of his mouth. An almost-smile. We clinked and drank.

Greg made his disgust manifest by bearing down upon his pencil, angry slashes like vengeful calligraphy marring the top of the page for round two.

Which, as it turned out, was a strange intersection of Chinese food and politics, during which Tyler and I had another beer each. An act that appeared fit to give Greg a stroke.

By round three and a beer of the same number, I was feeling downright jovial.

"And nooooow it's time for round three! Legal eagles. A category all about ruthless predators who feed off weaker creatures and also eagles!"

Cue amused laughter from everyone but me.

"Question one. What term is used to describe an improper fee taken by a lawyer?"

"Unconscionable!" Not only had I said it out loud, I shouted it, overcome by the rush of pleasure at knowing the answer.

The satisfaction was short-lived.

Much groaning and eye rolling from the other tables preceded the quizmaster's reminder that answers were *not* to be shouted out by the audience or participants.

Greg drove his nubby fingers through his orange-rind-colored hair. Doing a rather fine job of ruing the day he'd ever met me.

And truly, this made me feel the tiniest bit defensive for the people who actually had a *reason* to rue the day they'd met me. And there might have been a few more of those people than is altogether flattering to admit.

"I'm sorry, okay? I got a little excited."

"It's okay." Dagney gave me a watery smile. "It happens to everyone."

"Queeeestion number two!" The quizmaster's voice cracked everyone into silence like a whip. "What is the second smallest falcon in North America? The second smallest *falcon* in North America."

"Oooh!" Instead of blurting out of my mouth, the answer managed to travel all the way down my neck, up my arm and through to my hand, which flapped wildly in the air. "I know. I know!"

"Put your hand down and just tell him what it is." Tyler's spine seemed a little less like steel rebar. In fact, I might go so far as to say he actually *slouched* a little.

"Kestrel," I whispered.

"And how do you know that?" Greg regarded me from beneath brows that tried for imperious and landed somewhere closer to constipated.

"Because sometimes when it's been a stressful week and I need to unwind I like to watch reruns of *Mutual of Omaha's Wild Kingdom* with a glass or two of wine and who the fuck are you to judge me if I drink the whole bottle by myself because I'm a grown-ass woman and I can do what I want!"

The fact that my lungs hurt just a touch informed me that all of the words might have come out of my mouth in one breath. Never a good sign, this.

James cleared his throat. "Kestrel sounds good to me."

Greg glanced down at the page and quickly scribbled down the answer.

"Aaaand question number three, something every good lawyer would know: According to Illinois law, it is prohibited for men to have *what* in public?"

"An erection," I said.

Tyler choked on his beer. Alcohol had flushed his cheeks pink as a kitten's tongue.

James, Dagney, and I snagged gazes at exactly the same time. That kind of delicious collision that can't be planned. And then we laughed.

To my utter delight, Tyler joined in.

As it so often does, his laugh made us laugh even harder.

Laughter had long been something my mother trained me to pay attention to. One of the rare moments when people drop all artifice and cease to be self-conscious. Show you who they really are.

Caught in relentless mirth, Tyler let his head drop into his hands, driving his fingers into his own hair, mussing it irreparably. And my only thought was that Satan's ballsack must be shriveling back up into his infernal nether regions, because hell was surely freezing over.

Greg let go of a put-upon sigh, and for once I didn't feel the overwhelming urge to stab him with the fork.

It could have been the beer buzz talking, but for the briefest of moments, I had forgotten to hurt.

Looking around at the other tables, a feeling had begun to fill the rotting void that had grown around my mother's absence. Like water leaking into a cistern, reducing the scope and depth of its echo.

Friends.

These people were friends.

Nudging each other. Sharing stories and appetizers and simple acts of kindness. Busting each other's chops, then going right back to laughing.

Not a single one of them appeared to be squinting at their group mates through narrowed eyes, trying to determine exactly what kind of fuckery they would inevitably perpetrate.

All my life, this feeling had eluded me. I'd never known what it was like to sit down with a group of people without planning out potential defense strategies, trying to figure out what they wanted from me and what they might be willing to do to get it.

For the first time in my life, I *belonged.*

I had wandered into a place where people publicly delighted in being right. Where knowing odd things was more important than drawing people to you with the shine of your teeth or the batting of your lashes. People who accepted the kind of currency I had to trade.

My body was a catalog of unfamiliar but not entirely unwelcome sensations. A pleasant ache in my abdominal muscles. Tears wet in the corners of my eyes. Face stiff from smiling.

How long had it been since I'd laughed like this?

I dabbed at the corners of my eyes with a napkin.

"Dude," I said to my tablemates. "Speaking of erections." I jerked my chin toward the corner across from the bar.

It wasn't the erection I had noticed first, lest you think I spend all my time eye-humping random dudes' crotches. It was the way he stood. Tense and strange in a room full of people relaxed and chatting.

I looked again, sure I had to be mistaken. And this time, I followed what appeared to be a third leg all the way up to his waistband and saw the strange handle sticking out of his pants. A LARP sword, or so I suspected.

Which led me to additional discoveries. Like the leather vest hiding beneath his jacket. And the belt below his leather vest. And the small pouch attached to that belt. He scanned the room with squinted eyes, his gaze skipping from table to table.

I nudged Tyler with my elbow. "Do you know that guy?"

"What guy?"

"The one in the corner with the wicked overbite and the almost-mullet."

Tyler leaned closer to me than he might have had he not had several beers in him. His small ear wandering into wet willy range, were I less of a mature, grown-ass adult. "Nope," he said. "Don't know him."

"He looks like a LARPer. What if he's here to assassinate you?"

"What if he is?" Tyler shrugged. "It's just a bunch of pretend bullshit, anyway."

Greg's mouth dropped open, his tiny eyes going wide behind the blast door–thick lenses.

I picked up a coaster and fanned his reddening face. "He didn't mean that, Greg."

"Aaaaaand that brings us to the end of round three." The quizmaster closed his laptop. "Thirty seconds to turn in your score sheets. I'll be taking a ten-minute break to tally up the scores so far. Take a break, grab a drink, get your wiggles out"—here, he cast a meaningful glance at Tyler and the dude with the sword—"and we'll reconvene for round four."

"I suppose I'll take the score sheet up as I seem to be the only one with any interest in actually competing. It appears I was sorely mistaken in my decision to employ *outside* assistance." Greg speared me with a look of such disappointment and disdain that I almost expected someone to smack me with a rolled-up newspaper.

Dagney slid out of the booth so Greg could make his way over to the quizmaster.

"You can't take it personally," she said, plopping back down in front of me. "He just takes the scores a little more seriously than most."

"It seems that a lot of the people of his acquaintance have similar advice."

I glanced up at mystery LARP dude just as his eyes fastened on our table. He shrugged his jacket away from the hilt of his weapon, cool as a movie gunslinger. The only thing missing was the jingling of spurs as he began his journey across the room.

"Oh shit," I said. "Here we go."

Chapter Twenty-One

I reached over and took Tyler's beer from him, arresting its journey to his mouth. "Listen up, KongDong. Get your narrow ass off this bench and go assassinate that shitweasel before he gets over here."

"He can't." Greg had returned, a glass of amber liquid in his hand. "He doesn't have any of his weapons with him."

"Hold the fucking phone," I said. "Is that a beer?"

"It's ale," he said. "*Ginger* ale."

I resisted the obvious joke where the ginger was concerned, oak that I am.

"Greg, you wild man, you."

He flushed beneath his freckles.

LARP dude was halfway across the crowded room, temporarily blocked by a sudden reunion of squealing, bouncy girlfriends.

My mind was spinning now, the pump primed by trivia, my body beginning to tremble like a terrier with the arrival of an idea.

"Quick," I said to Greg. "Tell me the *exact* words in the LARP rule book regarding assassinations." I didn't bother to stop and ask myself precisely why I was so invested in the outcome of this duel all of a sudden.

"No warrior may attempt an assassination without a game-approved artifact on his person."

"A LARP artifact? That's all that's required?"

"That's what the rules say."

I reached into the neckline of my blouse and pulled out the Tears of Ysthelion. The delicate chain snapped easily as I yanked it from my neck. "Here," I said, sliding out of the booth as I pressed it into Tyler's palm. "Take this."

Tyler regarded the glinting silver amulet, his face a boozy mix of confusion and wonder. "You're still wearing it?"

The question dropped us into a pocket of silence. Around us, people talked. Glasses clinked. Laughter rose like the spatters of applause.

"You are Princess NightSpear's champion, goddamn it." I squeezed his hand, the sharp bite of the amulet passing between us like a shared thought. "Now go kick his ass."

Tyler slid out of the booth, eyes shining, hair ruffled, jaw set. "I command thee to stop!" he said, holding the necklace out in front of him.

The would-be assassin stopped where he was.

"Oh snap!" A rush of fever heated my cheeks. "Looks like homeboy is a level three or lower."

"How can you tell?" Dagney asked.

"Because holding someone is a level-*four* assassin ability. And if his opponent were of an equal level or higher, the spell wouldn't work on him."

Greg raised an eyebrow at me.

"Oh, don't look at me like that. Just because I did a little research doesn't mean I find this interesting or enjoyable in *any* way. Like, at all."

"How long does he have to stay that way?" James asked.

I knew that answer too, of course, but for reasons I would never understand, I turned to Greg, who I knew would be delighted to impart to anyone some of his wisdom. "Thirty seconds," he said.

"And then what?" Dagney leaned across the table, all shiny eyes and rapt expression.

"Then fur *really* starts flying." I rubbed my palms together, idly wishing I had some popcorn to munch on while I watched. "Teleportation, poisoned weapons. It's gonna get crazy up in here."

We all turned to watch.

"I cast veritas serum spell," Tyler said.

"What would you have me speak?" the assassin asked.

"The name of the one who sent you."

The assassin stood taller, his shoulders squaring. "I come on behalf of Prince DarkHelm DeadBlood, consort of Lord BoneSmuggler, who wishes me to avenge his beloved."

So Lucas Logan Bell's lover was a LARPer too. I made a mental note to ask Tyler what he knew of him just as soon as he was finished allegorically cutting a bitch.

"*His* beloved?" James asked.

"Yeah. Lucas—er—Lord BoneSmuggler wasn't an archaeological reference if you take my meaning."

They did.

People were beginning to look up from their tables, their antennae tuned to the signals of rising conflict.

I slid out of the booth and stood up behind Tyler.

"So, I hate to interrupt," I said, "but I have a question. Does this serum apply only to facts relating to the game, or can you ask him anything?"

"The rules aren't specific in that respect," Greg chimed in. "It only says that a player must answer any questions asked honestly and to the best of their knowledge."

"So, while this veritas serum thingy is still in effect, can I ask a question?"

"*If thou must,*" Tyler said, a gentle reminder that, if I insisted on interrupting, he would prefer that I did so in the language of the realm.

"I uh . . . musteth. 'Tis Lord BoneSmuggler's *death* thou art avenging, or his assassination?"

Both the assassin and Greg shot me dirty looks.

"Sorry," I said. "The dude in question was found dead in my bed. It's kind of an important distinction . . . eth."

"Answer her."

"'Tis the assassination that bade Prince DarkHelm send me."

"Right. So, this Prince DarkHelm guy, was he parking the meat-mobile in BoneSmuggler's garage in real life, or is that some kind of LARP thing as well?"

"They were of one flesh in the human realm, if this is thy reference."

"One last question. Did Prince DarkHelm ever mention anyone named RedWolf?"

The assassin's eyes narrowed but stayed focused on Tyler. "Wilt thou silence the wench? Or must I cast a silence spell?"

"Dude," I scoffed. "You can't cast a silence spell when you're frozen. Serious breach in protocol."

Tyler's grip on the necklace tightened, his knuckles going pale. I tried to imagine what his showdown with Lucas Logan Bell would have looked like. Would there have been triumph on his boyish face? Satisfaction?

Rage?

And what of the real murder?

What had gone through Lucas Logan Bell's mind before the bullet that stole his life? Had he known he was going to die?

"Shouldn't you poison your weapon?" I asked, leaning close to Tyler. "While he's still frozen, I mean."

Tyler flicked a sideways glance at me. "What, you read a couple of wikis and you think you can tell *me* how to play the game?"

"No," I insisted. "It's just that I read on the forums that it's an underutilized skill, and—"

"Really? The forums? You'd be better off tossing questions into a toilet."

"Assassinate!" Tyler's opponent whipped out his sword—foam, not flesh—and bopped Tyler on the sternum.

Apparently, the thirty seconds were up.

Tyler dropped to his knees in surrender just as Greg rose, then promptly fell face-first into the large platter of nachos our server had just delivered.

I turned from Tyler to poke Greg in the shoulder. "Dude. It's not that I don't appreciate your commitment to the game and all, but that spell was aimed for Tyler."

"Hey." Dagney shook Greg's shoulder. "Are you okay?"

I can access the images that came with and after those words with a clarity that isn't normal for me.

Shock does that.

Engraves odd details on the memory with uncommon specificity.

I remember the way Dagney's fingers looked against the sleeve of Greg's T-shirt. Her nails bitten down to the quick. Tattered cuticles chewed raw. I remember the way his head rolled to the side, his face toward me. Cheek smooshed against a pillow of refried beans and crushed chips. Sour cream and cheese smeared across the lenses of his glasses. Confetti of spring onions stuck to his forehead.

I remember Dagney's eyes. The way they widened. The pristine fringe of lashes mascara had never seen, magnified by her glasses.

And I knew.

I knew what she had seen. I knew what made her eyes do that.

A glance at the window behind them confirmed it.

A small, perfectly round hole. Created by a .22. The bullet not even large or forceful enough to break the safety glass. The muzzle signature not loud enough to tip off anyone not experienced with firearms.

I ducked down on the booth's bench, out of line of sight but close enough to press my fingers to the side of Greg's neck, searching for the subtle throb of a pulse, however faint. Nothing. His chest and back remained motionless. No rise and fall of breath.

Several things happened almost at once. Separated by a span of time both so infinitesimally small and cavernously large that they felt like they ought to occupy different dimensions.

Tyler rose to his feet, having satisfied the appropriate requirements for being LARP-dead.

I heard the signature slap of a rifle this time as Tyler's head rose into view.

Without thinking, I kicked Tyler's feet out from under him. One quick sweep and his sneakers slid to the side on the polished concrete bar floor. Him yelping in surprise as he went down. People just now noticing the commotion. Staring at us.

Staring at me.

"Active shooter!" I shouted. "Everyone get down!"

My words were swallowed up by Dagney's screams.

She looked at her hand. The hand she'd placed on Greg's shoulder when trying to rouse him. Staring at her palm as if she'd seen it for the first time, sticky and crimson in the bar's dim light.

The terrible sound of pure, primal terror that the human ear recognizes in its most elemental animal form.

Silence rode into the bar on its coattails, filling the room like a living thing, thickening the air to cement. No one moving. Frozen in place by panic's death grip. Brains sorting facts in elaborate Rube Goldbergian constructions. Making sense. Programmed, as we are, to believe these are the kinds of things that you read about in the paper. Not the kind of thing that happens when you're out for trivia night with your friends. Not the kind of thing that can happen when you have a beer in your hand and laughter in your throat.

The spell shattered in a sudden whoosh of sound as panic took over all at once. No one was moving, then everyone was.

Chairs overturned and plates broken. Silverware clattering to the floor. People jostling. Stepping on feet and hands, knocking each other to the ground in their race to be free of the danger themselves.

Always, my mother's words entered my brain like my own thoughts.

See, Janey? That's all people are at the end of the day. Animals. They turn on each other when threatened. And they'll all be threatened eventually.

And thus my spell was broken too.

The illusion that I could ever be part of a merry gathering. That I could, without consequence, bring people into my life and expect them to stay.

Now I knew why.

Not because I was my mother's daughter.

Because I was my father's.

Death followed me like a lady-in-waiting.

The bar was empty.

Strangely silent.

Tyler on his back, blinking up at the ceiling. Me on my stomach near him. Food crumbs and napkins beneath my palms.

"Are you okay?" I searched him for some sign of a wound I might have missed in my haste to get him out of the range of direct fire.

He ignored me, rolling over to his knees.

"Stay down." The fear in my own voice surprised me.

"Greg," Tyler said. "What's wrong with Greg?"

Shock had narrowed the gap between our IQs.

"Tyler, he's been shot. It's a head wound. You know what that means. I know you do."

"No." He rocked back and forth in the same overinsistent way he had that morning sitting on the cold marble bench. "No. I can heal him."

My heart broke then. Crumbled into pieces as dry as the warm desert sand as Tyler got up and sat in the booth, taking Greg's head and guiding it into his lap, pressing his hands against what remained of Greg's scalp. Muttering spells through his sobs.

"Stop, Tyler." I moved to pry his hands away from his friend's face, slick with blood still warm. Holding them by the wrists. "Tyler, he's gone."

"No." Tyler's hands clenched into fists, Greg's head still in his lap. "No, he can't be gone. He was my friend."

"Tyler, listen to me. It's not your fault."

I knelt on the carpet of broken glass at the booth's edge, shards biting into my knees as I reached out a hand to him.

Tyler only stared at it, eyes wide like it might bite him.

"Tyler," I repeated. "It's not your fault."

I said it because I'd learned that, for some reason, these were the first words humans always needed to hear in the wake of shocking violence. No matter how untrue they were or would continue to be.

"It was meant for me," he said, tears making tracks through the blood streaked like war paint on his cheeks.

And he was right.

I had known it from the second I saw the bullet hole in the glass at eye level, in line with where Tyler had been standing before he suddenly knelt.

His life had been saved by a LARP assassination.

The assassin himself was gone. Along with James and everyone else in the bar.

Almost everyone else.

There was Dagney, under the table.

Trapped in the booth by Greg's body, she had made her way to the floor, huddled into a ball with her back against the wall.

"Hey," I said, squatting as best as my skirt would allow. "Why don't you come on out of there?"

She gave no sign that she had actually heard me.

"I—I was just sitting there." Behind their lenses, her eyes darted toward the place where Greg's legs still were. His sneakered feet inches from her hands, a disturbing juxtaposition of the living and the dead.

He'd put them on with the simple faith all of us have when we get dressed in the morning. That we will also be the ones to remove our own clothes at the end of the day. The word *coroner* light-years away from our consciousness when we perform these simple acts.

"I know," I said. "Come on out. I'm calling 911 right now. Help is on the way." I pulled my phone out of my bra, held it up for her to see. Only then did I register that I had several text messages and several missed calls.

The missed calls were from Shook and Melanie.

The text messages were from Shook and Shepard.

When my stomach flipped, I couldn't be entirely sure whose name had been responsible.

I looked at Shook's message first.

Jane, please call me at your earliest convenience. I would like to talk about our conversation this morning.

I wasn't entirely sure I was ready for that conversation quite yet.

I then looked at Shepard's message, received only minutes earlier.

Threat neutralized. I got your six. U okay?

I got your six. Military speak for I have your six o'clock. Translation: *I got your back.*

Gratitude flooded me like melted wax, taking up the negative spaces not yet occupied by panic or fear. He'd been following me. Even after I had sent him away. Said terrible things to him, he was still there. Still watching. Busy being the reason the sniper had only gotten in three shots before ceasing.

"What if there are more shots?" Dagney asked.

"There won't be," I said.

"How do you know?"

"I just do. See? I'm calling the police right now."

"I've already called." A mustachioed bartender peeked over the edge of the bar, his face colored by the rainbow of bottles like lanterns on the bar behind him.

And for once, I was relieved.

There had been witnesses. The blood was not on my hands.

In the most literal sense, it was on Tyler's. I needed to get him off the bench. Get Tyler away from Greg before he compromised any potential evidence.

People need a task, Janey. You want someone on your side? Give them something to do.

"Dagney, can you help me? I need a hot washcloth. I bet that gentleman behind the bar could help us out."

"Sure thing," the bartender said, hurrying away to arrange it.

Dagney crawled carefully over toward me, head ducked beneath the table.

I helped her stand, then bent to brush the glass from my knees, dots of blood welling from the impressions below the hem of my skirt.

The bartender handed the hot towel to Dagney, who brought it to me. A strange ritual we had all agreed to in an even stranger environment.

Tyler stroked sticky strands away from Greg's face, his freckled forehead already going waxy as blood leached away, gravity now stronger than his heart.

I approached slowly, the rag sending curls of steam up from my cupped hands.

"He was my friend," Tyler said.

"I know." I seated myself on the leather bench next to him, slowly, slowly bringing the steaming cloth to his smooth cheek.

"We met in sixth grade. He was the only one who would sit at my lunch table."

That merciless landscape of partitioned trays, social customs, and pecking orders more complex than a Tudor court was instantly resurrected in my mind. Such was our need to move around that I had attended no fewer than eight junior high schools. I had learned the rules early and well.

"He taught me about Dungeons & Dragons."

Using gentle strokes, I wiped the blood away from Tyler's cheeks with strong, sure strokes. Picking up both flakes of blood and drying tears. "He sounds like a good friend."

That word again.

Odd to imagine two such antisocial people forging so delicate a social bond.

When I had one cheek cleaned, I gently turned his face toward me and cleaned the other.

His skin was almost poreless, impossibly smooth save for the places intersected by the fine scars I only noticed at this proximity.

When his face was clean, I turned my attention to his hands.

Carefully taking the washrag to his palms, then moving it along the length of each finger, paying special attention to the creases where the blood tended to gather.

I pushed up the sleeve of his hoodie and had to bite down on my lip to stifle a gasp.

Here, too, there were scars.

Of the self-inflicted variety. A ladder of pain crawling up his arm. Some white, some pink, some purple and barely healed.

No wonder he wore only hoodies, those long billowy sleeves hiding a multitude of secrets.

There are always two kinds of cutters, Janey. The ones who slice where everyone will notice. And the ones who cut where no one can see.

Saying nothing, I pulled his sleeves back down, tethering them with a gentle squeeze. His secret to keep.

The telltale wail of a siren in the distance. Precious seconds now before their arrival.

"Come on," I said to Tyler. "Let's get you up."

Because his hands were already clean, I took on the unenviable task of lifting Greg's head so Tyler could scoot out of the booth. When he was free, I gently set Greg back down, face turned toward the back of the bench.

And that's when I saw the small dark hole in the back of his head just below the downward slope of his skull's occipital shelf. The lack of exit wound told me that either Greg had a metal plate in the front of his skull, or the shooter had been at least a hundred yards away, near the rifle's terminal distance. The bullet would have lodged somewhere in the bone, but not before making scrambled eggs of his brain.

Or so I had learned over butterscotch pudding parfait at my mother's table.

I stared at that small hole, black as a pupil as the memory assembled itself around me.

My mother across from me, a stack of flash cards at her elbow, her own pudding in a chipped cereal bowl because she always insisted that I eat mine from the one pretty glass we owned.

"Are you ready, Janey?" she had asked.

"Ready," I had said around a too-large bite of buttery sweetness.

She had flipped over the first card then.

Pasted on the other side was a blurry photograph of a man's temple. His eyes covered by a black bar. His mouth open and slack. I remembered thinking that his bushy eyebrows looked like caterpillars. And the one on the right side of his face looked like it was going to crawl into a dark hole the size of a dime in his temple.

"Entrance wound!" I shouted proudly, holding my spoon aloft in triumph.

"Good girl. And how do we know?"

"Because it's a perfectly round circle," I parroted. "Exit wounds are much messier."

She narrowed her eyes at me in mock challenge. "Caliber?"

".22!"

"Very good. Extra credit?"

I had nodded enthusiastically.

"Was this wound inflicted at close range?"

"Nope! Close-range gunshot wounds have burnt gunpowder stippling around the edges," I recited.

Another fact my fourth-grade teacher hadn't been especially enthusiastic about my sharing with the class.

"Good girl." As a reward, she leaned across the table with the spray can of whipped cream and gave me an extra dollop.

"Momma?" I asked, scraping the muddy fudge in the bottom of my glass.

"What, sweetness?"

"Where'd you get all these pictures?"

My mother took a bite of her own pudding and swallowed slowly. She was always better than I was at savoring the rare treat of a dessert, usually reserved for very special occasions.

"That's a story for another day, Janey."

But that day had never come.

Chapter Twenty-Two

Those lights again.

Red.

Blue.

Red.

Blue.

Their blinking in the rearview mirror like the punctuation to a sentence. Two words repeated again and again.

The end. The end. The end.

If only I could make those colors belong to something else now. Some other memory.

But no.

This night would join them. Another drop in the ever-deepening well of events I neither wanted to remember nor seemed able to forget.

I pulled Tyler's car into his assigned spot in the apartment complex's lot.

The patrol car stopped behind us, effectively blocking us in. The officer in the passenger seat got out, thumbs hooked into his belt. Waiting to escort us up the stairs to Tyler's apartment.

When I had explained, albeit in an extremely abbreviated version, my thoughts on the shooting and how the bullet had surely been meant for Tyler, they insisted on seeing us home.

Tyler had been in no shape to drive, his eyes dull as a beached fish's.

I turned off the engine and nudged his shoulder.

"Shall we?" I asked.

He made no answer but mechanically reached for the door handle.

"Thanks a bunch for following us home," I said, threading my arm through Tyler's as we approached the officer. "I think I can take care of things from here on out."

"Not so fast, young lady." He wagged a finger at me in a fatherly gesture that left me—dare I admit it—a little nostalgic for Officer Bixby of the eighteen-inch biceps. "I still need to do a quick sweep of the apartment. Make sure the premises are secure."

"Right," I said. "Of course."

As we walked up the stairs, Tyler spoke his first words since Greg's head had been in his lap. "Don't let him touch anything."

I squeezed his forearm as affirmation of my understanding.

The officer wandered through the few rooms of Tyler's apartment with the entitled swagger of a landlord inspecting his tenant's holdings.

"Quite a collection." He reached a blunt index finger toward one of Tyler's figurines.

"It sure is." I rested my hands on his shoulders and aimed him toward the door before he could knock anything else over. "Thank you so much for coming all the way up."

"You sure you two will be all right?" He directed this question at me while keeping his gaze fixed on Tyler, who stood before the bank of blank black monitors. Staring. Swaying ever so slightly.

"Positive," I said. "Good night."

As soon as the door was closed, I engaged the series of security measures Tyler had installed, beginning with the dead bolt and ending with the security chain.

"Well," I sighed. "That was unpleasant."

Tyler sat down at the desk, the screens lighting up when he moved the mouse.

"What are you doing?" I asked.

"It was my fault," he said.

"What was your fault?"

"Greg," he said. "Greg is dead and it's my fault."

"Just because you happen to be the principal engineer on a project that's worth billions of dollars doesn't mean Greg's death is your fault. Whoever wanted Lucas Logan Bell and Sam Shook dead wants you dead too. Someone really doesn't want this lawsuit to go forward."

"I lied," he said.

"About what?"

"You remember during the meeting when Shook asked if there were any copies of the repository before it was rebased?"

"Yes."

"We *did* make a copy." Tyler rotated his chair around to look me in the eye. "The day we had our first meeting and Shook asked about it, Curt pulled me aside and asked me to destroy it. He said he didn't want to create more trouble for Jimmy."

"Jimmy?" Crammed as it was with facts, my brain refused to yield a match.

"You know. Horse-porn Jimmy."

"Riiight." How had I forgotten? "Why?" I asked. "Why would Curt do that?"

"The same reason people do lots of things," Tyler said. "Someone paid him."

"Is that a guess? Or do you know something?"

Benefit of someone incapable of controlling his facial expressions: muscles don't lie.

He knew something.

"But you didn't do it?" I nudged. "You didn't destroy it."

"I told him I did." Tyler looked down at his hands, perhaps imagining the blood that had been on them. "But I lied."

"You mean you still have a copy of the code?"

"No," he said, his earnest brown eyes finding mine. "*You* do."

———

My heart, that crazy internal barometer, had already begun to pound in my ears. Lefty had gone all humid. "What are you talking about?"

"You remember the flash drive I gave you?"

"Yes."

"Well, the copy of the codebase is on it."

My mind reeled back to the meeting. To opening the flash drive on the loaner laptop.

"Wait, you don't mean—"

"Princess NightSpear's Midreign Quest Blessing. I thought the title was kind of appropriate since this case is like your quest."

"Why the hell would you do that?"

"Because why else would your mother be meeting with Valentine that morning?"

Rarely had I been in the presence of a mind as sharp as Tyler's. The kind of machine that made leaps which left even me dizzy.

Brilliant beast that I am, I came back with the ever-so-clever "Wait . . . what?"

"Did you honestly think I would hand over those picture files without looking through them first?"

"So, yesterday morning, when you gave me the flash drive, you *knew* there was a picture of my mother and Valentine on it?"

"Yes."

"But she was in disguise."

"Pretty shitty disguise."

"Excuse me. That was a fucking *awesome* disguise."

"What does Valentine have to do with your mother's disappearance?"

"Who says he has anything to do with it?"

When he rolled his chair back, the screen was filled with the image that had upset me so in the dev meeting: Valentine and the diminutive mystery man, a.k.a. my mother.

"This picture. The search logs indicate that this is the image you were looking at right before you left the development meeting the other day."

"And?"

"And I did a little research on my own. That ad? The one you were calling the *Mile High Grapevine* about?"

"Yes."

"I made a couple calls of my own and got the IP address it was placed from."

"And?"

"And it was placed by a computer at Seventeenth and Welton in Denver, Colorado."

That buzzing feeling was back. The one that made my face feel like it was made out of billions of ants.

"But that's Valentine and Associates corporate headquarters."

"Exactly," he said.

"Quick, I need a pen and paper." I reached for his desk drawer only to have it nearly slammed on my fingers. "Jesus Christ. Sorry. I forgot. Don't touch anything."

Tyler cleared his throat, doing an okay job of pulling off sheepish, all things considered. "I . . . keep paper and pens in the junk drawer in the kitchen." He rose from his desk chair and returned with a ratty notepad and a pen lifted from some game store.

I sat down on the floor next to his desk and began scribbling hasty notes, jotting down the questions pinballing around my brain.

Access to Valentine HQ?

Maybe Miranda? Lure me to Seattle?

Mom at Valentine HQ after disappearance?

She had left me a note in the nightstand of his late mistress's suite in his private quarters, so it wasn't much of a stretch to think she might have visited on more than one occasion. I'd found it just a few days after she'd disappeared when Valentine, having had enough of my antics, decided that bringing me back to his private apartment was the only way to keep me safe. Whether it had been Valentine's moves she was anticipating or mine, it amounted to the same. She had known I'd end up there one way or another, as she'd indicated in her letter.

*All roads lead to Valentine. I think that's in the Bible.
Somewhere near the back.*

The rest of the letter was equal parts warning and apology. The warning pertained to ending up in Valentine's bed, and how I'd be totally grounded for life. The apology had more to do with my unusual upbringing and the inevitability of her departure from me.

And like those lines of her letter, the ad's words had been so . . . so . . . *her.* So something my mother would have said.

Whoever had placed it had to know her well enough to mimic her particular vernacular when it came to residents of Washington State.

Which brought me to the last and most disturbing possibility.

Valentine placed ad himself? Why?

I dropped the pen onto the pad and stared at the words, about as legible as the scratchings of a possessed chicken.

But the next question that popped into my head bypassed the paper and made its way straight to my mouth.

"Why?" I asked.

"Why what?"

"Why did you go looking for the IP address that the ad was placed from?"

He shrugged and looked down at his socks. "I thought it would be an interesting challenge."

I looked at him then.

Really looked at his face beyond deciding exactly where I'd punch him given a solid chance—where the bottom of his nose met his upper lip, in case you were wondering. For the first time, I observed just how sleek and fox-like that nose was. How his pillowy upper lip was almost exactly the same width. How his melted chocolate eyes, fringed in obscenely long lashes, were precisely the same distance from his eyebrows as they were from each other. And those eyebrows, equidistant from his hairline and his fine, angular nostrils. How understated this perfection was. I doubted if anyone ever took the time to notice.

"What?" he asked, glancing down at me from the lofty height of his chair. "Why are you looking at me like that?"

"Your face," I said. "It's very symmetrical."

"Yours isn't. Your eyes are too big."

Casting the pad and paper aside, I pushed myself up from the floor. "I know what you're doing. You're being deliberately insulting because you think it will push me away. Well, you're wrong. I know this game. I fucking invented this game, and if you want to play for real, I will leave your ass bloodied in the dirt."

Tyler stood from his chair, facing me, arms folded. "When have I ever insulted you?"

I blinked at him, openmouthed. "Please. Everything you've said to me since the moment we met was an insult."

"Example," he said.

"You said my skirt made my hips look wide."

"Did I say I didn't like wide hips?"

"Well, you didn't say that you *did*."

"That wasn't an insult. It was a lack of comprehension on your part. Next."

"Melanie," I said. "You said she was more attractive than me in every way."

"I didn't say who she was more attractive *to*."

"What about when you asked me what perfume I was wearing, and I said I wasn't and you asked me if I could? How is that *not* an insult?"

"Bodies release pheromones, and the smell of yours makes it impossible for me to think. And thinking is what I do. It's what I've always done. Every minute, every second of every fucking day until you showed up."

It was the first time I'd heard him swear.

My own potty mouth was extensive enough that such words were used interchangeably with conjunctions and adjectives and most often verbs.

But not Tyler.

The use of a pedestrian profanity represented a cracking of sorts. A lowering of levels.

Some chunk of mental bedrock shifted and suddenly, I knew.

Like that moment when, after years of studying a foreign language, you are suddenly inexplicably fluent. This is how I came to know Tyler Dixon. Immediately and all at once.

"Are you saying . . . are you saying that you *want* me?"

He shrugged, those dark eyes skating to the side. "I'm not saying that I don't."

You're not wrong.

My own words floated back to me. The admission that wasn't quite an admission. Saying something without saying anything. Because most expressions strike just left of the truth. Because it's not what *you* don't know that can't hurt, but what *they* don't know.

How intimately I knew the loneliness of such logic.

I took a careful step toward him. "Well? Do you?"

He looked at me, the air between us heavy with words unsaid. His. Mine. Ours.

"You know your nostrils flare when you're angry," he said. "And you get this line in the middle of your forehead."

"Yeah? And you're one hundred percent more attractive when you're not talking," I said, grabbing his shocked face and pulling it down to mine for a kiss.

Tyler came up for air, his cheeks reddening like he'd been slapped.

"Do you want to have sex with me?" he asked.

My mouth opened but failed to summon relevant words. Never in my life had I been asked this question straight out.

"Because I *think* you want to have sex with me, but I'm usually wrong about nonverbal cues. I mean your legs were crossed toward me earlier, which I remember reading is a subconscious sex invite, but then you also crossed your legs toward that Shook guy during the dev meeting, so you might just send out sex invites indiscriminately."

"Tyler—"

"Also, your pupils are dilated, which can be a sign of arousal, but it's also a side effect of certain drugs and you could have a habit of some kind." He was panting, his hands indicating various parts of me as he named them, trying to put me together like a puzzle. "And that could be a sex flush on your neck, but—"

"*Tyler—*"

"What?"

"Are you asking if I want to have sex with you as an isolated empirical fact, or are you extending an invitation?"

"Can't it be both?"

"Well—"

"Before you answer, I just want you to know that I don't feel rejection like other people do, so it's not a big deal if the answer is no to both. I do want you, but it's not like you're the most intelligent woman I've ever met, or the most conventionally attractive, so—"

I put my hand to his lips, still kiss-warmed and swollen.

"You've never done this before, have you?"

A half smile, almost-smile, bloomed beneath my fingers. He shook his head from side to side.

"Come on," I said, taking him by the hand and tugging him toward the bedroom. "I'm going to rebase the shit out of your repository."

———

Night in the strange cool dark of Tyler's apartment. Interrupted only by the intermittent flashing of the various power lights from his machines, glowing eyes staring me awake.

Next to me in the bed, Tyler snored softly. His face buried in the pillow, his breathing thick with sleep.

I carefully peeled back the covers and located his T-shirt, slung over the back of a chair. Which I guessed was the Tyler equivalent of high passion, still unable to completely discard it on the floor. The well-washed fabric enveloped me in a wave of his scent as I slipped it over my head. He wasn't large enough for it to dwarf me as, say, one of Shepard's would—not that I had thought about it—but enough to provide semidecent cover for my trip to the kitchen for a glass of water.

And while I drank it, I stared.

Stared at the desk drawer Tyler had so eagerly shut earlier, nearly relieving me of a finger. Not that there was anything wrong with missing fingers, I mentally amended for Bixby's benefit.

Setting my water glass in the sink, I wandered over to the desk and sat down in Tyler's office chair.

I paused.

I waited.

Tyler didn't come racing out of the bedroom, howling at me to stop, nor did the heavens crack open for a glowing finger to smite me dead.

Taking these as signs of the universe's complicit agreement, I slowly, quietly slid the drawer open.

I found nothing all that interesting at first. A few receipts. Copies of battle dialogue and costume sketches.

And then, my name.

Jane.

One word. Four letters. Written on the tab of a file folder in Tyler's precise, miniscule lettering.

I opened the folder, waiting for my eyes to adjust to the blue light of the digital clock in the shape of the Death Star on his desk.

Then I read.

I doubted if even D-Town himself could put together a more thorough dossier.

Bank statements. Credit card receipts. Dates. Times. Things only someone who had been watching me much longer than the few days we had been acquainted would know.

But the pictures . . . the pictures.

These weren't just from security cameras.

These were images from someone who had been following me. And not just following me in Seattle.

Following me in Denver.

Worse, I knew the day these had been taken.

The same day Lucas Logan Bell had been murdered. The day I'd read my mother's ad in the *Mile High Grapevine.*

Motive.

An idea, belief, or emotion that impels a person to act in accordance with that state of mind.

How often had this been drummed into my classmates and me as we sat in darkened lecture halls, our faces blue from the light of our open laptop screens?

It was the word around which entire cases hinged.

And I had ignored Tyler's this entire time.

No, not ignored. I had been aware of it but had tried to convince myself again and again that I had been wrong. That the strange twinges I'd had came from an overactive imagination.

The fridge compressor came on, startling me out of my thoughts.

Had this been a movie, it would have been the moment when I turned to see Tyler standing in the doorway behind me.

But he wasn't.

My throat closed.

My chest ached.

Don't touch anything.

Tyler's paranoia took on a new clarity now. Coming to life in vibrant, eye-frying color. What else might he be hiding?

I tiptoed back into the bedroom, slipping into my clothes before tucking the file beneath my arm and sneaking out the front door.

I knew what I had to do.

Chapter Twenty-Three

Mr. Smith blinked at me through the gap in the front door, one side of his face pillow-creased, his glasses slightly askew.

"Miss Avery. What are you doing here?"

Here was Mr. Smith's home—a midcentury ranch-style house in a gentrifying neighborhood on the outskirts of Seattle. It was an orderly affront to the lovely sprawling chaos of the city. Rows of houses all the same. The rhythmic spitting of sprinklers. Suburban paradise.

"I need your help," I said.

"How did you get my address?"

I shifted on my feet, one hand picking a chip of paint by the doorbell. Casual. Nonthreatening. The other hand hovering at my lower back, at the kitchen knife insurance policy I had lifted from Tyler's kitchen. "Mr. Smith, there are certain questions it would be better for you not to ask me. Now will you help me, or not?"

He considered me, a strange woman standing beneath the chandelier of moths batting at the porch light overhead.

After a moment far more tense for me than it was for him, he stepped back to grant me access.

I exhaled. Let my hand drop to my side after tucking the knife handle back under the hem of my blouse.

"This way," he said in the hushed tone of a man accustomed to accommodating a sleeping family. He looked too old to have kids still at home. A wife perhaps.

I followed him through the hallway to the step-down den, a shrine to knotty pine and unremarkable furniture reminiscent of the 1960s.

He clicked on a green glass desk lamp and took a seat behind his desk, gesturing to the chair in front of it with the authority of a school principal. Not an especially pleasant association for me.

"What is it you need help with, Miss Avery?"

I could taste my heart in my throat as I reached into my shirt and pulled out the zip drive.

"I need to know if the copy of the Oxbow Group codebase saved on this is real." I stared at it, hesitating in the final seconds before I handed it over.

Smith turned it over in his palm. "Where did you get this?"

"Remember what I said about those certain questions?"

He sighed grudgingly and booted up his laptop, the screen making blue rectangles of his lenses. "This will take a moment," he said, plugging the drive into the side.

He typed while I paced, moving along the walls of framed pictures like a museum patron, my hands knotted behind my waist to keep myself from touching anything.

Fingerprints, you see.

Smith, his average-looking wife, and two average-looking children posing in the backyard with an average-looking dog.

Years later. Same kids, different dog.

A whole unremarkable life.

The sight of them, their abundance, hit me with a wave of claustrophobia that made me want to run screaming through the front door.

"Just as I suspected," Smith announced, leaning back in his desk chair.

"What?" I rushed up behind him and stared at the monitor, not that the mosh pit of digital fuckery on the monitor meant anything to me.

"This is a mainline clone of the forensic repository we already have," Smith said.

"English, please."

"A fake," he diagnosed. "A very clever one. But a fake nonetheless." A dull ache woke in my chest as the roots of realization took hold. Tyler was lying.

———

Thirty minutes and several cycles of deep breathing later, I stood in the pool of light beneath a downtown Seattle streetlamp, my cell phone pressed to my cheek as I waited.

"Hello?" Shook's voice was groggy, thick with sleep.

"Hi," I said.

"Jane. I have been trying to reach you all evening. Is everything okay?"

"No." My throat closed over again, that feeling of choking that seemed my constant companion as of late. "Everything is not okay."

"What is it?" he asked. "What's the matter?"

"Could you meet me somewhere?" I hated the ragged sound of my own voice. The pathetic tears in it. "There's something I need to show you. I can't come to the hotel. I think they're watching it."

"Who, Jane? Who is watching it?"

"RedWolf's men. Can you get out without them seeing you?"

"Yes, I think I can, but—"

"I'll explain when you get here, I promise."

"You want me to meet you somewhere now? But it's"—a pause during which I could see him squinting at his phone—"two in the morning."

"I'm so sorry. If I had anyone else to ask, I would. Will you come?"

A sigh. "Of course. Where would you like to meet?"

I gave him the address.

"Give me half an hour and I will be there."

And half an hour it was down to the minute.

Shook stepped out of the taxi, looking fresh despite the ungodly hour, two cardboard coffee cups in hand. Only when the driver pulled away did I step out of the shadows.

"Jane? My God." He set both coffee cups on a concrete planter nearby and pulled me into his arms. Securing me to his chest. Securing me to the planet. And for the second time ever, I broke down in a man's arms.

Shook patted the area between my shoulder blades. "Shhhh. It's all right."

"Please don't fire me." I had meant to tell him everything I had learned first, but these were the words that found their way out of my mouth.

"Fire you?" Shook's hands were gentle on my shoulders as he held me back to look at me. "What are you talking about?"

"I know I've been completely unreliable lately. And I have no right to ask the firm to stand by me when I've been charged with a murder. But this job means everything to me, and I promise I'm going to solve this and be a solid employee again. Just please don't give up on me. Please don't give up on me. *Please.*" My tears were warm as they dropped onto my forearms.

"Jane. Look at me." When I didn't, he nudged my chin upward with fingers still warm from the coffee cups. "There's no need to worry about all that now. We'll get it sorted. It's like I told you yesterday. We just need to focus on finding your mother. Everything else will fall into place as it's meant to. All right?"

I nodded, resurrecting a badly used and pilled tissue to dab at my streaming nose.

"Now," he said, handing me one of the coffee cups. "What is this charming place you've brought me to?"

"It's where my mother has been hiding. At least recently." I sniffed at the warm steam curling up from the cup, redolent with spices.

"Chai," Shook said, taking a sip from his own. "I spotted a coffee shop around the corner and thought we might both be in need."

The liquid warmed me from the inside out.

He followed me into the dilapidated building, ducking under the fence with an agility that hinted at his yogic training.

We stopped in the grimy kitchen littered with trash and debris from the crumbling walls; we looked at the chairs but didn't sit.

"If I did believe in the zombie apocalypse, I believe this might be where it would start." Shook toed a used condom away from his shoe on the linoleum floor and folded his arms. "So what is it you wanted to show me?"

I untucked my badly wrinkled blouse from my skirt and pulled the file folder out.

Shook set his cup on the table and took the file folder, angling it toward the window where the streetlight outside sent in a filthy anemic beam.

"Where on earth did you get this?"

So I told him everything.

Okay, not *everything* everything.

But about Valentine and Miranda, my mother and RedWolf, RedWolf and Oxbow Group, and finally about Greg, the conversation at Tyler's apartment that followed, and the flash drive.

"It appears he had all the information he needed here to frame you," Shook said, still leafing through pages. "Your whereabouts, your habits. Even your security codes."

"I know," I said. "But why me specifically? Why would he want to frame me for the murder?"

"Perhaps he hadn't even intended to frame you for the murder." Shook took a sip from his cup, the warmth lowering his lyrical voice. "Perhaps he just needed to create enough suspicion around you that you would no longer be eligible to work on the case."

I thought about this for a moment. "If that's true, then why would he give me a fake copy of the repository before it was rebased?"

Shook looked up from the folder, eyes wide as he blinked at me. "How do you know it's fake?"

"Because I had Smith look at it."

The fine skin creased between Shook's dark brows. "When?"

I cleared my throat, drew a circle in the dust caked on the long-abandoned kitchen table. "Recently."

"Recently as in . . . tonight?"

"Indeed," I said, channeling Greg so effectively it made my chest ache.

The seed of a smile dimpled one corner of Shook's lips. Perhaps imagining the look on Smith's face when I showed up unannounced. "How did you get his address?"

"He had the same question."

"Which went unanswered, I suspect."

"You suspect correctly." I wiped a dusty fingertip on the back of a chair.

"And had you not considered that Smith might be the one lying to you?"

"Why would he do that?"

"The same reason Curt asked Tyler to delete the only existing copy of the codebase before the . . . equine pornography incident." Shook waited, his leonine eyes glowing in the gloom. His words like bread crumbs carefully sprinkled, waiting for me to follow.

My canine-loyal desire to impress snuffled ahead, even if my thoughts lagged slightly behind it. "Oh my God. What if there was never an *incident* at all? What if Curt only *said* that Jimmy had uploaded a bunch of horse porn as an excuse to cover his own tracks? Because if Oxbow Group really did copy BitSled's codebase . . ."

"Then it would be imperative to do away with any evidence of what the Oxbow Group codebase looked like before they copied BitSled's code."

My head swam. Whether with adrenaline or confusion, I couldn't be sure. I fished the small black stick out of my bra and squeezed it until the edges bit into my palm. "But if Smith is dirty, who else can we have look at this? Because if this *is* a real copy of the codebase, it's way too risky to engage some other random data forensics wonk to make the comparison."

"Preferably someone who has been working closely enough with Smith to know the chief points of comparison."

"Like who?"

"Like me." Shook patted the messenger satchel strapped diagonally across his chest. "Always prepared."

"A regular Boy Scout, you are."

Shook held out his hand, the buttery skin of his open palm a couple of shades lighter than the elegant fingers extended into the flophouse's gloom.

As I had with Smith, I hesitated a split second before handing it over, modern Maltese Falcon it had so far proved to be, before dropping it into his upturned palm.

Shook stared at the small black rectangle. "Jane, do you realize what this means?"

"It means . . ." A wave of nausea rose up on a foul current of moldy air. "It means that we'll be able to prove once and for all who owns the rights to the 3-D microchip printing technology."

"You're absolutely right," Shook said, dropping the drive into his shirt pocket. "It is a shame it will never see the light of day."

I staggered two steps backward, sat down hard when my knees gave out. Cold sweat bloomed on my upper lip and forehead, the already-murky atmosphere darkening around me. My limbs were heavy and dull.

Drugged.

"What did you do?" My own face felt like putty in my hands.

"I added a little something of my own to your tea." He reached across the table and picked up the chai. "Of course, it appears I was a little premature. I thought surely you were inviting me here to confront me."

"About what?" My words seemed to be sticking together, my tongue clumsy and thick.

"About my sabotaging the lawsuit."

"You . . . *you?*"

"I already have patents filed in India. My team of software engineers has been working on duplicating the technology for some time." Shook set the folder down on the table, tapped it once with his knuckle. "Of course, they received a better copy of the code repository than Oxbow Group did. Still, the longer I can keep the lawsuit going, the better chance there is that my team will solve the remaining issues first."

"So Oxbow Group . . . did copy BitSled."

"Oh yes," Shook said. "They most certainly did."

"But Tyler . . . how would Tyler not know?"

"I am fairly certain he knows *now*. But I doubt he knew what he was doing at the time he was doing it."

My thoughts scuttled forward with all the haste of an insect in molasses. "How?" was the most intelligent question I could muster.

"Because Tyler never saw the BitSled code. Curt Allen did."

The mere mention of his name sent the memory of the CTO's unassuming giggle and kind intelligent face swimming through my foggy brain. "Curt?"

"As the CTO, all he had to do was lay out a few patterns. Make it seem as if he was the one suggesting ideas and solutions. It was more simple than you might think."

"And Curt got the copy from Lucas?"

Shook nodded. "As did I. Unfortunately, Lucas neglected to inform me that I wasn't the only one he'd given a copy of his code repository to. He betrayed me, you see."

"How did he betray you?"

"He gave us all different copies. Me. Your mother. Curt. He was looking to make the best deal possible for himself. I made the mistake of trusting him. Just as your mother made the mistake of trusting me."

"My mother? How?"

"Valentine became aware that Oxbow Group was attempting to file for a patent for the same technology he had BitSled working on. So he brought your mother into the loop and she began investigating the case. It wasn't long before she figured out that RedWolf was in bed with Oxbow Group, which is when she came to me."

Even through the haze, I felt the sting of jealousy that came with other people describing the meetings they'd had with my mother.

Even her ghost was haunting other lives.

"When she first approached me to make it clear how important it was that BitSled win this lawsuit, we spoke of many things," he continued. "She mentioned that Oxbow Group was backed by a very dangerous man. Someone called RedWolf, and she had in her possession evidence that would make it clear exactly who owned the rights to the patent.

"But then, your mother disappeared, and I got *closer* to Lucas Logan Bell over the course of the lawsuit investigation, and we came up with a different idea about how we could make this whole affair more privately profitable."

And though my thoughts moved through my brain like cement, there was something about the way he said *closer* that stuck.

I come on behalf of Prince DarkHelm DeadBlood, consort of Lord BoneSmuggler, who wishes me to avenge his beloved.

I squinted to bring my doubling vision back into line. "You're Prince DarkHelm. You were his . . . his—"

"His lover," Shook finished for me. "Yes. We met when BitSled first engaged the firm to research the patent rights. Love at first sight, I suppose you could say."

"How did I not know you were gay?" I was really flying now. My limbs made of water. My head a helium balloon on a long string. Whatever miniscule verbal filter I had once possessed long since dissolved by the drugs.

"Wishful thinking, perhaps?"

"Pfffff," I said with far more lip flapping than I had intended. "Least I wasn't the only one."

Shook inclined his head. "What do you mean?"

"Melanie." My head bobbed forward. I stacked it back onto the stem of my neck with some effort. "Trying to take a ride on your baloney pony."

"Melanie?" Shook laughed. "Oh no. Quite the opposite. *I* was the one who came onto her. I thought perhaps if I made her *think* I was interested in her, it might widen the rift between the two of you. Lessen the odds that you might share information."

My mind reeled back to the night she had stopped by my room. The tense phone call yesterday evening. It felt like years ago.

Both times.

Both times she had been trying to tell me something.

Air escaped my nostrils in a horselike snort. "I am *such* an asshole."

"Now, Jane. You mustn't be so hard on yourself. You have been under a tremendous amount of pressure."

"Couldn't have anything to do with the fact that you left a dead guy in my bed. Which, *dude*, congratulations on his man-tackle. Homeboy was *pa-cking*," I said, breaking the word into syllables roughly approximating the length of Lucas Logan Bell's manly bits.

"Yes. Unfortunately, I wasn't the only one benefiting from those gifts."

"Huh?" Such was the diminishing quality of my speech, reduced to the verbal equivalent of primordial sludge.

"He was cheating on me," Shook said. "With one of his LARP compatriots, apparently. So, I convinced him we were to have a tryst elsewhere and we met at your apartment. When we got there, and I had him in a compromising position, I confronted him with the evidence I'd found in his trash can."

"Ohhh," I said. "You're talking about the used condom."

"Correct."

"Then you shot him?"

"Jane. I told you. I practice nonviolence. I had someone *else* shoot him. An acquaintance of mine who is lacking in both scruples and cash."

"But you used my gun."

"That was not the plan originally, but I thought it lent a certain realism to the scene."

"I still don't understand why all this had to happen in *my* bed." I attempted to point a finger at my chest but poked myself in the eye instead. Luckily, I felt no pain.

"I didn't actually expect you to be charged with murder. But because of your association with Valentine and your mother's involvement with the case, it made you a far more interesting suspect. And by defending you, I was able to ensure your gratitude to me while making you the center of the blame and myself the most unlikely of suspects."

His voice had the same pleasant lilt as always. His face still as kind. His manner just as polite.

I liked him.

Still.

This, at last, penetrated the anesthetic haze to puncture my heart. And so died any illusions of myself as a keen judge of human character. The tough, smart, savvy girl I'd always imagined myself to be.

Tyler, innocent. Sam, guilty.

And I, a fool.

Everything I knew, everything I thought, was wrong.

"*Why*, Sam?"

He scooted a chair close to mine and seated himself. Our knees brushing in the dark.

"It's as I told you before. I am *tired* of playing the puppet for men with money. Do you have any idea how many lives this technology would improve? What it would do for the town I come from? Instead, it's men like Valentine and RedWolf, looking to fatten already bulging pockets." Bitterness corroded his words, revealing the sharp metallic edge beneath.

"You *murdered* a man."

"Two men, if we are being technical." Shook glanced to the side in a deferential manner.

"And now you'll make it three?" The darkness was breeding in my field of vision again. Growing to overtake everything in my periphery.

Anger grew with it.

Not at him, but at myself.

For not having listened when my mother had told me I couldn't trust a single soul.

"I am afraid we must." Shook stood, reaching into his pocket and pulling out a rectangular object, setting it on the table. I knew it not by sight, but by sound.

A hollow sloshing.

Lighter fluid.

Breath frozen in my lungs. My stomach small, tight, and cold. A black hole below my heart. "Sam. Sam, please."

Shook picked up the file folder and began strewing the pages as he would flower petals at a wedding.

"He loves me. He loves me not. He loves me. He loves me not." His smile was still beautiful, even now. "You know English is my second language. Nursery rhymes were the first thing they taught us in school."

Another paper fluttered to the ground at my feet. I tried to kick it away and only succeeded in sinking down farther in my chair.

"It took me the longest time to realize that 'This Little Piggy' was talking about animals being driven to slaughter."

"Like 'Ring Around the Rosie' was about smallpox."

"Yes," he agreed. "Is that not barbarous? To teach this to children?"

That he could say this so calmly while scattering pages on the floor and pissing all over them with lighter fluid gave my fuddled brain a pinhole peek into the florid madness stretching behind his mild brown eyes.

I grabbed onto the edge of the table, tried to haul myself upright. Searching, searching for any kind of weapon. My fingers closed over a familiar shape. In my mind, I saw one of the burnout spoons scattered around the apartment. Slowly, I rotated my hand until the bowl was pressing into my palm as the shank jutted out through my fingers.

Shook leaned over me to reach for the pack of matches he'd left on the cluttered table.

My arm hung in suspended animation, making a great, slow arc through space. The pace of nightmares. The body's refusal to obey the laws of gravity and time.

The blow missed, barely grazing his ear.

Shook laughed as he easily pried the would-be weapon from my failing fingers.

"Jane, how I do love that rebel spirit of yours. This is something I have always appreciated about you." He set the spoon out of my reach and resumed his decoration.

Even a mind bifurcated by disembodying chemicals will still feel fear.

And I felt it now.

The scent singed my nostrils with the power of memory.

Happier times.

"Camping" with my mother.

Our bonfires out behind the trailer. Flashes of heat on my cheeks and my mother's smile, twice as bright beneath the desert stars.

"I do apologize, as shooting would be much more convenient for me and painless for you, but you didn't give me adequate time to plan."

"How much time does it take to plan a shooting?" I made the mistake of turning my head. The entire universe pitched hard and to the left. I was sliding down out of the chair now. Liquid limbed and fighting oblivion.

"More than you think, if you're not the one pulling the trigger. It's as I told you, my protégé, I practice nonviolence."

The subtle scraping of boot heels on debris caused Shook to look sharply to his right, where a patch of shadow moved . . . then spoke.

"She's not your protégé. She's my daughter."

The room descended into total, thunderous silence, and I could no longer be certain where life ended and dreams began.

That voice.

Her voice.

Its particular cadence as familiar as breathing. The tone hard and smooth as a polished stone. Driving into my chest like a piston, stinging tears to my eyes, my every molecule attuned to it since birth and before. My muddled mind swam with memories of lullabies, murmured comforts, shared laughter as past slammed into present.

The woman I had ached for. Cried for. Searched for. Lied for. Lied to.

She was alive.

She was *here*.

Shook turned but not fast enough. Her hand clapped across his mouth at the precise instant that the knife slid between his ribs.

Shook's eyes widened, whites on all four corners. Shock. Shock frozen to his face as his heart pumped blood into his chest cavity. She struck again, the knife burying itself where Shook's neck met his shoulder. His knees failing as the match in his fingers dropped to the floor.

And as he fell, I saw my mother.

"Mom?" A one-syllable prayer uttered with the last of my strength.

"Janey." My name stuck as her throat closed over, the distance between us gone fast as she rushed across the rubble and crushed me to her.

We stayed like that for time no man could measure. My face against her chest, her good heart wild against my ear.

"Oh, baby." Her breath was warm in my hair as she rocked me, her tears damp. "My baby girl."

Chapter Twenty-Four

One week later

When I had imagined this moment, it always happened over bowls of my mother's homemade butterscotch pudding. With extra whipped cream, because I had fucking earned it.

As it turns out, we ended up skipping the pudding and going straight for higher-octane fuel.

Margaritas.

And lots of them.

My mother and I sat there in our favorite Mexican joint near downtown Denver, haloed in the relentless bath of neon advertising various brands of cerveza, damp cocktail napkins twisted into fat worms between us. Salt gritty beneath our elbows. Shards of tortilla chips littering the table like shrapnel. Kicky mariachi music the most absurd soundtrack to tales of multiple murders and maiming.

And so far, we'd only covered the resolution of the BitSled patent dispute—much to Oxbow Group's dismay—and the subsequent dropping of all charges against me in the murder of Lucas Logan Bell, much to my delight. Sidenote: suck it, Vick Wiggins.

We'd been winding our way through this forest of glasses, letting the alcohol work before I felt the dialogue cut closer to the bone.

"So, about your father. Shall we pause here for a dramatic sigh?" My mom offered the sigh herself. She had always been pretty bitchin' when it came to recounting a narrative. "Your father. I need you to know a couple things about him. First, I didn't know about the other side of him when I fell in love. Second, I did love him. Sociopaths are charming as fuck, as it turns out."

"So I've been learning."

Shook's face shivered through my thoughts. The surprise in his eyes as the knife sank into his neck. The rattling sound he made moments later. Blood on his white teeth. The smile I had thought so beautiful lost to the world.

Lost to me as my mother was found.

Found, and now sitting right across the table.

A state of affairs that still didn't feel real because in ways, she was not my mother. Not the same woman I had lost.

Her skin was no longer pale like mine, but tawny and glowing. Her once coffee-colored strands had been bleached and bobbed at her jawline, the dark roots just beginning to push through.

I stole sneaky sips of her face anytime she looked away. Looking for the mother I knew in the woman sitting across from me the way I'd looked for *her* in the wide world.

Her.

The way the corners of her mouth drew back like theatre curtains just before she smiled full blast.

Her.

The subtle lowering of her lashes to the right, like she was always on the verge of telling a dirty joke.

Her.

The softness of her earlobes against her jaw, the elongated holes in them a testament to a lifelong obsession with hoop earrings.

I memorized a new detail each time, some part of me storing them up against the eventuality of her absence.

"How did you meet my father?" I asked.

Our whole exchange had been marked by this pattern. Long currents of dialogue from her steered by the occasional eddies of my questions. For once in my life, I listened more than I spoke. I'd been trying to reconstruct the timeline, plug memories into the empty slots.

The specter of a smile haunted her lips, slicked as they were in her favorite shade of bluish red. "That part of the story is embarrassingly pedestrian. We met at a bar. We fell in love. We got married. We got pregnant. We had you. We were happy. Really happy. *Stupid* happy. *Hallmark movie* happy. For a while, anyway."

"What happened?"

"He started to change. And we're not talking about leaving his socks around the house or refusing to take out the trash. We're talking about disappearing for days at a time. Locking himself in his study with a flashlight and a firearm. The more I tried to find out what was wrong, the more violent he became."

I licked the salty, citrusy rim of my glass. "Violent toward you?"

"Lord, no. He'd *better* have known I'd have had his balls for earrings if he tried that shit with me. But he liked to break stuff. Put his fist through walls. That kind of thing." Mom scraped the bottom of the salsa bowl with a handful of chip crumbs and brought it quickly to her lips. Her talent for doing this without anointing her T-shirt with a blob of tomato spooge was another skill I wished I'd inherited.

Me, I would have just poured the salsa over the remaining flakes, pronounced it salsa cereal, and eaten it with a spoon.

Were I not a paragon of good manners and shit.

"You want to know the worst thing?" She ducked her head and smirked as she always did when she was laughing inwardly at herself. "I was actually *relieved* when the feds showed up on our doorstep. I thought he was having an affair. That's how naïve I was in those days. Here I was, worried about him putting his dick in stuff, and he was having people killed on the reg and laundering money for the mob."

She tossed back the remainder of her margarita, setting it to the side so she had a new napkin to mangle.

My mother had developed nervous habits.

"That had to have been a pretty big shock still." I picked up the heavy pitcher, beaded with moisture, pouring the last of the frozen oblivion into my mother's empty glass.

"It was. Of course, I said all the things that tragically naïve wives of serial killers and career criminals usually say. There had been signs. Things I had seen but explained away."

"As you do," I said, offering absolution to us both.

"They asked me if I'd be willing to testify." She stared at the table's battered wooden surface, pushing around flakes of salt with the tip of her finger. Her features hardened into that look I knew never to argue with. "I had to face him, Jane. I had to sit on the witness stand and look him in the eye and let him know that I wasn't afraid."

"I thought Valentine was the only one who testified against him." I still couldn't quite dodge the dart of ire that poked me at the mere mention of his name.

My mother shook her head. "Valentine and me."

"Wait, how old was I when this trial happened?"

"Not quite four."

"And Valentine was?"

"A brawny sixteen. Your father was no respecter of age, as it turned out. Opportunities abounded for anyone with talent." She raised a dark brow at me. "Especially talents as remarkable as Valentine's were."

"Twelve years." I leaned back in my uncomfortable wooden chair. "Somehow I hadn't realized he was that much older than me."

"He entered the witness protection program at the same time you and I did, emancipated minor that he was. I lost track of him for a while after that." My mother's slender fingers traced the garish green cactus arms sprouting from the glass's stem. "Then the assassination attempts started, and oh, what fun those were. No one was supposed to be able to find us, but somehow they always did."

And what volumes of pain lived in that blank, flat stare. When she remained silent, I knew she'd drifted too far into the sea of her memory. Lost somewhere in the ocean of time.

I tugged her back to me with words. "What did you do?"

She blinked once like a shutter click, and she was there again behind her eyes.

"Those government wonks shuffled us from agency to agency. It was harder for them to place a woman and a young child, they said. And do you know what that wank-weasel of a caseworker suggested? He suggested, he *actually* fucking hinted, that maybe I should consider giving you up for adoption. Cut ties with you permanently. It was me they were after, anyway. You would grow up safe and far away from all this shit."

"What did you say?" I signaled to the waiter, pointing both to the empty margarita pitcher and the denuded chip basket with its paper gone translucent from oil. He nodded and cut a swift right into the kitchen.

"Well, after I bitch-slapped him, I went home and I thought about what he'd said. I stayed up all night, sitting by your bed, watching you sleep. You were having one of your nightmares. And then you woke up, and you saw me. You opened those gray-blue eyes of yours, and you crawled into my lap. I touched your buttery neck. You looked up at me, and you saw that I was crying, and do you know what you said?" She waited. Like if she stared at me long enough, the years would fall away like leaves and there I'd be at four years old, ready with whatever words I had given her on that night.

I shook my head no.

"You said, 'Don't worry, Momma. I'll protect you.'"

Her throat clenched, making the words sound strangled from her rather than spoken.

Our eyes met then, mirror reflections of a gray that wasn't blue or a blue that wasn't gray.

"And my God, Janey. My heart." She pressed a hand to her chest like she was staunching a wound, dimples whitening in the newly tanned expanse of her skin above the black half-moon of tank top. Black like her leather jacket. Black like her boots.

This, too, was new. This preference for monochromatic attire.

"I could actually feel my heart breaking," she said. "I knew that even after everything I'd tried to keep from you, you'd still seen. You'd seen enough to *know*."

The waiter arrived and replaced our provisions. In addition to the margaritas and fresh chips and salsa, he'd augmented the tray with a squat stone mortar filled with guacamole. Perhaps to tempt us into eating some booze-absorbing fat.

I gave him a grateful smile.

Or what I hoped was a grateful smile.

My craniofacial muscles weren't exactly spot-on by this point.

If my mom had noticed any of these happenings, she gave no indication.

"I couldn't do it," she said, reaching across the table to take both my hands in hers. "I couldn't give you up."

And to both our great shock, I yanked mine back.

"But you did," I said. "You did give me up." Heat gusted through my body, stealing my words and leaving a strange film of sweat in its wake. My nails bit into my palms inside my clenched fists. The sprightly trumpets died away in the face of the far more primal song of blood pounding in my ears.

"Janey—"

"The day of my graduation. You left. You left me there. Just like you left me at the trailer when I was ten years old. You left me, and I was alone and scared."

My mother's cheeks glowed a vivid red, as if I had reached across the table and slapped her. Which, in a way, I had.

With words instead of hands.

"I left you a letter."

"Right. A letter. Just like you left me an envelope when you were arrested. Do you honestly think that's supposed to make everything okay?" I wrestled words away from the sobs threatening to crush my throat. "My whole life you lied to me about my not having a father. You lied about *everything*. Is it any fucking wonder I grew up to be what I am?"

My mother ventured first into the silence left by my impassioned speech, slow and deliberate as steps through a minefield.

"What you are is a brilliant, compassionate, capable woman who doesn't need anyone—"

"But I *do*. I do need people. I may not be all that great at making them like me, and I might want to cave in their heads with a polo mallet most days"—here, a brief but exceedingly vivid image of Melanie Beidermeyer's perfect blonde melon sprang to mind—"but I need them. And I don't want to spend the rest of my life running."

Mom looked down at her hands, finally surrendering the corpse of her most recent napkin worm. "If that's true, then we only have one option."

"Which is?"

Her eyes hardened into that bright glacier blue that usually preceded someone having to run for cover under a hail of bullets. "We take down RedWolf," she said. "Once and for all."

"Fuck yes." The voice that spoke these words was close, deep, and decidedly male.

So enrapt had we been in our high-drama *Terms of Endearment* moment that Mom and I had both failed to notice the two extra "waiters" until they flanked our table.

The one who had spoken was tall and broad enough to make most doorways nervous, his tray-bearing arm covered in military-themed tattoos.

The other, lean like a mink and slightly pigeon-toed, untied the white apron covering his Pac-Man hoodie and tossed it on the back of the nearest chair. "When do we start?"

Epilogue

"Morocco or Venice?" My mother traced her finger along the antique map—a good find, but not an unusual one in the Victorian seaside hamlet of Port Townsend, Washington.

Around us, the Sunday-morning coffee shop regulars settled into their well-worn butt grooves on the battered leather couches. A band of local pluckers warmed up on the banjo and harmonica against the charmingly steampunk hiss of the espresso machine.

"Neither," I said. "I still don't get why it is that we feel the need to go looking for that shitweasel in the first place."

Shepard hunched on the sofa between us, trying to lean back far enough so as not to be in the direct line of conversational fire while Tyler slouched on the couch opposite.

"Because that *shitweasel* risked everything to infiltrate RedWolf's organization because *I* asked him to."

The shitweasel in question, one Archard Everett Valentine, had dropped off the grid the day after I'd seen him canoodling on the boat with his not-quite ex-wife. A.k.a. the Great Red She-Whore, in Shepard's parlance.

"So you're saying all that schmoopy-doopy stuff with Miranda was just an act?" A small flame of hope flickered somewhere in the recesses of my brain.

"That's what I'm saying. But wherever they're headed, Miranda is driving the show."

"They're headed to Morocco." Tyler's fingers skittered over the laptop balanced on his knees. Through means both miraculous and highly illegal, he'd hacked into the navigation system on Valentine and Miranda's yacht and was now tracking the complicated GPS triangulations as they set their course. "We're wasting our time," he said. "I already told you that Customs and Border Protection Pleasure Boat Reporting System has his yacht checking in at the Costa Rica port of call. He's headed for the Panama Canal. And according to my database of navigational charts and fuel sources, he'll have to stop for fuel in Morocco before going on to Venice either way."

Shepard turned to me. "You turned me down for casual sex, but you bang this guy?"

Heat flooded my face. "*Jared* Shepard, I am not going to discuss that with you." Okay, maybe not the best time to drop a fishing hook out there but worth a shot.

"Nice try," he said. "But nope."

"Jacob?"

"Also nope."

"Jamie!"

"Negative."

"Well, whatever the fuck your name is, I am not discussing this with you."

"Why not?" he asked.

"Because I'm a lady, assface. Also, it's none of your damn business."

"That's where you're wrong." Shepard leaned in closer, the heat of him scorching my arm. "If you're going into battle, you need to know all of your team's dynamics. And if you polished his knob, this is vital information."

Tyler only halfway looked up from his laptop. "And is your first name vital information as well, J—"

A blur of motion.

Shepard had Tyler pinned to the coffee table, one hand on his throat, the other clenched into a fist and hovering above his face.

"This isn't some LARP game, kid. You ever so much as *breathe* the rest of what you were about to say, and I will punch your teeth down your throat quicker than you can roll a pair of dice."

A banjo note died a quick and painful death as people stared, coffee cups hovering halfway to their mouths.

"Boys." Mom hoisted herself out of the overstuffed armchair and pried them apart. "We're not going to accomplish anything with you two pecking at each other like this."

"Knuckle-dragging scope monkey," Tyler muttered under his breath.

"Joystick-jerking data nerd," Shepard shot back.

"Hey!" I clapped my hands at them like a pair of dogs prone to scrapping. "You've both done shit that could be construed as creepy as hell. As I've already explained to you both, Tyler was trying to help Valentine find out who was framing me, and Shepard was trying to keep me from eating a bullet. I find you equally irritating and undesirable. Now hug and make up."

The conversation had taken place in the hospital, where I'd wound up despite my own protestations and thanks to my mother's insistence. There, against the backdrop of beeping monitors and bustling nurses, Tyler had told me all. Or at least, all he was comfortable with. Namely, that he—Tyler—had been roped in by Valentine with orders to find out everything possible about who had been setting me up to take the fall for Lucas Logan Bell's demise. And Tyler, thorough soul that he was, had elected to excavate even further, investigating days long before LLB's murder in hopes of uncovering who had targeted me in the first place.

Shepard had been less forthcoming.

Shocking, right?

Stonewalling me against all questions as to how much he knew about Valentine's decision to involve Tyler, as well as my well-meaning but ill-received inquiries about the status of the investigation into his ex-wife's lover's homicide.

His offer of casual, commitment-free bones jumping, however, he'd bring up at every opportunity.

Not that I'd thought about it.

Not that I was thinking about it *now*, this second, in this very coffee shop with the sagging leather couch beneath my thighs and Tyler and Shepard squaring off within humping distance.

My mismatched would-be colleagues and corescuers eyed each other with all the affection usually reserved for moldering piles of camel shit.

My mom folded her arms and shifted her weight, her round hip in its buttery black leather pants drawing more than one admiring look from the hard-bitten fishermen sitting at the counter. "We're not going anywhere until you two make nice."

They each leaned in slightly and gave each other a brusque pat on the back. I was mildly surprised when they didn't wipe their hands on their pants afterward.

"You call that a hug?" I said. "Come on now. Scrote to scrote. Show me how it's done."

Predictably, they leapt apart like someone had kicked a bomb between them.

"Progress." My mother shrugged and turned to me. "So are we agreed on Morocco? We're meeting the flight crew in a little under an hour, and we need to tell them where exactly we'll be going."

My mother's ability to wrangle Valentine's own private jet in his absence simply because they'd been working together spoke to the true measure of her talents in the persuasive regard.

"Venice," I said.

"You're sure?" My mother's eyes bored into mine. Letting me cast the deciding vote was an act of deference. An act of grace. "You're sure you want to do this?"

And that's the moment I fell off the bandwagon.

Maybe those aren't the right words. How about *leapt off* the band-wagon? How about *threw myself off it with the gusto of a flying squirrel*?

The lie tickled the back of my tongue before rolling effortlessly off my lips.

"I'm sure," I said. *See Jane lie.* "Let's go get Valentine."

ACKNOWLEDGMENTS

I know people a lot cooler than I am. And for some reason, many of these people are willing to put up with my endless questions, frequent whining, and bottomless need for emotional validation and support while I'm writing a book.

Here they are, in no particular order.

My deepest thanks to Cody Ainge, who, over avocado toast, introduced me to the term *scrote to scrote* when describing the complicated rituals of bro-bonding and who contributed significantly to my research on all things LARP and gaming related.

To Nathan and Cindy Barnett, proprietors of the Old Consulate Inn in Port Townsend, Washington (where you should totally stay), for providing delightful accommodations, exquisite conversation, and copious amounts of scotch during the writing retreat responsible for large swaths of this book.

To Sarah Hegger, fellow author and darling friend, and her lovely daughter, Olivia, for being the kind of people you can count on to enthusiastically take on the task of coming up with potential names for horse porn so I didn't have to worry about yet one more problematic entry in my browser history.

To Kari, an exceedingly sane human who is useful for music, much-needed adventures, and for spouting so many excellent one-liners and agreeing to allow me to shamelessly thieve them like the conversational magpie I am. "I like to surprise people with my competence"—yep, that's all her.

To the talented trio of gentlemen who make up the band Magic Giant—introduced to me by the aforementioned Kari—whose album *In the Wind* was the only thing I could listen to while I finished this book. If *Lying Low* has a soundtrack, they wrote it. #MagicalMisfits4Life

To Sir Charles Allen, who provided wise counsel, sorely needed levity, a patient ear, and a willing shoulder. And also cool wooden things made with a magic laser. Every lady should be so lucky as to have a knight-errant, and every knight-errant should be as gallant as you.

To Kent, who has the best giggle in the free world and inspires wicked loyalty in his software development teams as well as his former executive assistants. Thank you for being the best of bosses and the most loyal of friends.

And lastly, but never leastly, I owe my everlasting thanks to Kerrigan Byrne. My plot guru. My kite tail holder. My anchor. My person. You are, quite simply, everything.

ABOUT THE AUTHOR

Photo © 2017 Jason Coviello

USA Today bestselling author Cynthia St. Aubin wrote her first play at age eight and made her brothers perform it for the admission price of gum wrappers. A steal, considering she provided the wrappers in advance. She never quite gave up on the writing thing, even while earning a mostly useless master's degree in art history and taking her turn as a cube monkey in the corporate warren.

Because the voices in her head kept talking to her—and they discourage drinking at work—she started writing mysteries instead. When she's not standing in front of the fridge eating cheese, she's hard at work figuring out which mythological, art-historical, or paranormal friends to play with next. The author of The Case Files of Dr. Matilda Schmidt, Paranormal Psychologist series and the Jane Avery mysteries, *Private Lies* and *Lying Low*, Cynthia lives in Texas with two surly cats.

Cynthia loves to hear from her readers.

Like her: www.facebook.com/cynthia.saintaubin
Friend her: www.facebook.com/cynthia.st.aubin
Follow her: www.twitter.com/CynthiaStAubin
Visit her: www.cynthiastaubin.com
Email her: cynthiastaubin@gmail.com